DANGEROUS *CURVES*

Peter Cheyney

DANGEROUS
CURVES

A Slim Callaghan Mystery

COLLIER BOOKS

Macmillan Publishing Company

New York

First published in 1939
Copyright reserved Peter Cheyney Limited

Collier Books
Macmillan Publishing Company
866 Third Avenue, New York, NY 10022

Library of Congress Cataloging-in-Publication Data
Cheyney, Peter, d. 1951.
    Dangerous curves/Peter Cheyney.
       p.   cm.
    "First published in 1939"—T.p. verso.
    ISBN 0-02-031050-1
    I. Title.
PR6005.H48D327   1989   89-477   CIP
823'.912—dc19

First Collier Books Edition 1989

10 9 8 7 6 5 4 3 2 1

PRINTED IN THE UNITED STATES OF AMERICA

For my stepdaughter
Maureen

At the tender age of fourteen, **Peter Cheyney** (1896–1951) persuaded his parents to let him drop out of school so that he could become a writer. His first published story followed within the year. Between that auspicious beginning and his untimely death, Cheyney went on to publish 150 more short stories, thirty-five novels, and a host of radio dramas. His series characters included Lemmy Caution, an American G-man stationed in Europe during World War II; Sean Aloysius O'Mara, a smooth-talking secret agent; Alonzo McTavish, gentleman jewel thief; and Slim Callaghan, the wise-cracking Sam Spade of London's criminally laden East End. Slim is the only British private eye, from the hard-boiled school of hard knocks, still surviving in print from the golden age of detective writing. Cheyney was an inveterate storyteller, which is suggested by his favorite working method: He preferred to *tell* his books, rather than write them—dictating to his faithful secretary, Miss Sprague. Devoted readers of Peter Cheyney will be long in her debt as they relish the spontaneous, tough quality of her boss's delicious prose.

CONTENTS

CHAPTER ONE

Friday

One in the bag

Callaghan awoke and looked at the ceiling. The fire sent grotesque shadows flickering across the white expanse above him. He yawned, turned over, kicked off the bedclothes, swung his legs to the floor. He sat, his tousled black head in his hands, looking at the fire.

His lips were dry and his tongue felt like a yellow plush sofa. Outside he could hear the rain pattering on the windows. He looked at his wrist-watch. It was eight o'clock.

He got up and began to walk to the bathroom, when the telephone bell jangled. It was Effie Thompson. He growled into the receiver.

'All right,' she said primly. 'Is it my fault if you've got a head? Forgive me for troubling you, but are you ever coming back to this office? Things are happening down here.'

Callaghan ran a furry tongue over dry lips.

'Well, why the hell didn't you phone up, Effie?' he asked. 'What's the matter with you? Why do I have my apartment two floors above my office? If you wanted to get at me, why didn't you telephone?'

'Don't make me laugh,' she said. 'I've been ringing you most of the day – you've just been unconscious.'

'I was on a jag last night,' said Callaghan. 'I feel like hell. What's happenin' down there?'

'The Riverton case is happening,' she answered. 'It's breaking out all over the place. If you want to hold on to those clients you'll have to make something happen. I think . . . '

'I'm not askin' for your advice,' snapped Callaghan. 'When I want you to run my dam' business I'll ask you.'

'All right, sir,' Effie's cool voice came back accenting the 'sir'. 'Let me give you the details. First of all I'd like to point out to you that you haven't been here for two days. There's a pile of correspondence on your desk that'll take you a week to answer. But that's not all. There have been eight calls from the Manor House. I think the Colonel must be getting a little bit annoyed with Callaghan Investigations. And there's a letter here from Selby, Raukes & White, the Riverton solicitors. Would you like me to read it?'

'No, thanks,' said Callaghan. 'I'm comin' down. Anything else?'

'Yes. A man who owns a cinema came in this afternoon. He employs a woman manageress who banks the takings. He says there's a shortage somewhere and wants you to investigate. What do you want done?'

'Did you ask him why he hasn't been to the police?' asked Callaghan.

'Yes,' she answered. 'I don't think he wants to. He sounded a bit nervous when he talked about the manageress.'

Callaghan grunted.

'It sounds like the old story,' he said. 'Charge him fifty pounds retainer and put Findon on the case. He likes movies.'

'I know,' said Effie. She paused for a second. 'He also likes women. I thought Nikolas was the man for that job. So I put him on to it. And I charged a hundred.'

Callaghan grinned.

'Nice goin', Effie,' he said.

He hung up. He walked across the long luxurious bedroom towards the bathroom. He was wearing the top half of a pair of red silk pyjamas. When he walked he put his well-shaped wiry legs on the floor like a cat.

He took off the pyjama jacket and stood under the shower. He started the water very hot, ran it through to luke-warm, then to cold. Then he put on a bathrobe, sat down on the stool and began to rub hair-dressing into his tousled hair. He thought about the Riverton business and began to curse quietly, systematically and comprehensively.

The telephone rang in the bedroom. It was Kells. Callaghan, who, still wet, had picked up the receiver with an oath, toned down when he heard the Canadian accent on the line.

'Hallo, Slim,' said Kells. 'How's it going?'

'All right, Monty,' said Callaghan. 'I've got a hangover, that's all. What is it?'

'I've got that skirt,' said Kells. 'The Dixon dame. Her name's Azelda Dixon and they call her "Swing-It". And by God does she! She's got something, this baby, except she looks tired to death.'

Callaghan grinned.

'Nice work, Monty,' he said. 'Will she talk?'

'Not a crack,' said Monty. 'She's as quiet as a goddam grave. I don't even know where she lives. She's a tight one, that doll.'

'They're all tight,' said Callaghan. 'Those women either talk too much or say nothin'.'

'You said it,' said Kells. 'I've fixed it this way: I'm seeing her again, so maybe she's going to fall for my sex appeal an' come across. If she don't, I'll have to think up something else. I'll be seeing you.'

'All right, Monty,' said Callaghan. 'Listen, I'm going over to Martinella's place tonight. I want to see that fight. I'll finish up at Perruqui's. Effie says the Manor House has been telephonin' all day. They're gettin' dam' excited about something. Maybe they don't think I'm doin' enough for that £100 a week. It looks as if we'll have to get a ripple on.'

'I like that,' said Kells. 'For Jeez' sake, what do they think we've been doing?'

Callaghan hung up.

He dressed himself. He put on a white silk shirt, a low, stiff double collar and a black, watered silk bow. His double-breasted dinner-jacket was well cut. His clothes looked good and expensive.

He put on a black soft hat and lit a cigarette. After the first few puffs he began to cough and went on coughing for quite a while. He walked over to the cupboard in the corner and poured himself out four fingers of rye whisky. He drank it in one gulp.

He went into the corridor and rang for the lift. On the window at the end of the long passage – the window at the Berkeley Square end – the rain was beating hard against the window pane. He stood there waiting, thinking about the Riverton business.

Callaghan was five feet ten inches high; his shoulders were broad, descending to a thin waist and narrow hips. His arms were long; his face was thin with high cheekbones, a decided jaw, ears that lay flat against his head. His eyes were of a peculiar blue, his hair black and unruly, and women liked the shape of his mouth. Looking at him, one got an impression of utter ruthlessness and a cynical humour.

The lift came up. Callaghan went down to his office two floors below.

Effie Thompson was at the filing cabinet in the inner office. She was of medium height, well rounded. Her hair was red, her eyes green. Her clothes fitted her as clothes ought to fit. She looked trim and efficient.

Callaghan sat down behind the big desk. He began to open the letter from Selby, Raukes & White. He said suddenly:

'Has Kells been in?'

She nodded.

'He was in this morning, and I wish he'd keep his hands to himself!'

She shut the cabinet with a bang.

Callaghan grinned. His eyes lit with an impish humour.

'So he's been pinchin' you again?' he said. 'It's dam' funny, but women always seem to get pinched by the wrong man . . . eh, Effie?'

She flushed, walked into her own office. He heard her typewriter begin to clatter.

Callaghan read the letter:

> Selby, Raukes & White, Solicitors,
> 478 Lincoln's Inn Fields, W.C.
>
> 15th November, 1938.
>
> Dear Mr Callaghan,
>
> We are instructed by Colonel Riverton, who, we regret to say, is now seriously ill, to write you again in the matter of his son Mr Wilfred Eustace Riverton.
>
> It is now eight weeks since you were originally asked to provide our client with comprehensive information about the whereabouts of his son, his mode of living, the names of his immediate associates and, if possible, some definite indication where the large sums of money which Mr Wilfred Riverton has been spending – or losing – have gone.
>
> We hope that you will be able to report within a few days, and in this connection would remind you that your retainer of £100 per week is, in our opinion, a generous one, and should enable you to proceed more quickly in this matter than has been indicated up to the moment of writing.
>
> We are,
> Truly yours,
> pp Selby, Raukes & White,
> T. J. Selby.

Callaghan swore softly. He rang the bell-push on his desk. Effie Thompson, her book open, came in.

'Write to these people, acknowledge receipt of their letter, and tell 'em if they don't like the way I handle my cases they can go to somebody else. Sign it for me.'

He threw the letter across the desk. She picked it up.

'You were supposed to be having dinner with Juanita tonight,' she said primly. 'Are you, or do I telephone as usual?'

'You write that letter an' go home,' he said. 'I'll do the telephonin'.'

She nodded.

'Mrs Riverton came through at six o'clock,' she said. 'She sounded as if she was rather fed-up with Callaghan Investigations. She seemed to think we were all asleep round here. She's in town. She's at the Chartres Hotel. She'll be back there at eleven o'clock tonight. She said I was to tell you to telephone her at eleven-fifteen.'

He nodded.

'Good night, Effie,' she said.

Five minutes later he heard the outer door close behind her. He took off the telephone receiver, dialled a Park number.

'Hallo, Juanita,' he said. 'Sorry I've got to miss that dinner we arranged. I'm busy. . . . Now, it's no dam' good crackin' on . . . that's how it is. . . . Yes . . . I'll call you tomorrow.'

He hung up the receiver. Then he leaned down and opened the bottom desk drawer and took out a quart bottle of rye whisky. He pulled the cork and took a long swig. Then he opened another drawer and took out a Mauser automatic. He looked at the gun for a moment and then threw it back into the drawer.

He got up, switched off the lights, walked through the centre and outer offices, which were still lit, closed and locked the outer door. The electric lift took him to the ground floor. He waited until a cab from the Berkeley Square rank appeared. He hailed it.

'Go to Joe Martinella's place,' he told the driver, 'and step on it.'

Callaghan stood at the end of the long white-washed passage that ran from the street entrance, and looked round Joe Martinella's place. A pall of cigarette smoke hung in the air above the ring. The tiered seats, rising on steps set behind the six rows of ringside seats, were packed with men of every description and a few women. One or two of the women in the ringside seats – ladies who liked occasional, pugilistic slumming – were in evening frocks.

In the ring two reputed lightweights banged each other about in a desultory fashion, punching as if they meant it only when some raucous voice accused one of them of being a sissy. A babel of sound echoed throughout the place, hitting the white-washed walls at each end of the old-time gymnasium, echoing back.

Callaghan walked through the narrow gangway. He put his soft black hat on one of the ringside seats in the second row. Then he walked round the ring, through the opposite gangway, along the passage that ran to the dressing-rooms and turned off into Joe Martinella's private bar.

The room was small. It smelt of stale tobacco smoke, horse oil embrocation and sweat. Leaning up against the bar, talking to Joe and one or two bookmakers and professional gamblers, was Gill Charleston.

Callaghan thought that Charleston looked like a fish out of water. His tall, well-built body, dressed in a well-cut dinner coat, expensive linen and quiet jewellery, added a touch of distinction to a nondescript collection of near-toughs.

Charleston looked up and saw Callaghan. He smiled and his eyes lit up. Callaghan sent him a heavy wink. Then he went outside and stood round the doorway, in the passage, lighting a cigarette. Charleston came out.

'Well, you old horse-thief,' he said pleasantly. 'Who are you after this time? How's business – or are the clients getting wise?'

Callaghan knocked the ash off his cigarette.

'Gill,' he said, 'I'm in a bit of a jam an' I'm goin' to put my cards on the table. Maybe you can help me. It's about Wilfred Riverton – The Mug.'

Charleston nodded.

'Go ahead, Slim,' he said.

'The family's gettin' on my tail,' said Callaghan. 'The old boy – the Colonel – is pretty sick, an' he's worryin'. I'm gettin' a hundred a week to find out where his little boy is throwin' the family money – who the women are, or – if it's not women – who's runnin' the roulette board or whatever is separatin' The Mug from the Riverton cash. I haven't done so well.'

Charleston nodded.

'How've you played it, Slim?' he asked.

'We've been hangin' around all the usual joints,' said Callaghan. 'I reckon we've been into every high-class, low-class and lousy *spieler* in London. We're still dam' cold. Whoever's got little Wilfred on a hook is keepin' it nice an' quiet.'

Charleston lit a cigarette.

'Look, Slim,' he said quietly. 'You know me. I like to keep out of trouble. I do a little gambling and I make a little money. I'd hate to get myself up against something I couldn't handle. See . . . '

Callaghan grinned.

'I see . . . ' he said.

Charleston looked about him, dropped his voice.

'Raffano's the boyo,' he said. 'He's the black in the woodpile. He's as crooked as a couple of corkscrews an' he's getting away with it. He sells 'em everything. He's got a boat somewhere in the country, and I hear there's some sweet money dropped on it. He's got other interests, too. One or two nice little dumps outside London with one or two nice little girls with charming habits to get back the money off the boys who're lucky enough to win. He's half American and half Italian, and he's as tough as they come.'

Callaghan sent a cloud of smoke out of one nostril.

'Thank you, Gill,' he said. 'I'll do somethin' for *you* one day.'

He was silent for a moment. Then:

'Did you know I was interested in The Mug?' he asked.

Charleston laughed.

'Everybody knows it,' he said. 'All the clever boys, anyhow. But I reckon that they've all had a cut at the Riverton Mug, so they weren't letting you in on anything.'

He paused and looked at the glowing end of his cigarette.

'Look, Slim,' he said. 'You said you'd like to do something for me. . . . '

Callaghan looked at him and smiled.

'I'll do anythin' for you, Gill,' he said softly. 'What is it?'

'It's Juanita,' said Charleston. 'I'm crazy about that girl. I've never been so nutty about a woman in my life. I'd give something to get Juanita.'

Callaghan grinned.

'Well, why not, Gill?' he asked pleasantly.

'Why not!' echoed Charleston. 'I like that. You've got your hooks into her so hard that she don't even look at anybody. I've tried everything I know. Flowers and invitations and everything else on the menu, and she's as cold as a snowball. She'd rather be kept waiting by you than have a good time from me. . . . '

'Don't you believe it,' said Callaghan. 'Juanita is a clever girl. She's not really stuck on me . . . she only thinks she is. I think you're the

15

sort of feller she'd really go for.' He thought for a moment. 'I'll have a little talk to her, Gill.' He lit another cigarette. 'And thanks for the tip-off about Raffano.'

'There's your boy,' said Charleston. 'I've heard it said that he's taken the Riverton Mug for thousands, and that he's not through with him yet. But you go easy, Slim . . . Raffano's poison . . . and he's got some tough boys working for him around the place. He takes no chances.'

Callaghan nodded.

'So he's a tough worker?' he said.

'Very tough,' said Charleston. 'Look at this fight tonight – the big fight after this cuddling match is over. You try and get a bet on the black . . . just try . . . you can't do it. Nobody'll look at it. They all had their money on three days ago with any mug who'd take it . . . before Raffano put the fight in the bag. . . . '

Callaghan looked up. There was a gleam in his eye.

'So it's in the bag, Gill?' he said.

Charleston nodded.

'Lonney—the white boy—could murder that black if he wanted to,' he said. 'But he's been told to lie down in the third round, and he'll do it. He'll do it because he'll get a hundred that way and some more easy money in the future. All the wise boys here know that, too.'

Callaghan nodded again.

'An' I suppose The Mug will be backin' Lonney,' he said. 'I suppose that Raffano's given him a sweet price an' The Mug thinks he's on a good thing.'

He leaned against the passage wall.

'Where does this Raffano feller hang out, Gill?' he asked.

Charleston shrugged his shoulders.

'He keeps out of the way most of the time,' he said. 'He's not over here tonight. If things are goin' all right he just doesn't trouble. I believe he lives somewhere in the country.'

Callaghan ran his tongue over his lips.

'I see . . . ' he said quietly. 'He just turns up when things are goin' wrong.' He straightened up. 'Thanks for the information.' He grinned. 'I won't forget about Juanita,' he said. 'I'll see if I can get her sort of interested in you. So long, Gill.'

He walked down the passage. Charleston went back into the bar. Half-way down the passage Callaghan stopped and stood for a minute or two thinking. Then he walked on and turned down the short flight of stone steps that led towards the dressing-rooms.

There was nobody in the short passage. Callaghan walked quietly to the door at the end. He opened it far enough for him to put his head round. On the other side of the room, sitting on the rubbing-down table, was Lonney, the fighter. His hands were already bandaged. He was looking at the floor. Callaghan went in, closed the door behind him.

'Hallo, Lonney,' he said. 'You don't look very happy.'

Lonney looked up.

'I'm all right, Mr Callaghan,' he said. 'How are you?'

'Pretty well,' said Callaghan.

He smiled, showing his white teeth. He reached back to his hip pocket and took out the thin gold cigarette-case that Cynthis Meraulton had given him two years before. He took out a cigarette, lit it. He did everything slowly. He was watching the fighter.

'I have got a £10 note in my hip pocket that says you're going to kill this black,' he said softly.

There was a pause. Then:

'I dunno, Mr Callaghan. I'm not feeling so good. Maybe I've overtrained a bit.'

Callaghan grinned.

'Like hell,' he said.

He blew a smoke ring out of his mouth and watched it. Then he walked over and stood beside Lonney. He dropped his voice.

'You listen to me, Lonney. Don't make any mistakes. I know all about this fight. It's been ready-eyed. It's in the bag. You're getting £100 to lie down in the third round. You're getting it just so's that cheap skunk Raffano can clean up over this fight. I know what I'm talking about. You can't get threepence on that black outside because everybody knows he's going to win.'

Callaghan sat down on the table beside Lonney.

'Lonney,' he said, 'I'm goin' to tell you something. Jake Raffano's finished. He's been doin' pretty well over here, but he's not goin' on doin' well. I'm fed-up with that feller.'

'I'm goin' to make a suggestion to you, Lonney,' he went on, speaking in the same quiet, even voice. 'You get into the ring and kill that dam' black. You know you can do it. You've forgotten more about fightin' than that boy'll ever know. All right, then. You take the

17

winnin' end of the purse, don't you? That's £50. And tomorrow my office sends you another £100. So you get £150 instead of the £100 that Raffano was goin' to pay you, and you win another fight. You put yourself one rung up the ladder to that championship that there is somewhere in the distance. Well, what are you goin' to do?'

Lonney looked at the door. His eyes were scared.

'It ain't so easy,' he said. 'If it was as easy as that it'd be all right. But if I cross him up and win this fight – and I can do it – what's Raffano goin' to do to me? Somebody's goin' to wait for me one night with a razor; and I like my face in one piece.'

Callaghan smiled.

'I wouldn't worry about that, Lonney,' he said. 'I told you I was lookin' after Raffano, didn't I? Well, now, you have it which way you like. You can go out and lie down in the third round and get that £100 he promised you, in which case you're goin' to have me on your neck for the rest of your life. Or you can go out there and kill that black, in which case I'm tellin' you that nobody's goin' to get at you with a razor, now or at any time; and that's a promise.'

Callaghan drew a great gulp of smoke into his lungs and began to cough. He coughed for quite a while. Then he got up.

'Well?' he asked.

The fighter raised his bandaged hands and folded them behind his head. His shoulders and chest muscles stood out.

'All right, Mr Callaghan,' he said. 'I'm winnin' this fight. I can kill that black any day I want to. I'll take the winnin' end of the purse and your £100. I'm standin' on you, but I don't want no trouble.'

Callaghan smiled.

'Good goin', Lonney,' he said. 'You're goin' to be all right.'

He walked over to the door.

'Put him down for ten in the first round,' he said. 'So long, Lonney.'

Callaghan got back to the ringside in time to see the end of the light-weights' performance. Seated in front of him, three men in dinner coats were smoking cigarettes and telling each other dirty stories. Callaghan tapped one of them on the shoulder.

'Is there any bettin' on the big fight?' he said.

They looked at each other. One of them, whose wilted collar seemed to be strangling him, looked at the other two with a grin before turning round.

'Who wants to bet on this fight?' he said. 'That black boy's going to

18

do something to Lonney. Lonney ain't in the same class.'

'You don't say,' said Callaghan. 'Well, I don't think so. I think Lonney's as good as that dam' black any day.'

The three looked at each other again. One of them, from whose hatchet face a pair of slit Asiatic eyes glowed, said:

'Do you want to back Lonney, Callaghan?'

Callaghan thought for a moment.

'Well, why not?' he said eventually. 'If the odds are right.'

He noticed the almost imperceptible flicker of an eyelid between the man with the jowl and the hatchet-faced man.

'The odds would have to be good,' said Callaghan.

'The odds are all right,' said the hatchet-faced man. 'I'll lay three to one as many times as you like.'

Callaghan grinned.

'All right,' he said. 'I'll take £300 to £100 from you, and if I win I want payin' after the fight. Have you got the money?'

The hatchet-faced man looked at Callaghan for a moment. Then he pulled out a pocket-book. It was crammed with tens and twenties.

'What about yours?' he said.

Callaghan felt in his hip pocket. He produced a note-case. He took out ten £10 notes. He handed them to the hatchet-faced man. Then he sat back in his chair.

Five minutes after Lonney had knocked out the black in the second round, Callaghan stood in the passage that led towards the dressing-rooms. He lit a cigarette and leaned up against the wall and waited. He straightened up as the hatchet-faced man came down the stairs and turned into the passage-way. He stepped into the middle of the passage, blocking it.

'I'll take £400 from you,' he said.

He was smiling. The hatchet-faced man felt in his pocket. He produced the fat note-case, handed over the money. Callaghan still stood in the centre of the passage.

The hatchet-faced man began to smile too. His eyes almost disappeared and his mouth became a very thin line.

'You had a nice win, Callaghan,' he said. 'I hope the money's going to do you some good. And you might get out of the way. I want to have a few words with Lonney. Somebody's been teaching that boy to get clever.'

Callaghan did not move.

19

'Listen,' he said, 'you look to me like an intelligent feller. I'm goin' to give you a tip. You go home. You don't want to say anythin' to Lonney. You only *think* you do.'

The hatchet-faced man didn't say anything. Down the steps behind him came the other two – the man with the jowl and the short man. Callaghan raised his voice a trifle.

'You boys ought to have a word with Jake,' he said evenly. 'Somebody ought to tell Raffano that people are gettin' on to the way he's playin' it. I think he's losin' his grip.'

He smiled amiably.

'It was too bad for him Lonney decidin' to win that fight,' he said. 'It looks as if Raffano will have to pay the Riverton Mug some money for once. It'll be a nice experience for him.'

'You think you're good, don't you, Callaghan?' said the man with the jowl. 'All right, you've had a nice win. You wait till we get through with you.'

Callaghan grinned, his teeth showed like a dog's. With a swiftness that was amazing he brought up his right hand and, using it like a sledge-hammer, smashed it into the face of the man with the jowl. He went down like a log. Callaghan was still grinning.

'Now start something,' he said to the other two, 'and in about half an hour I'll have the whole dam' lot of you where I want you. Another thing, maybe this big air-balloon Raffano would like to have a little talk to me. I believe he uses the Parlour Club. I'm goin' there now.'

Nobody said anything. Joe Martinella came down the steps into the passage two at a time. There were beads of sweat on his forehead.

'Joe,' said Callaghan, 'I'm goin' over to the Parlour Club. Maybe I'm goin' to have a little talk with Jake Raffano. I want you to keep an eye on Lonney. Just see he gets home all right. I'm holdin' you responsible, see, Joe? And,' he continued evenly, 'you do it, Joe, otherwise I'll close this place for you tomorrow.'

Martinella ran a finger between his neck and his tight silk collar.

'Don't be silly, Slim,' he said. 'You've got this all wrong. Everything's fine. I'm glad Lonney won.'

Callaghan laughed. The big man with the jowl had got up. He was leaning against the wall. A thin stream of blood had trickled down his chin on to his white shirt front.

'Good night, boys!' said Callaghan.

20

CHAPTER TWO

Friday

Be nice to a lady

It was ten-forty.

Callaghan paid off his cab in Regent Street and walked to the Parlour Club.

The Parlour Club was a nice spot if you liked it. It was operated by a high-yellow black called Kennaway, who had got out of America three jumps ahead of the 'G' men and landed in a motor-boat via France, on a foggy night, near Dymchurch, without any Customs formalities.

It was on a third floor and had originally been decorated in pastel shades by a young gentleman with long hair, indeterminate sex and a *penchant* for cocaine. The pastel shades were faded, but the cocaine was still going strong. You could get anything you liked at the Parlour Club provided you had the money. Sometimes you could get it without the money, but credit facilities were usually extended only to ladies who were prepared to listen to reason.

Raffano was sitting at a little table in an alcove at the far end, away from the bar. He was alone.

Callaghan ordered a double whisky, paid for it, picked it up, walked to the alcove. He sat down.

'How's it goin'?' he asked pleasantly.

Raffano began to laugh softly. He was a short, square-built person with coal-black hair, bushy eyebrows and a pleasant expression. His clothes were perfect and he wore too much jewellery. He was very intelligent.

'Say, Callaghan,' he said when he had finished laughing, 'I reckon I like you. I go for a guy like you. When the boys told me about you gettin' around an' crossin' me up over that fight over at Martinella's I sorta saw the funny side. *I* think you're smart.'

He picked up a little glass of *creme de cacao*, gulped the cream off the top and tossed it down.

'I'm glad to meet you, Callaghan,' he said. 'An' where do we go from here?'

Callaghan drank his whisky.

'Listen, Raffano,' he said. 'Don't make any mistake about me. I'm not out for any trouble an' I'm not goin' to have any trouble . . . '

Raffano raised one eyebrow.

'No?' he said pleasantly.

'No,' said Callaghan. He leaned across the table towards Jake and his face wore that peculiarly frank expression that he invariably used when lying. 'I'm givin' you a good tip, Jake,' he said, 'an' if you're the feller I take you for you're goin' to take it.'

'OK,' said Raffano. 'Well . . . I'm listenin'.'

He bit off the end of a cigar.

Callaghan said: 'You know as well as I do that private detectives can't afford trouble in this country. In America a private investigator means something, but over here he is just nothin' at all. That's why I'm puttin' my cards on the table.'

Raffano said nothing.

'Maybe you know I've been workin' for this Riverton business,' Callaghan went on. 'The old boy, Colonel Riverton, has been payin' me £100 a week to get a line on little Wilfred. Well, they want a report, and up to now we haven't had anythin' to report. The way that feller's covered himself up is nobody's business. I've tried everythin' I know. Two or three weeks ago I got the idea in my head that whoever it was who was takin' the boy for all this money was pretty clever – somebody with a very nice technique and enough money an' pull to keep the boys' and girls' mouths shut.

'Well, tonight I found out. I got a tip that it was you.'

Raffano drew on his cigar.

'Too bad,' he said. 'An' where did you get that, Callaghan?'

'Oh, just around the place,' said Callaghan. 'Now you know why I fixed with Lonney to win that fight. I worked it out that if somebody crossed you up over that fight you'd want to talk to 'em. I knew that if you wanted to talk to 'em you were takin' this thing dam' seriously. Well, you got here pretty quickly, and you got here because you wanted to talk to me, so you are takin' it seriously, and I know the reason why.'

Raffano chewed on his cigar.

'Ain't you the clever guy?' he said, 'An' what's the reason?'

'You're scared,' said Callaghan. 'And why not? This isn't America. I bet you're thinkin' it's about time you pulled out of here. You know we've got a dam' efficient police force in this country an' you can't bribe 'em, Jake.'

22

Jake smiled reminiscently.

'You're tellin' me,' he said.

'Well, now, look at it my way,' said Callaghan. 'I don't know much, but I know enough to report *something* to my clients. I know enough to tell 'em that I've heard that your gamblin' syndicate is responsible for takin' The Mug for all that money he's been gettin' rid of.

'That's all I can say. Mind you, I could make a few guesses. I could guess that before you got at that boy you had to get him pickled in alcohol first – not that that would be difficult – an' you had to use one or two pretty ladies just to get him thinkin' the right way for you to get to work on him. But they're only guesses.'

'Well, supposin' I put this report into the Riverton lawyers – what's the next move? You know what the next move would be.'

Raffano nodded.

'The cops,' he said.

'Correct,' said Callaghan. 'Directly the lawyers get that report they're goin' to get in touch with Scotland Yard, and you've got to remember that this Riverton family are important. Before you knew where you were, Jake, you'd be cleaned up, and the best thing that would happen to you would be that you'd get your marchin' orders. You'd be back in the States in no time, with a feller from Scotland Yard to wave you goodbye.'

He paused for a moment to let his words sink in.

'Maybe you don't want to go back to America just now. They tell me those Federal Agents are pretty good these days.'

Raffano pushed out a mouthful of cigar smoke with his tongue.

'You're a nice accommodatin' bastard,' he said. 'You cross me up on a prize-fight that I'd got in the bag – a business that is goin' to cost me a few thousands – an' then you come around here an' start givin' me advice. If this had been in Chicago in the old days . . .'

Callaghan grinned.

'I know,' he said. 'I'd have been taken for a nice little car ride and found in the local ash-can. But this isn't Chicago, Jake.

'All right. You want to know why I'm bein' so nice to you, takin' such an interest in you and advisin' you. Well, I'll tell you. Supposin' I put that report in to the lawyers. Well, I'm through. My £100 a week stops; and I can use £100 a week. My puttin' that report in will mean that I step out and the police step in.'

Raffano nodded.

'So what?' he asked.

'Well,' said Callaghan – he smiled expansively – 'I thought we could play it this way. Supposin' you lay off The Mug. Let the boy alone for a few weeks. Let me get at him and try and do a little dry-cleanin'. That way I can spin the job out for another couple of months. I can get another £1,000 out of it – and you don't get pinched.'

Raffano stubbed out his cigar. He signalled to the waiter on the other side of the room. He ordered two double whiskies and sodas. When they were brought he pushed one over to Callaghan.

He said: 'I'll think about it.'

Callaghan drank his whisky and soda. He got up.

'You'll think about it all right, Jake,' he said, 'and you'll do it. There's just another little thing – that boy Lonney. He's a nice boy. I think he's goin' to be a good fighter one of these fine days, and I'd just hate to think that any of the boys who were disappointed tonight at losin' their money would try to get at him – you know – rough stuff. If they did I might get the idea that you were behind it. If I got that idea I'd find a way to fix you, Jake.'

Raffano looked up at him and smiled.

'I wouldn't do a thing like that, Callaghan,' he said.

He took another cigar from his waistcoat pocket, offered it to Callaghan.

'No, thanks,' said Callaghan. 'Good night, Jake.'

Callaghan walked to the call-box in Cork Street. He looked at his wrist-watch and rang through to the Chartres Hotel. He told the reception office to tell Mrs Riverton that Mr Callaghan would be coming round at eleven-fifteen. Then he began to walk round to the hotel.

Women were a nuisance, thought Callaghan. They just had to stick their noses into things, and in the process they messed things up. He wondered about Mrs Riverton and concluded eventually that it was normal that the mother of Wilfred Eustace Riverton should be worried about her offspring. He hoped she wouldn't entreat him to get a move on and do something quickly. First of all, he did not like being entreated by old ladies, and secondly, he had his own ideas about the speed with which he worked.

The rest of the time, until he walked through the dignified portals of the Chartres Hotel, was spent in wondering about one or two other things that interested him.

The lift took him up to a room on the first floor. The page-boy opened the door and Callaghan stepped inside. He stood just inside the doorway looking at the woman who was standing by the fireplace. He looked at her for a long time.

'I'm Callaghan,' he said. 'I came here to see Mrs Riverton.'

'I am Mrs Riverton, Mr Callaghan,' she said.

She noticed his raised eyebrow.

'The fact seems to surprise you,' she said coldly.

Callaghan was still looking at her. His lower lip was caught between his teeth. He was thinking to himself that wonders would never cease, wondering how old man Riverton – grey, grizzled and sixty – could have got himself a wife like this.

She was about thirty years of age. Her hair was black as night and her eyes sombre. Her face was oval, with features perfectly carved, and Callaghan, who liked to find words to match a situation, found himself at a loss for an adequate description of the tremulous beauty of her mouth.

Callaghan liked women. He liked women who walked beautifully, who knew how to move, how to dress – women who *were* beautiful. He believed that being a woman was a business, and that if you were in a business you ought to try and be damned good at it.

And he was, in the main, intrigued with a certain evasive something that emanated from the woman he was looking at – some quality of mind or breeding that was worth even more than mere looks.

She was a beauty, he thought . . . a thoroughbred . . . and thoroughbreds meant high breeding and damned bad tempers, and wilfulness, and trouble, generally. You were supposed to handle them cleverly, otherwise they kicked out just because they were feeling like that.

He stood there, his hat in his hand, a half-smile playing about his mouth, looking at her, saying nothing at all.

'Mr Callaghan,' she said. 'You seem surprised at something.'

Callaghan put his hat on a chair. He smiled.

'Life can be funny,' he said. 'I was expectin' to see an old lady. You see, I met the Colonel when we started on this job, an' I thought

25

his wife would be somewhere about his own age. I didn't expect to see anyone like you.'

His eyes moved over her from the top of her hair to the small, exquisite foot that rested on the edge of the fireplace.

'I hope you approve after your lengthy examination,' she said. 'I didn't expect to see you here tonight, because I have an idea that I instructed your office to tell you to telephone me. But perhaps it's as well that you are here. I want to talk to you.'

Callaghan nodded. As cold as ice, he thought, and as tough as hell. He was still smiling.

'Do you mind if I smoke?' he said.

'By all means,' she answered. 'Won't you sit down?'

He walked over and stood on the other side of the fireplace.

'I'll stand up, if you don't mind, Mrs Riverton,' he said, 'at least while you're standin' up – and that's not so much a matter of good manners as psychology.'

His smile broadened.

'*I* always like people to sit down while I stand up when I'm puttin' them through the hoop. It sort of gives them an inferiority complex . . . sometimes,' he added pleasantly.

She flushed. She did not move.

'Mr Callaghan,' she said, 'I do not think I particularly want to discuss inferiority complexes with you. I want to talk to you about my stepson. The fact that he is my stepson will possibly explain to you the surprising fact that I am *not* an old lady. I am Colonel Riverton's second wife. Because I am Wilfred Riverton's stepmother, because I am considerably younger than my husband, and much nearer the age of his son, I feel all the more responsible in this matter.

'My husband is seriously ill. I don't suppose the fact has perturbed *you*, but during the last six or seven weeks he has been rapidly becoming worse. The reason is not far to seek. He is worried to death about Wilfred.

'Up to now I have kept out of this business. First of all because my husband's solicitors are very efficient, and secondly because I believed that any firm of investigators that they employed would also be efficient. During the last six months my stepson has got through over £80,000. I believe that most of that money has been lost by gambling. That, Mr Callaghan, is a large sum of money; and the sort of people who win money like that from a weak, stupid and vacillating young

26

man of twenty-four are not the sort of people to keep the information to themselves. I should have thought it would have taken an investigator two or three weeks at the most to find out who these people are and to give my husband the information he desires so urgently to have.'

Callaghan said nothing. There was silence for a moment. Then: 'Well, Mr Callaghan?'

Callaghan opened his cigarette-case and took out a cigarette. He lit it. He looked at her through the smoke.

'Well, what am I supposed to say, Madame?' he asked. 'Am I supposed to say that you're perfectly right – that we've just been kickin' around London coolin' our heels, taking £100 a week from our clients and doin' nothin' for it? That's the suggestion, isn't it? And do you know what I think of it? I think it's a dam' rude one, and it is just the sort of suggestion that a woman like you would make.

'If I wanted to say anything,' said Callaghan coolly and not unpleasantly, 'I could say a lot. I could say that it looks as if you think you're an expert on private detectives and the gamblin' mob in London. If you know such a lot about it, why didn't you save that £100 a week and get out and do the job yourself, or why didn't Selby, Raukes & Co. do it? Well, *I'll* tell you why.

'First of all, this job isn't easy. There are lots of clever people in London who can do with the £80,000 odd that they've taken off The Mug – because that's what we call him – and if you think those people are goin' shoutin' the odds about it all over London, you're wrong. And there is another thing, and it is rather more important,' – Callaghan paused for a moment in order to let his words sink in – 'You seem to think, Madame,' he said, 'that the only crooks in this game are the ones who have been takin' your beloved stepson for his money. All right. Well, you said he was weak and stupid and vacillating. Well, let me ask you something: How do you know he's not a bit of a crook, too?'

He waited for her reply but she was silent. She stood, one foot on the fender, one hand resting on the mantelpiece. Callaghan thought that she was regarding him with a certain curiosity, as if he were some new sort of animal. Her eyes – he saw now that they were not black but blue – rested steadily on him.

Callaghan said: 'I'm not a fool. When a good firm of lawyers, representin' a good family, comes to me with a case like this, the first question I ask myself is, why they didn't go to Scotland Yard. Well, I know the answer to that one. It is because they're not quite certain as to what's been goin' on. Just as you're not quite certain as to what your precious stepson, Mr Wilfred Eustace Riverton, has been up to.

'Another thing,' he concluded, 'what's £100 a week against £80,000?'

'*I* think £100 a week is a great deal of money, Mr Callaghan,' she said. 'Much too much money to be wasted on an impertinent private detective.'

Callaghan grinned.

'Keep cool, Madame,' he said. 'We shan't get anywhere by losin' our tempers. You know' – his voice was casual – 'I like a woman with a bit of a temper.'

'I'm not interested in the women you like or dislike,' she replied icily. 'And it is just as well that we understand each other.'

She went over to the settee and sat down. Callaghan watched every movement. He thought she moved like an empress. It fascinated him to watch her.

'You already know that my husband is seriously ill, and whilst this worry about Wilfred continues there's little chance of improvement,' she said. 'I don't know whether Mr Selby told you that in just over a year's time, on his twenty-sixth birthday, my stepson inherits £200,000. Until that time his father is trustee and can, more or less, control the money. He can, if he thinks fit, appoint another trustee. He wishes to resign from this trust, to appoint me in his place, because he believes that he may not live for many years, and because he believes that unless there is a decided change in the character and mode of life of his son, Wilfred should not be allowed to handle that money. You understand that, Mr Callaghan?'

Callaghan nodded.

'I do not want this trusteeship,' she went on. 'Stepmothers and stepfathers are invariably unpopular as trustees. I have no particular respect for my stepson. I want nothing to do with his affairs. I would prefer that your investigation is concluded quickly so that whilst my husband is still well enough to deal with this matter he can make his own decisions. In the ordinary course of events the solicitors would have informed you of this, but during the last two days our efforts to get you at your office have been useless. Nobody knew where you were. I hope I have made the position plain. You understand, Mr Callaghan?'

Callaghan nodded. His eyes wandered about the well-appointed room, noted with appreciation the black crêpe-de-chine evening bag with the initials 'T.R.' lying on the chair, the black gauntlet gloves, the luxurious ocelot cloak with its fawn crêpe-de-chine lining. Nice clothes, he thought. He wondered what the initial 'T' stood for.

'I understand, Mrs Riverton,' he said. 'At least I understand what you say. I'm sorry you couldn't get me at my office; but, then, you see, I'm out a lot—' He looked at her and smiled. 'As a matter of fact, I was on a jag,' he said; 'but possibly you wouldn't know what that means.'

He threw his cigarette end into the fire, walked over to the chair on which he had put his hat and picked it up.

'It's very nice to have this little understandin', Mrs Riverton,' he said. His smile became mischievous. 'It probably amuses you and it doesn't do me any harm. There's just one thing I'd like to say. You don't like me very much, and I don't know that I particularly like you, but so far as this case is concerned, while I'm handlin' it I'll take my instructions from Colonel Riverton or his lawyers.'

Her eyes flashed suddenly. Callaghan noted with an internal chuckle that her lips were trembling. She was very angry.

'I see, Mr Callaghan,' she said. 'Then I think I can promise you that tomorrow you will receive instructions either from my husband or his lawyers to retire so far as this investigation is concerned.'

Callaghan shrugged.

'I don't think so, Madame,' he said. 'I think that once again you're wrong, but I'm not goin' to satisfy your curiosity by tellin' you why. I'll tell the lawyers *if* and *when* they tell me to get out, and then you'll find they *won't*, for a very good reason. Selby, Raukes & Company know that I'm the best investigator in London. You can't be expected to know it, because you probably don't know anything.'

He paused with his hand on the door-knob.

'Did you ever read the history of the French Revolution, Madame?' he asked. 'There was a woman in that revolution who looked – I should think – like you. She had everything an' she

29

could afford to be dam' superior. When somebody told her that the common people were starving and hadn't got bread, she said, "Well, why don't they eat cake?" She was what the Americans call dumb.

'Good night, Madame.'

He went out.

Callaghan stood for a minute outside the Chartres Hotel. Then he looked at his wrist-watch and saw it was eleven forty-five. He began to walk slowly down Knightsbridge in the direction of Piccadilly.

He lit another cigarette and began to think systematically. First of all he thought about Mrs Riverton. Callaghan had decided that she was going to be a little difficult. He wondered why Riverton had married a woman who must be nearly thirty years his junior, to say the least of it. For some unknown reason he found his mind bucking away from the things that ought to occupy it and concerning itself solely with the physical attributes of Mrs Riverton.

She certainly had something, thought Callaghan. She stood and moved like a woman ought to stand and move. The poise of her head with its almost imperial angle, the unconscious sensuousness – the ripple – of her body when she had moved over to the side of the fireplace, the sudden and hot intensity of her eyes when she had begun to be angry – all these things intrigued Callaghan.

And she knew about clothes. He remembered the exquisite workmanship of her bag that was on the chair – the bag with the initials in fine diamonds – and the ocelot cloak. . . .

There was something incongruous about that cloak. Callaghan found himself thinking that a woman who had been to a show or visiting, and wearing a frock of the kind that she had worn, would not be wearing an ocelot cloak. It was the sort of cloak she would wear for driving a car. Possibly she had driven up to town and changed for dinner.

He realized, with a grin, that she *had* probably driven up for the sole purpose of telling him just what she thought of him. . . . She was cold as ice. Callaghan conceded that it was right that she should be cold. She was the type that attracted for the excellent reason that she didn't give a damn whether she attracted or not; the sex-appeal was there; it wasn't acquired or aped or even thought about. She had something all right, and she was going to be very difficult. She was the type of woman who'd throw a spanner into the works and not give a hoot in hell. Well . . . why not? The best women were always like that.

She had sense, too. She was going to keep her eye on the Riverton money all right.

Callaghan pulled his brain back to the more mundane businesses of life and Jake Raffano. He wondered whether Jake was going to fall for the line of talk that he had handed out to him at the Parlour Club. Callaghan realized that if Jake analysed the talk it would sound a bit thin. It ought to be as plain as daylight that the one thing that Callaghan wouldn't do would be to report on the case at the moment – when he had practically nothing to report except the bare fact that he had a strong suspicion that Jake was the person who had separated The Mug from the eighty thousand and introduced him to the high-spots, the pretty ladies, the drink and the rest of it.

But maybe he had thrown a scare into Jake – and that was all that mattered. If Jake got scared and got out, Callaghan thought he could handle the rest of the business on his own lines and in his own time.

It was dam' funny being a detective, he thought. Cases were always taking a turn. There wasn't such a thing as a straight case with a straight, cut-and-dried line to it and a straight solution. People who wrote detective stories always knew just what their people were going to do. They established characteristics, and their characters acted up to them. But life was never like that. People never did what you thought they were going to do. Something turned up, and they got frightened or tried to be tough; they lost their nerve when they came to the dangerous curves in the road and took them either too fast or too slow.

He threw his cigarette stub into the gutter and lit another. He turned into Berkeley Square, and in a minute or two walked into the side entrance to his apartment building. Wilkie, the night porter, a youth of nineteen with a strong admiration for Callaghan, came out of his little glass office.

'Your office telephone's been going, Mr Callaghan,' he said. 'I switched it down here last time. It was Mr Charleston. He wants you to give him a ring when you come in.'

Callaghan nodded and went into the lift. He went straight up to his own apartment on the fifth floor. He threw his hat on the bed and rang a Mayfair number.

Charleston came on the line.

'Watch your step, Slim,' he said. 'I've been listening a lot tonight, and Raffano hates your guts. For God's sake go easy, Slim. His boys are damned dangerous. . . . '

'That's very nice of you, Gill,' said Callaghan. 'I had a little talk with Jake at the Parlour tonight. He seemed all right. He took things very nicely.'

'Like hell,' said Charleston grimly. 'I've told you he'd twist his own mother on her deathbed, haven't I?'

Callaghan laughed.

'What're you tryin' to tell me?' he asked.

Charleston hesitated for a moment.

'I wouldn't go out too late at night for a bit, if I were you,' he said. 'You remember that fellow they found up against the Park railings with his face slashed to ribbons five weeks ago . . . you remember that boyo they found down in Epping Forest . . . '

Callaghan grinned into the telephone. He opened his cigarette-case with one hand and lit a new cigarette from the stub of the old one.

'That was Jake, that was . . . ' he said softly. 'Anything else, Gill?'

'Yes,' said Charleston. His voice softened. 'About Juanita . . . I think it's pretty swell of you to try and put me in with her. I'm nuts about her, Slim, an' I know she's damned keen on you. I wish to hell I knew what it is you've got that makes women go for you like they do . . . and you don't even try. . . . '

'No,' said Callaghan. 'You never do any good if you try. Good night, Gill . . . you leave Juanita to me.'

He hung up.

He went into the bathroom and poured some eau-de-Cologne into his hands. He sluiced his face with the spirit and fanned it with a towel. Then he rubbed eau-de-Cologne into his hair until his scalp tingled.

He put on an overcoat and his hat and went down in the lift. He walked out of the side entrance, turned the corner, made for Berkeley Square. He had walked ten paces when he spun round, waited.

Coming towards him was the figure of a young man in evening tails. He wore no hat and his fair hair was rumpled. One long lock hung over his forehead. His face was flushed. As he came under the street lamp-light, Callaghan noticed that the pupils of his eyes were contracted to pin-points and that he was near-drunk.

'An' how is Mr Riverton?' asked Callaghan pleasantly.

The Mug seized the iron railings with one hand. He stood there swaying.

'Listen, Mr bloody-clever-Callaghan,' he said in a thin, uncertain voice. 'Just do me a favour, will you? Mind your own damned business and keep that long, ugly nose of yours out of my affairs . . . otherwise . . . '

'Otherwise nothin',' said Callaghan evenly.

He took a loose cigarette out of his pocket and lit it.

'So they got you on dope now, have they?' he said, smiling. 'Cocaine . . . I'll bet . . . an' in a few weeks you'll be takin' morphine to get over the hangovers.'

He drew in a lungful of smoke and sent it out through his nostrils slowly.

'Why don't you go home an' get some sleep, Mug?' he said civilly. 'Hasn't somebody told you about your father? He's dam' ill . . . but I suppose that wouldn't bother you. . . . An' your stepmother's worryin' about you, too . . . an' you don't deserve a stepmother like the one you've got. . . . '

The Mug let go of the railings. He moved towards Callaghan.

'I've warned you,' he said. 'I've told you . . . damn you. . . . You mind your own business an' tell that clever stepmother of mine to mind hers. You . . . '

He called Callaghan by a very rude name, then, in a sudden surge of temper, lurched towards him, his fist raised to strike.

A cab came round the corner. Callaghan put out one hand and caught The Mug's fist. With the other he signalled the cab.

The driver opened the door. Callaghan shifted his grip from the fist to the shoulder, propelled The Mug towards the cab, pushed him into it like a sack of coal, slammed the door.

'Take that to wherever he wants to go,' he said to the driver. He gave the man a pound note. 'An' you can keep the change.'

The cab drove off. As it went Callaghan noted the number, stood under the lamp writing it down in a little black leather book.

Then he began to walk towards Bond Street.

CHAPTER THREE

Friday

The ticket

Callaghan, standing on the low, gilt and red balcony that ran round three sides of the Yellow Lamp, felt in his jacket pocket for a loose cigarette, lit it, stood watching the dancers. He was busy coughing when Perruqui, sauve, plump and immaculate, came over to him.

'Too mooch smoke, Meester Callaghan,' he said. 'You still got the smoker's t'roat, eh?'

Callaghan nodded.

'One of these days I'm goin' to give up smokin',' he said. 'How's Juanita?'

'She's fine,' said Perruqui. 'She make a beeg success. She's got a new number tonight. And she's been asking for you, Meester Callaghan.'

Callaghan walked round the balcony, through the pass-door on the right, along a passage. He tapped on a door. Somebody said, 'Come in.' He went into the dressing-room.

Juanita, already dressed for her number, was powdering her face. She turned as he came in, threw the powder-puff on to her make-up table. She was of middle height, well-curved, supple, full of vitality – a brunette with big lustrous eyes that could promise a lot. Her figure was perfect.

Juanita, who was supposed to be Spanish, had been born in Chicago. Callaghan thought she was a little slow and not very clever about men.

She liked Callaghan. She liked him because he didn't care whether she did or not, and because she could not fathom what went on behind his casual eyes. She was used to men who fell quickly; could not understand one who did not.

Callaghan stood just inside the door looking at her. He was wondering just how far he could use Juanita . . . just how much she would stand for without becoming too curious.

'So you finally got here!' she said.

She put her head on one side and looked at him half seriously.

'Are you a heel or are you?' she said. 'Why do I waste my time on you?'

Callaghan began to grin. She sat down on the stool, crossed her legs and lit a cigarette.

'You've had four dates with me this week, Sherlock,' she said, 'an' you've stood me up each time. What's the matter with you? Am I losin' my appeal?'

'It's business,' he said. 'I've got a tough case. Has anybody ever told you that you've got a perfect figure, Juanita? I think it's amazin'.'

'Like hell you do,' she said. 'You're so interested in my figure that you don't care whether you cuddle it or take the fast train for Saskatoon.'

He sat down.

'I'm putting on a new number tonight, Slim,' she went on. 'A Mexican solo dance. Will you tell me what you think of it?'

He nodded.

'That's what I came round for,' He lied easily, 'I've been thinkin' about you, Juanita. . . . '

'Oh, yeah . . . ' she said. 'An' I've been thinkin' about you, Mister Callaghan. You'd better make up your mind what you're goin' to do about this baby while there's still time. . . . '

She looked at him out of the corners of her eyes. She saw he was still smiling.

'You mean Charleston?' he said. 'Well, he's a good feller, an' you could do worse. You're too nice a girl for this lousy racket. You've got some money an' so has he. Why don't you get out of it an' marry Gill?'

She looked at him with her red mouth open. She bit her lip.

'Well . . . for crying out loud!' she said. 'So I'm getting the air, am I? So I've been wasting my time an' sex-appeal on a human iceberg? Have you got your nerve! Another thing . . . have you forgotten last Tuesday night? What about last Tuesday?'

Callaghan grinned wickedly.

'That was last Tuesday, that was,' he said. 'Today's Friday.'

He lit a cigarette.

'I was serious about Charleston,' he went on. 'He's nutty about you, Juanita.'

'Well, that's something,' she said. 'Gill's all right, except I've never thought about him like that. Still,' – she threw a sharp look at Callaghan – 'it might bear thinking about.'

Callaghan said: 'He looks good in evenin' clothes, an' he's got some money, an' he opens doors for women an' all that sort of thing.'

'You don't say,' said Juanita. 'Well . . . a hall-porter opens doors, too, but where does that get him? I like Gill. He's a swell guy and he's got some dough . . . but for how long? I know these gamblers. Even if they're as straight as he is, they're like their money — here today and gone tomorrow—' She shot a quick sideways look at him. 'I'd just as soon think of marrying a private detective,' she said. 'Maybe I'd like that better.'

Callaghan grinned.

'They're worse than gamblers,' he said.

She came over to him.

'You're telling me,' she said. 'Don't I know?'

She put one hand under his chin, bent down and kissed him on the mouth.

'I don't know what it is about you,' she said, 'but you've got *something*, you so-and-so! Now you get out of here and tell me what you think of the new number. I'll be on in a few minutes. That'll give you time to have a drink and get in the right frame of mind. And listen, you come round and see me afterwards. I want to talk to you.'

Callaghan got up.

'All right,' he said. 'I'll be back.'

He went back to the balcony. The band had stopped playing. Waiters were serving food. Across on the other side of the dance floor Callaghan saw what he was looking for. At a table in the corner sat a burly man, with a round face, and a dinner jacket that was a little too small for him. The woman with him was well dressed, weary, and in an odd way rather fascinating.

He walked slowly round the balcony and approached the table. He said:

'Do you mind if I sit here?'

The burly man looked surprised. His eyes wandered round the room, took in half a dozen empty tables.

'If you *have* to sit here, all right,' he said. 'But there're lots of vacant tables.'

'I know,' said Callaghan, 'but I want to sit at this one.'

He looked at the woman, sat down, stubbed out his cigarette end, lit a fresh one. Then he said to her:

'What about a little drink, sweet?'

The burly man smiled unpleasantly.

'We've got drinks, thank you,' he said slowly.

Callaghan grinned.

'You have,' he said, 'but hers is finished. What do you say, honey?' He looked at her wickedly. She shot up her chin.

The burly man began to grin ominously.

'Say, listen, punk,' he said. 'Are you tryin' to start somethin'? You take a tip an' get outa here while the goin's good.'

Callaghan got up.

'Who do you think you're talkin' to?' he said.

He leaned over the table and smacked the burly man across the face with his open hand. There was an ominous pause. People in the vicinity were looking round, waiting for the fun to start. The women spoke:

'You get me out of here,' she said. 'I'm not getting mixed up in any free fights.'

As the big man began to get up the lights went out. A spot lime shone on the band platform. Perruqui appeared.

'Ladees an' gentlemen,' he said, 'I have a lot of pleasure to present to you the one and onlee Senorita Juanita – fresh from her triumphs in New York – in a new dance creation . . . Mexican Fandango. . . . '

The band went into a rumba.

The big man looked at Callaghan across the table.

'So you're looking for a little trouble,' he said. 'All right, you can have it. I'm going to put this lady in a cab, then I'll deal with you . . . that is—' he grinned – 'if you're not quite yeller.'

Callaghan sent some cigarette smoke out of one nostril.

'That suits me,' he said.

They began to walk out. The woman first, then the burly man, then Callaghan. Juanita made her entrance to a house that was busily engaged in looking over its shoulder at the departure . . . slightly disappointed that there hadn't been more trouble. Juanita, who had stopped the band with a gesture, stood in the middle of the dance floor looking at Callaghan with eyes that were more expressive than any language. He threw her an apologetic grin over his shoulder. As he passed through the door curtains he heard the orchestra begin the *ad lib* again.

The big man was waiting in the cloakroom.

'There's a Mews around the corner,' he said.

'I'll fix you . . . you . . . !'

Callaghan didn't say anything. They walked out into the quiet street, Callaghan a little way behind. The woman was talking fast under her breath, complaining. Just up the street a few yards away was a cab rank. The burly man gave an instruction to the driver and opened the door of a cab. As he did so Callaghan jumped forward, swung a badly aimed blow at his back, cannoned into the woman, sent her handbag flying on to the pavement.

The big man moved quickly for a man of his size. He turned, side-stepped, grabbed Callaghan's collar with his left hand, brought a short hook to his stomach, knocked him against the railings.

'You lousy punk!' he said.

Callaghan leaned up against the railings gasping for breath. The big man began to pick up the things that had fallen out of the handbag. When this was done he handed it to the woman.

She was leaning against the open door of the cab. Callaghan saw that her frock was well-cut, that she looked tired to death.

'I hope you ain't gonna hold this against me, honey,' the burly man said plaintively. 'Can I help it if some rat starts insultin' you? But don't worry, I'll fix him. You go on home . . . I'll be seein' you . . . '

The cab drove off. The burly man walked over to Callaghan who was still standing against the railings. He took him by the right arm and yanked him upright.

'So you want to get funny, hey?' he growled. 'Well – walk around the corner an' we'll start playin'. This way, feller.'

He dragged Callaghan along the street, into the Mews. Round the corner, in the darkness, he loosed Callaghan's arm. Callaghan said:

'Dam' you, Monty, do you have to hit so hard?'

He felt for his cigarette-case.

'Did you get anything?' he said.

Kells grunted.

'I don't know. I grabbed off every visitin' card and bit of paper and that there was in the bag. But she was watchin' me, I didn't get much.'

Callaghan said:

'Let's go and look at what you've got.'

They walked through the Mews, turned down into Conduit Street, began to walk back towards the office.

Callaghan sat at his desk and went through the bits and pieces that Kells had found in Azelda's handbag. There were two or three bills from West-End shops, a receipt, an advertisement for a new system of hair-waving, some unused notepaper and the return half of a first-class railway ticket.

He opened the bottom drawer of the desk and took out the whisky bottle. He took a drink and passed it to Kells.

Callaghan said:

'Tell me about Azelda, Monty.'

Kells eased his large bulk back in the chair. He opened the box on the desk, helped himself to a cigarette and lit it.

'It was just one of those lucky things,' he said. 'This mornin' I was playin' around with a floosie who hangs about Willie's Bar off Regent Street. Somebody told me she might know somethin'. I bought her a cocktail or two an' we got talkin'. Pretty soon in comes Azelda an' buys herself a drink. She sits there on a high stool an' I say to my girl friend that she looks to me like a tasty dish an' that I have seen worse figures in my time.

'OK. Well this don't go over so well, an' the baby starts talkin' about Azelda. She tells me a lot of stuff an' then she lets out that she has seen Azelda gettin' around with some guy who is young an' nutty an' with too much dough. My ears start flappin' because I reckon this guy is the Riverton Mug all right.

'I do a bit of thinkin' and then I take the girl friend for a walk, give her the air an' get back to Willie's. Azelda is still there. She is still all on her own. I go up to her an' tell her that I've met her some place before an' she don't seem to want to argue about it. So I do my stuff an' we have an early lunch an' I arrange to meet her tonight an' take her along to Perruqui's place. I think that maybe when she has had a little drink she will start talkin'.'

Kells reached for the bottle.

'There won't be anything else from Azelda after that little act you put on tonight, Slim,' he said.

Callaghan nodded. Then he picked up the return half ticket that had been in Azelda's handbag. It was a first-class return half from Malindon. He got up, went into the outer office. When he came back he said:

'You listen to me, Monty. You've got to work fast and I don't want any mistakes.'

He blew a stream of smoke out of one nostril.

'I had a tip-off tonight,' he went on. 'I heard that Raffano has got a gamblin' boat somewhere in the country. Well, it sounds like sense to me. If he's been usin' a boat that explains why we've never been able to get a line on where he's been operatin'.'

He threw the return half ticket on the desk.

'That's a return half ticket from Malindon,' he said. 'It's dated today. I just had a look an' I see that Malindon is the station for Southing Village an' Southing Village is where the Riverton Manor House is. See . . . ?'

Kells whistled softly.

'What's on your mind, Slim?' he asked.

'Nothin' much,' said Callaghan. 'But it looks to me as if Azelda might have gone down to Malindon today after she left you. Maybe Azelda was wise to you this morning. Maybe she knows you work for me an' she played you along, made a date to meet you again tonight an' then went down on the train to tell Raffano how the cat was jumpin'.'

He took a long draw on his cigarette and began to cough. After a minute he said:

'She didn't use the return half of the ticket because somebody brought her back to town by car. Maybe that was Raffano.'

Kells grunted.

'If she's one of the Raffano dames she'll know who you are,' he said. 'She'll be wise to that act we put on tonight. We'll never get a goddam thing out of her.'

'That's not worryin' me, Monty,' said Callaghan. 'Now you look at this.'

He opened a drawer and took out an AA map. He laid it flat on the desk.

'Here's Malindon an' here's Southing Village an' here's Pinmill,' he went on. 'An' Pinmill's a great place for boats. It would be a joke if Raffano had that boat of his down there somewhere, because it's the sort of place he would have it. Harwich an' the open sea are right on his doorstep an' he can make a getaway any time he likes.'

'I got it,' said Kells.

'We've got to get a move on,' said Callaghan. 'The Riverton family are beginnin' to get excited about that Mug. I had the stepmother on my neck tonight. She's a woman who could make a whole lot of trouble if she felt like it. . . . '

Kells grinned.

'Say, Slim, did I ever tell you that the reason I got out of the States was that my old man wanted to get me a stepmother? Yeah – he wanted to marry some dame with nifty curves who was singing in a night club. When it looked like I might have to call that baby Momma I just packed my grip an' scrammed. Stepmothers can be hell!'

'You go home an' get some sleep,' said Callaghan. 'An' you get away tomorrow mornin' at six o'clock. Hire a car. Get down to Malindon, put up the car and get round the district. Take in all the places where there are moorings in quiet spots. Get round Falleton, Laything and all round there. Try an' find a boat that's big enough for play to go on aboard, a boat that's been about for five or six months, that's owned by an American. An' work fast, Monty.'

'You're the boss,' said Kells.

He got up. 'I'll call through if I get anything.' He picked up his hat. 'So long, Slim,' he said.

Callaghan sat looking at the return half ticket on the desk. He began to piece together one or two incongruities, little straws that might show the way the wind was blowing. First of all, why hadn't Charleston tipped him off about Raffano before? Callaghan had had his eye on Raffano for weeks. Charleston must have known about him for months. Charleston was a professional gambler and must have known about Jake.

He thought he knew the answer to that one. Charleston was no fool. When Callaghan brought up the subject of The Mug he had guessed that somebody was going to start some fireworks and he knew that when the fireworks began Jake would probably get out. He had volunteered his information just at the right moment. Jake out of the country meant there would be no trouble, and Callaghan would be grateful and might pull a string or two with Juanita. . . .

Callaghan thought that Raffano was going to get out while everything was nice and quiet. Why not? Having got the £80,000 odd out of The Mug he could afford to think of quitting before the game got too hot.

The second interesting point was the obvious annoyance of The Mug at having his recent career investigated. Callaghan thought back to the scene off Berkeley Square. He took a piece of notepaper from his desk and wrote on it the number of the taxicab into which he had bundled The Mug. Underneath he wrote:

Dear Effie,

Get Findon to walk round to the Berkeley Square rank, find this taxicab and ask the driver where he delivered young Riverton last night. If he comes across give him £1.

He signed the note and put it in the right hand drawer of Effie's desk, into which she looked for possible instructions first thing each morning.

Then he began to think about Azelda Dixon. If she was one of Raffano's women, it was a certainty that she would know that Kells was on Callaghan's staff. It was more than probable that she had gone down to the country to tell Raffano. Because, thought Callaghan, it was not at all improbable that Raffano's boat was somewhere in the Malindon district. Maybe it was because the boat had been there in the first place that Raffano had heard of The Mug.

Callaghan put the ticket in his desk drawer, and lit another cigarette. Then he reached for the telephone. He dialled the number of the Yellow Lamp, asked for Perruqui.

'Perruqui,' he said, 'this is Callaghan. I want to have a little talk with you – a private talk. I'm comin' round now. I'll be with you in five minutes.'

Perruqui, seated behind a walnut desk in the corner of his beige and black office, smiled expansively at Callaghan.

'At your serveece,' he said.

Callaghan looked at the tiny pin-point of fire made by the diamond stud in Perruqui's shirt-front.

He said: 'I wanted to say I was sorry about that little upset I caused on the floor tonight. I hope it didn't do any harm.'

Perruqui shrugged.

'I don't like any troubles round here you know, Meester Callaghan,' he said. 'But you are a good client—' he shrugged expressively – 'it doesn't matter one leetle bit. It is all right,' he concluded.

'That's fine,' said Callaghan. 'And it wasn't any trouble really, Perruqui. It was an act I put on. The man was an operative of mine – Monty Kells. The woman's name was Azelda Dixon. Do you know Azelda?'

Perruqui looked blank.

'I don't know nozzin' at all,' he said. 'I don't know nozzing.'

Callaghan grinned.

'Don't tell dam' lies, Perruqui,' he said.

He got up, walked across to the desk, stood looking down at the Italian.

'The fact is,' he said, 'I met young Riverton tonight. You know I've been chasin' round after him tryin' to find out what he's at. You know it because half the crowd here know it, and what you *don't* know about what goes on in this district could be stuck under a postage stamp and lost.'

Perruqui shrugged again. His smile had vanished.

'When I was talkin' to The Mug tonight,' said Callaghan, 'I got my first good look at him. Somebody's feedin' that boy dope. Tonight, when I had a look at Azelda I thought that she looked as if she knew what cocaine smelt like too. I wondered if Azelda was the woman who put young Riverton on the stuff. Maybe *you* know?'

'I've tol' you, Meester Callaghan, I don't know nozzin'.'

Callaghan did not move. He stood quite still, his lips smiling pleasantly. But his eyes were not smiling. They rested steadily on Perruqui's face.

'That's all right, Perruqui,' he said. 'Maybe you don't know anythin', and maybe you can start findin' out somethin', because *I* do know somethin'.'

He reached for his cigarette-case.

'Last year,' he said evenly, 'some people gave me a job to try to find out where that Lallen girl got to. You remember her, Perruqui? That good-lookin' blonde girl, the one who used to come here with the saxophonist from the Hop Club band an' pay the bills? Well, we found out where she went to, but the information wasn't very much good to her people by the time we handed it over. The Lallen girl was too far gone. Maybe she's got as far as Buenos Aires by now.'

He stopped talking. Two little beads of sweat had appeared on Perruqui's forehead.

'The one interestin' point in the job,' Callaghan went on, 'was the number of the car that took that girl down to the coast the night she disappeared.' He grinned. 'Monty Kells got that number,' he said, 'and he traced the car. It was that big green one of yours, Perruqui.'

He put the cigarette which he had been holding in his fingers into his mouth, lit it.

'Now you tell me about Azelda,' he said.

Perruqui kept his heavy lidded eyes on the desk before him. It was a full minute before he spoke. Then:

'I don't know much about her, Meester Callaghan,' he said. 'Not much. I think she uses a leetle dope. I think she gets around with some of Mr Raffano's friends. I don' know any more.'

'Just think a bit, Perruqui,' said Callaghan. 'See if you can't think up a little more. Where does she get the dope?'

Perruqui still looked at the desk.

'There is a leetle night bar in Soho,' he said. His voice was low and truculent. 'The Privateer.'

'I know!' said Callaghan. 'Who's runnin' that place now?'

'They call him Henny The Boyo,' Perruqui answered.

Callaghan picked up his hat. 'What time does Henny The Boyo close up?' he asked.

Perruqui got up. 'He's open till about four, Meester Callaghan,' he said.

Callaghan walked to the door. Perruqui began to talk.

'Meester Callaghan . . . '

Callaghan grinned.

'It's all right, Perruqui,' he said. 'I'll forget about the number of that car of yours. Good night.'

Callaghan walked through the pass-door on to the club floor. The Yellow Lamp was nearly empty and only two or three tired couples sat at the gilt tables. In the hall he met Charleston on his way to the cloakroom. Charleston smiled.

'Hallo, Slim,' he said. 'Are you a fast worker! I had supper with Juanita tonight. You weren't exactly popular. She says you killed her dance!'

Callaghan grinned. He said:

'There was a little trouble while her dance was on. I don't think she likes me as much as she did.'

He began to move towards the entrance. Then he said:

'Listen, Gill, you work hard on Juanita. I believe she thinks a lot of you, an' she's fed up with the dancin' game. I think she'd like to get married an' if you find yourself a new business I think she'd do it. Good night, Gill.'

He went out into the street. He walked until he met a crawling taxicab. He stopped it, told the driver to take him to Soho.

The Privateer Bar was one of those places that changed hands about every three or four months. When the police decided that they would like to interview the proprietor they had to do plenty of legwork, and when they eventually got him – as they always do – he never knew anything about 'it'. It was the manager's fault anyway, and he, the boss, had been in Paris the night 'it' happened and so on. . . .

There was one bar on the ground floor and one down a flight of narrow stairs in the basement. At the end of the basement-bar a tired young man used to play the piano and think about the days when he wasn't feeling quite so old.

The place was usually crowded upstairs and not so full downstairs. Every now and then one of the CID men from Tottenham Court Road used to take a look round, and the occupants of the downstairs coffee bar would look at each other and wonder who the 'blue-inks' were after this time. . . .

It was always full of smoke and smelt of stale coffee and very often of that peculiar acrid stink that comes from Marihuana cigarettes that only cost sixpence and make things so much easier for half an hour.

Callaghan bought himself a cup of coffee in the upstairs room, drank it slowly and smoked a cigarette. When he looked at his watch he saw it was half-past two. He realized suddenly that he was tired out.

He got up and went down the stairs. At the bottom he stood still and began to grin. At the other end of the room, past the piano on its little platform, was three steps leading to a door. Azelda Dixon was just coming down the steps.

There were only three men in the room. They were seated, with their heads very close together, at a table near the piano.

Azelda was looking at the floor as she walked towards the stairs. She did not see Callaghan until she was almost on him.

'Hallo – Azelda,' he said quietly.

She looked at him. Her face was very white, very strained, and there were dark shadows about her eyes. Azelda had been good-looking once, Callaghan thought. And she still had something. She was well-shaped and in an odd way she looked like a lady.

'What do *you* want?' she asked shortly.

'Nothin' at all,' said Callaghan evenly. 'How's Henny The Boyo?'

Her lips tightened. For a moment Callaghan thought she was going to scream with temper.

'You go to hell!' she said. 'And stay there. And you look out, Mr Callaghan.'

'All right, Azelda,' said Callaghan pleasantly. 'I'll look out, and who do I have to look out for?'

'You'll see,' she said hoarsely. She pushed past him. 'I've got one or two friends – still—'

'I'm glad,' he said. 'Well, Azelda – when you want another one you come round an' see me. The Berkeley Square cab rank'll tell you where my office is. Good night. . . . '

She began to walk up the stairs. He heard her high heels tapping towards the street entrance upstairs.

He began to walk towards the door that led to Henny The Boyo's office, then he changed his mind, sat down, smoked another cigarette. After ten minutes he got up, walked upstairs and out into the quiet street.

Twenty yards down the street he turned into the dark passage that twisted through into the Tottenham Court Road – near the cab rank. Half-way down the passage he stopped to light another cigarette. He took some time about it because, through the flame of his lighter he could see the shadow that lay across the passage at the end, where the street lamp stood just round the corner.

Callaghan put his hands in his overcoat pockets and began to walk along, keeping close to the wall. He put his feet firmly on the ground so that his footsteps were quite audible, and he walked with a careful speed.

He came to the end of the passage, his eyes on the shadow. Just before he reached it it moved slightly.

Callaghan put his foot forward for the next step. But it did not reach the ground. He sidestepped, jumped back a pace, and then, as the shadow lurched forward, his right foot shot out, thigh high.

His foot caught the man who had been waiting round the corner in the stomach with the full force of the kick. The man gave a funny sort of half-yelp and fell flat on his face. He lay there squirming for a moment before he passed out.

Callaghan looked to see if there were any more of them. Then he turned the man over with his foot. Then he bent down and dragged the inert body of the tough under the lamp-light and took a long look at the face. He wanted to remember it.

Then he looked at the man's hands. The left one was bare, but on

46

the right there was a glove. It was a thick brown kid glove and fixed across the front of it, edge upwards, were three safety razor blades.

Callaghan felt for his cigarette-case. He took out a cigarette and lit it.

Then he began to walk towards the Tottenham Court Road cab rank.

CHAPTER FOUR

Saturday

Goodbye Jake!

The mechanical bells in the Chinese clock on the mantelpiece struck four.

Callaghan woke up. He yawned at the ceiling, then reached out for the telephone.

'I'll be down in fifteen minutes, Effie,' he said. 'Get some tea ready.'

He got out of bed and stretched, went into the bathroom, took a shower and rubbed eau-de-Cologne into his hair. Then he dressed, took a short drink of neat whisky, lit a cigarette, indulged in a spell of coughing and went down to the office.

Effie Thompson came in from the outer room with a cup of tea.

'Findon's been round to the cab rank,' she said. 'He found the taxi-driver. The driver said that young Riverton stopped the cab at the Piccadilly end of Down Street. He walked up Down Street. The driver couldn't see where he went. Findon gave him the pound. I've charged it to the Riverton expense account.'

Callaghan nodded. He began to drink his tea. Out of the corner of his eye he was watching Effie. She had a new coat and skirt on and a white silk shirt-blouse. Callaghan thought that Effie had a nice line to her hips. . . . He began to think about Mrs Riverton's figure – it was a dam' shame that a woman with a figure like that should be wasted on a sick sixty-year old husband and a stepson who was a dope. . . .

Effie went on:

'Mrs Riverton rang through at three o'clock from Southing. She wants to speak to you. She says it's urgent. I said you'd get her on the phone when you came into the office – that you were out. Wilkie told me you were asleep. I wouldn't disturb you.'

'Quite right, Effie,' said Callaghan. 'You'd better get her on the phone now.'

She was half-way across the office when he changed his mind.

'Don't bother,' he said. 'I'll do it another way.'

He drank his tea, smoked a cigarette. He sat there in the darkening office thinking. After a while he picked up the telephone, dialled Gill Charleston's number. The operator at Linley House told him that Mr

Charleston was out and would not be back till later. Callaghan waited a moment, then he rang through to Juanita. The maid said she wasn't in. Callaghan grinned.

'Mr Charleston called for her, didn't he?' he asked.

'Yes, sir,' said the maid, 'and she said that if you came through she'd go straight back to the Yellow Lamp tonight.'

'Thanks,' said Callaghan.

He hung up.

When he looked at his watch it was twenty to five. He rang the bell on his desk.

'I'm goin' down to the Manor House,' he said. 'Wait for ten minutes, then ring through. Tell Mrs Riverton I haven't been back to the office, but I came through on the phone, that I told you to tell her I was goin' down to see her, that I'd be there between six and half-past.'

He got up, walked out of the office. Effie heard the door of the outer office slam. She raised her eyebrows and shrugged. Then she sat down by the telephone.

It was twenty past six when Callaghan stopped his car before the portals of the Manor House. It was raining hard. As he walked towards the pillared entrance he looked over his shoulder at the bare trees that lined the long carriage-drive that led from the gates to the house. A nice place in the summer, he thought.

He rang the bell.

Mrs Riverton was standing by the drawing-room fireplace when he was shown in. Callaghan's quick eyes swept round the room, taking in the fine furniture, the tapestries, the atmosphere generally.

He saw that she was tired. There were blue shadows under her eyes, and there was no vestige of even a formal smile of welcome. He stood quite still in the middle of the polished floor, his hands hanging down by his sides looking at her, thinking that there was the same cold antagonism showing in her eyes. He wondered if anything would remove it; just what the formula was that would soften Mrs Riverton. Perhaps there wasn't a formula. Perhaps she was just one of those born-cold women who didn't react to anything at all.

Callaghan thought that it would be pretty good to get a smile out of her. She was the sort of woman who ought to smile a lot.

His eyes moved over the folds of her black frock down to the small feet in the superbly cut shoes. She had something all right.

They stood looking at each other. Each perfectly poised and like a pair of fencers waiting for an opening.

Callaghan thought: She hates my guts. She'd throw me out any minute she could do it. She'd have done it before, but I'll bet old Selby told her that it wouldn't be a good thing to do. She broke the silence:

'You're a surprising person, Mr Callaghan,' she said. 'The last time I tried to get you on the telephone, nothing happened for two days. Now, within a few hours you appear after a long and quite unnecessary drive into the country when the telephone would have done just as well. Won't you sit down?'

Callaghan sat down.

'I didn't think the telephone would have done as well, Mrs Riverton,' he said. 'I wanted to see you—' he grinned – 'I get a certain amount of pleasure from lookin' at you,' he said casually, 'an' although I know *that* wouldn't interest you, there are one or two things I wanted to tell you – things I thought were better not said on the telephone. But maybe you'd like to talk first?'

She gave a little shrug. Callaghan knew that she was annoyed because he had said that he got pleasure from looking at her. She considered the remark personal and unnecessary. She resented it. Well that was better than nothing. Callaghan believed that if a woman didn't like you she might just as well actively *dislike* you. Anyway there was some sort of kick to be got out of making her feel *something*.

She moved to a little table and brought a cigarette-box over to Callaghan. She opened it, offered him one and took one herself. He got up and lit both cigarettes. He was rather pleased at the fact that she was, at any rate, feeling sufficiently good-natured to give him a cigarette. Probably she was merely being polite.

'I'm sorry to tell you, Mr Callaghan,' she said, 'that my husband is very much worse. This morning it became necessary to move him to a Nursing Home at Swansdown. The doctors are very worried about him.

'I'm sorry for more than the obvious reason, because before he was moved he executed a deed which places the whole of the responsibility of handling the Riverton Estates, and of deciding the issue about my stepson, on my shoulders.'

She stopped for a moment. Then:

'The process also makes it necessary that you should find it agreeable to take your instructions from me, Mr Callaghan, much as you seem to dislike that.'

50

Callaghan smiled and sent a thin stream of cigarette smoke out of one nostril.

'I don't know that I dislike it,' he said. 'I think you could make a nice boss, Mrs Riverton. I don't mind who I take my instructions from – providin' they're intelligent people, providin' they realize the sort of things that private detectives are up against.'

He looked at her. He was smiling. In spite of herself she could not help noticing the evasive charm of that smile or the fact that his lips were well carved, his teeth and jaw strong and regular. She found herself thinking that he was the strangest man.

'In fact,' said Callaghan, 'I think I rather like takin' instructions from you.'

'I don't think it matters who gives the instructions,' she said coldly, 'providing they are properly carried out. You have something to report?'

'Yes,' said Callaghan. 'I think we can say we've got a bit of a move on. I've found out one or two things – nothing much, but enough to show me which way the cat's jumpin'. I think in a matter of weeks I'll be able to tell you all about this business; who it was had that money, or most of it, from Wilfred Riverton, who it is he's gettin' around with, and who is responsible for gettin' him the way he is.'

'Precisely what do you mean by that?' she asked.

'He is takin' dope,' said Callaghan. 'I had a few words with him last night. He was waitin' for me outside my offices. He told me to mind my own dam' business and he suggested that his clever stepmother – clever was *his* word – might like to mind hers too. I don't think we're either of us very popular. Anyhow,' he went on, 'he is takin' dope. He was full of cocaine when I spoke to him.'

She didn't say anything. She moved over to the fire, put her two hands on the mantelpiece and stood looking into the flames.

'How awful,' she said.

She raised her head and turned towards him.

'Mr Callaghan,' she asked, 'why should it take a matter of weeks? Why is it necessary for this process to be so long drawn-out – or are you still thinking of that £100 a week?'

Callaghan drew on his cigarette.

'I hoped you wouldn't start talkin' like that,' he said seriously. 'I don't like you when you talk like that. I think it'll take a couple of months to clear this job up if it's done in the way I'm goin' to do it.'

She sat down in the big carved chair by the side of the fire. Callaghan got up, walked to the fireplace, leaned against it, stood looking down at her.

'You listen to me, Mrs Riverton,' he said. 'Why don't you try trustin' people a little bit instead of bein' so suspicious and cynical? I think this job will take two months to clean up, and I've got my reasons for thinkin' that way. Your stepson has got himself in with a very nasty crowd of people – the sort of people who aren't above doin' a little blackmail. If he waves goodbye too quickly to that crowd some of them may try a come-back.'

'Suppose they do, Mr Callaghan?' she said. 'I believe Scotland Yard is very efficient.'

'Scotland Yard is dam' efficient,' he said. 'You take it from me – I know 'em. If you want to make a complaint to Scotland Yard, you make it. They won't be interested in wet-nursin' Wilfred Riverton, but they'll be interested in the gamin' angle, and they'll be interested in the dope angle. They'll get out after that bunch so quickly that the boys will wonder what's hit 'em.

'All right. An' what good does it do you, the Colonel or Wilfred? You see, Scotland Yard aren't private detectives. They're servants of the State. When they prosecute the job's got to be an open one. We've got newspapers in this country too. Even if you and the Colonel don't mind the publicity, I should think The Mug might. They *might* have to charge him too. He'll hate you more than ever, an' if you're in charge of the estates and money from now on, you're not goin' to make things any easier for yourself by gettin' up against him now.'

She got up.

'That is a matter which I think does not concern you, Mr Callaghan,' she said. 'And I think that you and I have said all we need say to each other about this business at this moment. I am not prepared for this case to drag on for another eight or nine weeks. I have my own reasons for that.'

Callaghan shook his head.

'That's how it'll have to be, Madame,' he said.

'That is how it will *not* have to be, Mr Callaghan,' she replied. 'This is my last word. Today is Saturday. So far as you're concerned this investigation must finish in a fortnight – by Saturday week. If it is not concluded satisfactorily, Mr Selby will have to look for another firm of investigators if further investigation is necessary.'

Callaghan got up.

'I see, Madame,' he said. He grinned. 'In fact I'm bein' given two weeks' notice. I don't think I like that.'

She smiled. Her hand went towards the bell-push.

'I rather hoped you wouldn't, Mr Callaghan,' she said.

Callaghan looked at her. His grin had broadened into a smile.

'I don't know that I dislike you even now,' he said. 'In an odd way you're rather like I am. You get a kick out of bein' dam' rude. Good evenin', Madame, an' thank you for the cigarette.'

It was after eight o'clock when Callaghan got back to the office. Effie Thompson, an expression of patient resignation on her face, sat smoking a cigarette in the outer office, her hat on, her handbag and umbrella on the desk.

'Get me Darkie on the telephone,' said Callaghan as he passed through her room, 'an' then you go home, Effie. Have a nice week-end.'

He grinned at her, noticed the pout on her pretty lips.

He took the call in his own room.

'You listen to me, Darkie,' he said. 'There's a young feller called Riverton – Wilfred Riverton – five feet nine about – thin an' sick lookin'. His face is a bit bloated from too much liquor an' he's takin' dope. He's got blond hair a bit long an' he's short-tempered. You got all that?'

Darkie said he had.

'Last night he was dropped near Down Street. He was cock-eyed an' full of cocaine,' Callaghan went on. 'I reckon he's livin' somewhere around there. You find out where he is. If you've got to use half a dozen of the boys to do it, use 'em – the expense sheet will stand it. Another thing, keep your eyes open for a woman name of Azelda Dixon. Ordinary height, nice figure, dresses well – a brunette – maybe she's gettin' around with young Riverton. Get busy, Darkie. I want to know where those two birds are livin' an' I want to know quickly. Understand?'

He hung up.

Effie Thompson appeared in the doorway. She held a copy of *The Bystander* in her hand.

'I'm going now,' she said.

She came into the room and put *The Bystander* on his desk.

'There's a picture of Mrs Riverton on page seven,' she said. 'Mrs Thorla Riverton' – she shot a quick look at him – 'I think she's very beautiful,' she said.

'Yes?' said Callaghan. 'So what—?'

She looked over her shoulder from the doorway. Her smile was a little acid.

'That's what I was wondering,' she said. 'Goodnight!'

She shut the door quickly.

Callaghan was still thinking about Mrs Riverton when the telephone jangled. It was Kells coming through from the country.

'Hallo, Slim,' he said. 'Say, am I the little sleuth or am I?'

Callaghan straightened.

'What have you got, Monty?'

'I've found that boat,' said Kells. 'I'm talkin' from Falleton – half-way between Southing Village an' Pinmill. The boat's called the *San Pedro*. She's a nice bit of work too. Nice an' big, but not too big, an' fast. She looks like one of them gamin' lay-outs they useta have around the Californian coast before the Feds got so busy.

'She's moored out here on the broad that runs down to the end of this Falleton dump. She's about sixty yards out, an' from where she is she can move out on to the river an' make the open sea off Harwich in no time.'

Callaghan looked at his watch.

'I'm comin' down,' he said. 'Where are you stayin', Monty?'

He heard Kells chuckle.

'I'm staying at some one-eyed dump called The Goat Inn,' he said. 'I told 'em I was a travellin' salesman. The liquor ain't bad down here, an' the barmaid looks as if she might fall for my line in due course. Where do I go from there?'

'You stay there,' said Callaghan. 'I'll be down about twelve-thirty. I've got a feelin' that Jake is goin' to get out an' I want to have a little talk with him before he goes. I'll drive past The Goat about twelve-thirty an' pick you up.'

'OK,' said Kells. 'You better bring a gun with you. I reckon that Jake ain't very fond of you. If he's goin' he might like to rub you out first.'

Callaghan grunted.

'I don't like guns,' he said. 'You have to explain too much when somebody gets shot in this country. This isn't Oklahoma.'

'You're tellin' me,' said Kells. 'But I'd still bring a gun. I'd rather do a lot of explainin' than be dead for ever. OK. Twelve-thirty. I'll be seein' you.'

It was ten o'clock when he stopped his car in the Mews just round the corner from the Yellow Lamp. He went in, drank a cocktail, said a word to Perruqui and walked round the balcony, through the pass-door to Juanita's room. She was smoking a cigarette, reading an evening paper.

Callaghan put up his hand. His face wore a rueful expression.

'I know . . . ' he said. 'An' I'm very sorry about it. It was just one of those things. It just happened.'

She stubbed out her cigarette.

'Like hell it was,' she said. 'For God's sake why do you have to pick the minute my act begins to start a free fight out on the floor. Ain't you got a heart at all?' She got up. 'And who was the dame?' she asked.

Callaghan shrugged his shoulders.

'I don't know. I've never seen her before,' he said. He began to grin. 'How's Gill?' he asked. 'Did you have a good time?'

She tossed her head.

'Not so bad at that,' she said. 'Gill's got a helluva way with him. An' he showed me some very nice fresh air an' a marvellous dinner with a bottle of champagne. Which is a bit better than some people do.'

She looked at him cynically.

'Gill's a great feller,' said Callaghan. 'I knew you two would hit it off.'

Juanita took two cigarettes from the box, put them both in her mouth, lit them, brought one over to Callaghan and sat down on the stool in front of her dressing-table. She said:

'Look, Slim, you're a funny guy but I'm sorta fond of you. I don't know why, but I am. Gill says that you've got to keep your nose clean. He says that you're musclin' in on some guy called Jake who is pure poison. That this guy Jake don't sorta like you. That he's liable to get some of his mob workin' on you.'

Callaghan smiled.

'Yes, I know,' he said. 'They started in last night. Some feller tried to mar my beauty with a kid glove fitted up with the latest thing in razor-blades.' He grinned. 'It didn't get him anywhere,' he concluded.

'Is that the guy they found in some alley near Tottenham Court Road?' she asked. 'I was just reading about it. He's in hospital. The paper says that it's a gang war or something. . . . '

Callaghan nodded.

'*I* was the gang,' he said. He got up. 'So long, Juanita, I'll be seeing you soon. I've got a date. Good night.'

He went out.

She twisted round on the stool as the door shut behind him. She sat there thinking, looking at the door.

The moon came out from behind the clouds as Callaghan swung the Jaguar into the narrow main road at Falleton. He switched on the headlights, slowed down to twenty. Half-way down the road the lights picked up Kells standing, his hands in his pockets, a cigarette hanging from the corner of his mouth.

He got into the car.

'Straight on an' take the right fork,' he said. 'Twenty-five yards from there, there is a landin' place. The *San Pedro* is moored out opposite.'

Callaghan nodded. He turned off the headlights.

Kells said:

'You ain't playin' this by yourself, Slim?'

Callaghan nodded again.

Kells shrugged.

'You're the boss,' he said.

Callaghan stopped the car. They got out. Before them, the grass ran down to a landing stage. Out across the sheet of placid water Callaghan could see the riding lights of the boat, and the lights showing through half a dozen portholes.

'There she is,' said Kells. 'An' a very nice job too.'

Callaghan looked round.

'Park the car over in that shrubbery, Monty,' he said. 'I don't want some country policeman gettin' too interested. Another thing,' he went on, 'you're goin' to stay down here an' look round. This boat looks the perfect set-up for a gamblin' joint an' if that's right, then Jake has got to have a house somewhere round here, a place where the people come down to an' leave their cars an' get a drink before they go aboard – you know the usual thing. Wherever it is it's got to be near here because the boat's here. See?'

'OK,' said Kells. 'I'll start in tomorrow. If it's here I'll find it.'

'You put that car away now,' said Callaghan. 'I'm goin' aboard the boat. Come through to the office when you find that house.'

'What about my stickin' around for a bit, Slim?' said Kells. 'Supposin' Jake's aboard there in a bad temper. Maybe he'll start something. Have you got that gun?'

Callaghan grinned.

'No,' he said. 'People with guns always get shot. An' you don't have to stick around either. Good night, Monty.'

'I'll be seein' you,' said Kells.

He turned towards the car.

Callaghan walked down, over the grass, to the landing stage. There was a dinghy tied up there. He got into it, untied it, shipped the sculls and began to pull out towards the *San Pedro*. A shore tide was running and he had to pull hard.

On the lee side of the yacht there was an accommodation ladder, with another dinghy tied to the bottom of it. Callaghan tied up his own boat and began to walk up the ladder. He moved soundlessly like a shadow. Upon the deck he stood and looked about him.

There was nothing to be seen or heard. He moved towards the stern, found the companionway, began to creep down into the darkness.

At the bottom he felt in his pocket for his electric torch, switched it on and moved along the narrow passage in front of him. He was working towards the saloon whose lighted portholes he had seen from the shore.

At the end of the passage was a closed door. Underneath a crack of light showed. Callaghan opened the door and went in. He found himself in a small saloon. There was a bar on one side with bottles and glasses set out. Opposite the bar was a steel-legged table, and underneath the table was a wastepaper basket. It was empty except for some torn scraps of paper.

He listened for a moment but heard nothing. He looked into the paper basket, picked it up, took out the pieces of paper. There were the eight torn pieces of an ordinary sheet of notepaper. On one piece the letters IOU showed plainly.

Callaghan put the pieces together on the top of the table. He stood looking at them, frowning. He read:

To Jake Raffano Esq.
IOU £22,000 (Twenty-two thousand pounds).
                                                    Wilfred Riverton.'

Callaghan heard something. He put the pieces of paper into his pocket and stood quite still, listening. The noise was peculiar. It was an irregular sucking noise, a peculiar heavy sound. It was unpleasant.

On the left of the table opposite the door through which he had come was another door. Callaghan opened it gently. He found himself in another passage six feet long. At the end was a drawn velvet curtain, behind it a door half-open, through which a shaft of light cut into the darkness of the passage.

Callaghan pushed open the door and went in.

He was in the main saloon. The electric lights were lit. At the end, opposite Callaghan, was a big walnut desk; behind it, slumped back in a chair, the front of his white evening shirt soaked red with his blood, was Jake Raffano. His left arm hung down by his side. His right hand, on the desk before him, grasped a heavy automatic pistol.

Callaghan looked over to his right – at the place where the unpleasant sound was. He saw what was making the sound. It was The Mug.

He was lying against the angle formed by the walls of the saloon, opposite the desk. His breathing was heavy – stertorous. Callaghan knew, almost without looking, that he had been shot through the lung. A stream of blood had trickled down over his shirt-front and leg on to the floor.

His right hand lay across his left thigh. In it was a .32 automatic.

Callaghan stood looking at him for a minute. Then he went over and looked at Jake. Jake was dead all right.

Callaghan lit a cigarette. He felt in his pocket for his gloves, put them on. He began a systematic search of the saloon. In the wall behind the desk, concealed by a picture, was a locked wall-safe. Callaghan turned his attention to Jake, but he might have saved himself the trouble. Jake's pockets were empty and a search of The Mug's clothes yielded only the remains of a packet of cigarettes.

He went into the small saloon where he had found the IOU. There

58

was a cupboard let into the wainscoting with the door half-open. He looked into it. Hanging on a peg was a thick woollen dressing-gown. He went through the pockets. They were empty. He noticed that the dressing-gown was damp. He wondered why.

Callaghan sat down on a chair and smoked for a minute or two. Then he got up, went back through the passage and up on to the deck. He went down the ladder, got into the boat, pulled towards the shore. The tide made it easy.

He tied up the boat at the landing stage, walked over to the car, started the engine and drove slowly along the fork through Falleton and out the other side.

Three miles farther on he saw the telephone box.

He stopped the car, got out, lit another cigarette, went into the box and dialled 999. He stretched his handkerchief over the mouth of the transmitter and spoke through it. He said:

'Police? Listen carefully please. There's a motor-yacht moored off Falleton. Name of *San Pedro*. There's been a little trouble aboard. In the main saloon is a feller by the name of Jake Raffano – an American – he's dead. There's another feller there shot through the lung – name of Wilfred Riverton. He's in a pretty bad way. That's all. Good night!'

CHAPTER FIVE

Sunday

A day of rest

Callaghan went down to his office at one-thirty.

Effie Thompson, in a fur coat, a smart hat over one eye, and with a preoccupied expression, was sitting at his desk reading newspapers.

'What are you doin' here?' he asked. 'I didn't phone you.'

'I saw the papers this morning,' she replied. 'I thought there might be something to do.'

Callaghan slumped down into the big chair by the side of the fireplace. He was wearing a grey pinhead lounge suit, a blue silk shirt and collar, a navy blue silk tie. Effie looked at him sideways, hungrily.

He sat looking into the fire, drawing on a cigarette. At last he said:

'What do they say?'

'There's not much,' she answered, 'but apparently last night, in response to an anonymous telephone call from a call-box somewhere near Falleton, the police went aboard a boat called the *San Pedro* at Falleton, and found Jake Raffano shot dead. I suppose you wouldn't know that?' she concluded with a small smile.

Callaghan said nothing.

'Wilfred Riverton was on the boat too,' Effie went on. 'He was shot through the right lung. They think he is going to die. The doctors think there's just a chance he may live.'

'What else?' said Callaghan.

'Colonel Riverton died last night,' said Effie, 'at eleven forty-five. He was in a Nursing Home at Swansdown Poulteney.'

'Exit the male members of the Riverton family,' Callaghan said. 'Not so good. How long have you been here?'

He threw a cigarette over to her. She caught it, produced a lighter from her handbag, lit the cigarette expertly.

'About two hours,' she said. 'Wilkie said you were asleep, so I switched the phones down here.'

'Has Kells been through?' said Callaghan.

'No,' she answered. 'Nobody's been through.'

Callaghan got up. He began to walk up and down the office, his hands behind his back.

'Get Darkie, Effie,' he said.

She put the call through. He took the receiver from her hand.

'Hallo, Darkie,' he said. 'Have you seen the papers?'

Darkie said he had.

'All right,' said Callaghan. 'Well that doesn't make any difference to you. What you've got to find out is this. I'm interested in this killin' aboard the *San Pedro* – never mind why. I believe young Riverton went down there some time yesterday afternoon or evening. Well, you've got to find out when, an' you've got to find out where he left from, an' you've got to find out how he got down there. If he went by car, somebody else was drivin' him. You got that, Darkie? All right. Now I tell you how you set about it.

'You remember that feller Mazely – the feller that came out on that drugs charge, three months ago? Well, get hold of him, show him a five pound note, and get him to drop in at the Privateer Bar in Soho. Let him stick around there for a bit and make out that he's done some sort of house-breakin' job out in the suburbs, that he's waitin' for it to blow over. Tell him to try to get next to Henny The Boyo or any of the other people round there who knew The Mug. Tell him to find out where he was yesterday – what he was doin'. All right, Darkie, go to it.'

He hung up the receiver.

Effie Thompson, who had gone to her own office during the conversation, came to the doorway. She looked a little worried.

'Do you want me any more?' she said. 'Is there anything I can do?'

Callaghan rubbed his chin.

'No,' he said. 'Did you send that £100 to Lonney?'

'Yes,' she said, 'that went off yesterday.'

'All right,' said Callaghan. 'You go home.'

She nodded.

'I shall be in all day,' she said. 'If you want me just give me a ring. I'll come round.'

Callaghan raised his eyebrows.

'Why should I want you?' he said. 'Listen, what's the matter with you? You're not tryin' to be a detective or anything, are you, Effie?'

She smiled.

'I'll leave that to you,' she said. 'I'm no good at problems. The only things I can ever solve are the "Are you a good detective?" things in the Sunday newspapers. But I thought it funny your going down there last night – being around that district – and that telephone call to the police. I wondered . . . '

Callaghan dropped his voice.

'Look, honey,' he said, 'you don't get paid to wonder. You stick to the "Are you a good detective?" series in the newspapers. Go home. Go and see a movie and forget the Riverton case. If I want you, I'll phone through.'

He grinned at her.

Callaghan lit a cigarette, went back to the leather armchair, lay back in it, looked up at the ceiling, thinking. The buzzer sounded in the outer office. He went through into the other office. It was Wilkie from downstairs.

'There's a gentleman to see you down here, Mr Callaghan,' he said. 'Detective Inspector Gringall from Scotland Yard.'

The telephone bell began to jangle in Callaghan's office. He let it ring.

'Did you tell him I was in, Wilkie?' he asked.

'I said I thought you were asleep, Mr Callaghan,' Wilkie answered.

'That's all right,' said Callaghan. 'You tell him you'll go up to my apartment and wake me up. Ask him to wait. Hang about upstairs for a couple of minutes, then go down and say I'm in the office. Give me four or five minutes before you bring him up.'

The telephone bell was still jangling.

Callaghan went back to his own office, took the phone call. It was long distance. After a minute Kells came through.

'Hallo, Slim,' he said. 'Findin' that house was easy. There's a place half a mile back of Falleton – about three-quarters of a mile from where the *San Pedro* was lying. There's grounds, an' shrubberies, kitchen gardens, flower gardens and what-have-you-got. But is this a screwy dump! There's nobody there. I've been in the place this morning. I got in through a back window. It's pretty swell inside – there's a big bar stocked with all sorts of liquor, food all over the place, and it looks as if somebody's got out of it in a hurry.'

'How did you find out about it?' asked Callaghan. 'And be quick, Gringall's comin' up in a minute.'

Callaghan heard Kells whistle.

'Does he know you were down here last night, Slim?' he asked. 'That's a sweet story they're runnin' in the papers. They got it pretty quick too. I've never known Sunday newspapers get a story that broke at half-past twelve at night as quick as that in this country.'

'Don't be a fool,' said Callaghan. 'They got that story because Gringall wanted them to have it. He probably dished it out himself.

'Now where did you find out about that place?'

'It was easy,' said Kells. 'The barmaid at The Goat wised me up.'

'Have you been over the place?' asked Callaghan.

'I haven't had a chance,' Kells replied. 'Do I go back there?'

Callaghan thought for a minute.

'No, lay off it,' he said. 'I bet the police are goin' to be pretty busy around Falleton. Besides I want to have a look at that place. I'll meet you down there in a quiet spot near to the entrance of that house some time tomorrow. You hang about, find out what you can. Find out what the police are doin', but keep quiet an' keep out of the way. If I can't get down by ten o'clock tomorrow night I'll phone through to The Goat and let you know. You got that?'

'Yeah,' said Kells. 'I got it. Just a minute, I've got a nice little tit-bit for you.'

'Well, be quick about it,' said Callaghan. 'What's the tit-bit?'

'There was a dame on that boat last night,' said Kells. 'Just at the Falleton end of that fork – we went down the right hand side of it – by the landing place, is a cottage. Some old guy lives there called Jimmy Wilpins. This bozo can't sleep – he's about sixty and he's got insomnia. I was talkin' to him in the bar this morning at The Goat. He says that last night about a quarter to twelve he got out of bed because he couldn't go to sleep. He went and looked out of the window of his cottage. There was a swell moon last night – remember, Slim? Well, from the upstairs room in his cottage he can see the landin' stage – he's got good sight. He says a boat pulled up to the landin' stage and a woman got out. She was wearing a tiger-skin cloak.'

Callaghan stiffened.

'What did he say she was wearin' – an ocelot cloak?' he asked.

'What the hell's an ocelot cloak? He said a tiger-skin,' said Kells.

'It's the same thing,' said Callaghan. 'All right. So long, Monty. Ten o'clock tomorrow night.'

He hung up.

He got up and picked his still smouldering cigarette out of the ashtray. He began to grin. He was remembering the ocelot cloak – Jimmy Wilpins would call it tiger-skin – that he'd seen thrown over the settee in Thorla Riverton's room at the Chartres Hotel the first night he'd seen her. Here was a nice one! He threw his cigarette end into the fire.

He began to laugh.

Callaghan was lying back in the leather armchair smoking a cigarette, with all the newspapers draped around him, when Detective Inspector Gringall arrived.

George Henry Gringall was forty-three years of age. He had a small bristling moustache, a quiet, direct and spontaneous manner. He was the youngest Detective Inspector at Scotland Yard, and, like most detective inspectors who serve in that institution, he had a great deal more brains than people credited.

Callaghan said:

'It's good seein' you, Gringall. It must be nearly two years since I've seen you. Sit down – the cigarettes are on the table.'

Gringall put his hat on the table and took the other armchair. He began to fill a pipe.

'Pretty good offices, Callaghan,' he said. 'You've been getting on in the world.'

Callaghan shrugged.

'This is a bit better than that fourth floor office off Chancery Lane,' he said.

'I saw Cynthis Meraulton* the other day,' Gringall said. 'I thought you handled that case pretty well.'

Callaghan grinned.

'I thought *you* handled it pretty well, Gringall,' he said. 'I thought I was goin' to finish up inside over that job.'

Gringall nodded.

'I thought so too,' he said, 'but the main thing is you didn't. You just took a chance and it came off. Funny thing,' he went on, 'I always

---

*Urgent Hangman

had a vague sort of idea in my head that you'd marry Miss Meraulton.'

'You don't say,' said Callaghan.

He looked at the ceiling. There was a silence. Callaghan was still grinning. He knew what Gringall had come to see him about and he knew that Gringall knew.

Gringall looked at the newspaper littered floor.

'It's interesting, isn't it?' he said.

Callaghan took the cue.

'Dam' interestin' for me, Gringall, but I don't like it. When I looked at the papers this mornin' I saw £100 a week floatin' away into the distance.'

Gringall shook his head. He made a clucking noise with his tongue.

'Too bad,' he said. 'So that's what they were paying you.'

Callaghan nodded.

'It was a nice job,' he said. 'Anything I can do for you?'

Gringall leaned back in the chair and folded his hands in front of him.

'You might be able to help me, Callaghan,' he said. 'I had a talk with Mrs Riverton – young Riverton's stepmother – early this morning. She said you'd been doing an investigation for them. I thought you might be able to give me one or two points.'

Callaghan raised his eyebrows.

'You don't want any points, Gringall,' he said. 'And you know it. The case is in the bag.'

Gringall's eyebrows shot up.

'How do you know?' he said. 'There is nothing in the papers except the fact that Raffano is dead and Riverton badly wounded – and he'll die too, I think,' he added glumly.

Callaghan said:

'Work it out for yourself. I was instructed by old Riverton through Selby, Raukes & White, his solicitors, to find out who was takin' young Riverton for a lot of money. We called Riverton The Mug, and believe me he was one. They had pretty well everything off him that he'd got. Somebody had got him takin' dope and he was cock-eyed most of the time.'

He paused and lit another cigarette. He coughed for a little while. He was thinking hard.

'Still got that smoker's throat, Callaghan?' asked Gringall.

'Yes,' said Callaghan. 'I'll have to give 'em up one day. I smoke too many.'

'Go on,' said Gringall.

'It's not goin' to take a Sherlock Holmes to decide this case,' said Callaghan. 'I hadn't been able to make a report to my clients because I hadn't got any facts. I'd got theories and theories aren't much use when you're gettin' £100 a week to report.

'Work it out for yourself,' he went on. 'I'd just got goin'. I'd just found out that Raffano was the boy who'd been takin' Wilfred for a nice walk down the garden path. Well, this feller Raffano was pretty well organized over here. He must have had some brains because although his technique was American he used it very nicely. Did you ever hear about him?'

Gringall shrugged.

'We heard rumours,' he said, 'but we don't deal in rumours. We never had a complaint.'

'You bet you didn't,' said Callaghan. '*This* was a complaint, only unfortunately for him The Mug complained to the wrong people. It looks as if he complained to Raffano.'

'Meaning just what?' said Gringall.

Callaghan blew a smoke ring. The frank and open expression which invariably accompanied a lie came over his face.

'I'll tell you how I worked it out, Gringall,' he said. 'I thought this way. If I went back to Selby, Raukes & White or old Riverton an' told 'em my theories about this business they could do one of two things. They could let me handle it my way – which I thought would be the best way – or they could make a complaint to the Yard. I advised Mrs Riverton that I thought that would be the wrong thing to do. I told her that if you got busy and started pullin' these boys in, you might have to pull The Mug in too. After all if it is a criminal offence to sell dope, it's a criminal offence to buy it.'

Gringall nodded.

'You think of everything,' he said. 'Mrs Riverton told me about that. And what was your idea, Callaghan?'

'My idea was this,' said Callaghan. 'I let Raffano know that I was wise to him. I had a little talk to him at the Parlour Club on Friday night. I gave him the tip to pack up an' get out while the goin' was good. I warned him that if he didn't he'd get it pretty soon, that the

66

best thing that could happen to him was to be seen off back to America by a feller from the Yard, an' I happen to know that Jake isn't too popular in the States. I believe Mr Hoover's boys have got something on him.

'It seemed to be workin' all right,' Callaghan continued. 'Young Riverton waited for me the other night outside here, told me to mind my own dam' business. He was full of cocaine an' so cock-eyed that he hardly knew what he was doin'.

'After that I was happy, because it looked to me that Jake would realize that things were goin' to get too warm for him, that he'd pack up an' clear out, that there would be a chance of gettin' The Mug back to a more or less normal mode of life nicely an' quietly with no scandal.'

Gringall nodded.

'It was an intelligent idea,' he said. 'The only thing was it didn't work.'

'I know,' said Callaghan. 'Can young Riverton talk?'

Gringall shook his head.

'He's unconscious. They've got him in the Cottage Hospital at Ballington. He may recover consciousness and he may not. I'd like to know why he went down to that boat. He might have known he'd be no match for Raffano,' Gringall concluded.

'He wouldn't worry about a thing like that in the state he was in,' said Callaghan. 'I reckon he heard that Raffano was packin' up and gettin' out. Maybe he stayed sober for long enough to realize that Jake was walkin' away with £80,000 odd. He didn't like the idea so he went all wild-west, got himself a gun an' went down there to get a little of it back before Jake went. Jake didn't like the idea so they shot it out an' by some chance The Mug had his gun pointin' in the right direction when he pulled the trigger.'

'It was a nice shot,' said Gringall. 'He got Jake clean through the heart at twelve yards.'

He got up.

'Well, it's nice of you to have helped, Callaghan,' he said.

He walked over to the desk and picked up his hat.

'I suppose it'll be murder,' said Callaghan.

Gringall nodded.

'If he gets better we'll charge him,' he said. 'It's murder all right. What else can it be?'

Using his arms as levers, Callaghan pushed himself out of the armchair.

'It can be self-defence, Gringall,' he said. 'If The Mug went down to have a show-down with Raffano, and he believed that Raffano might make an attempt on his life, I think a jury might say that he was entitled to have a gun on him. How do you know Jake didn't fire first? Maybe The Mug fired after he was hit. If that was so it would be homicide – justifiable homicide.'

'Well, you never know,' said Gringall. 'Goodbye, Callaghan. See you again.'

He went out of the office. Callaghan stood in front of the fire looking at the pile of newspapers round his feet.

Callaghan sat in the dark office, looking into the fire. Life was dam' funny, he thought. It depended on such little things. If he'd done what Thorla Riverton intended him to do on Friday night he would have telephoned her. He would not have gone to see her at the Chartres Hotel. He would not have seen the ocelot cloak. If Jimmy Wilpins hadn't had insomnia he would have been asleep on Saturday night. He wouldn't have seen the ocelot cloak. It was also dam' funny that Jimmy should have been at his window at the right time – the time he saw Thorla Riverton doing her landing act from the dinghy – and not at the wrong time – in which case he would have seen Callaghan coming off the *San Pedro*.

Callaghan, who never came to illogical conclusions, realized that of course there was a possibility that it hadn't been Thorla Riverton, that it had been some other woman. But this was a mere possibility.

He got up, switched on the light, got the telephone book from Effie's room, looked up the number of T. J. Selby, the Riverton solicitor, called him. Selby was in.

'It's a pretty bad business, Mr Selby,' said Callaghan. 'An' perhaps it's as well that the Colonel died before he heard of it. I suppose you've been through to the Nursing Home at Swansdown Poulteney and heard all about it?'

Selby said he hadn't. He was going down tomorrow. Callaghan talked about nothing in particular for a few minutes and then finished off the conversation.

After he had hung up he got through to trunk enquiries and got the number of the Swansdown Nursing Home. He called through, asked for the matron.

'Good afternoon, matron,' said Callaghan in a sombre voice. 'I'm Mr Selby, of Selby, Raukes & White; Colonel Riverton was my client. I'm terribly distressed to hear about his death. I can only hope that his passing was an easy one. In any event he must have been glad that Mrs Riverton was able to get there in time.'

'No, Mr Selby,' said the matron. 'It was terribly unfortunate, but she couldn't get here until twelve-thirty. When I telephoned her through at eleven o'clock to tell her that the doctor didn't think the Colonel could last the night, she had already left the Manor House. They said she was on her way here. Then she had engine trouble and was held up. She didn't arrive here until twelve-thirty. The Colonel died at eleven forty-five. *So* unfortunate.'

Callaghan's grin was almost satanic as he hung up the receiver. That clinched it. The woman that Jimmy Wilpins had seen *was* Thorla Riverton. Outside in Effie's office, with the AA map spread out on her desk and a slide rule, he worked it out. She'd left the Manor House and driven over to Falleton to keep an appointment on the *San Pedro*. She hadn't known then that the old man had taken a turn for the worse. She'd intended to drive straight back to the Manor House after she'd left the boat. She'd had her car parked somewhere near that landing stage.

Probably she'd called through from a wayside telephone soon afterwards, had spoken to the Manor House, had been told that the Matron had been through. She'd cut across country driving like hell, trying to make it before the old man passed out and probably she had run short of petrol. She'd lost a few more minutes getting some and by going like the devil had got to the Nursing Home at Swansdown Poulteney at twelve-thirty, just about the time that Callaghan was going aboard the *San Pedro*.

Callaghan flopped into the big armchair again, and began to turn over the interesting points in his mind, the unconsidered trifles which mean so much, the straws that show the way the wind is blowing. He began to find a possible explanation for the torn up IOU for £22,000 that Callaghan had found in the wastepaper basket in the small saloon on the *San Pedro*. He began to find possible explanations for two or three odd things.

He got up, lit a cigarette and rang a Mayfair number. He asked for

Mr Eustace Maninway. When he heard the cultured, drawling voice of that young gentleman on the telephone he said:

'Maninway? Do you want to make a quick twenty pounds? You do. All right, you listen to me. There's a woman livin' at a place called the Manor House at Southing. She's the second wife of a feller who died last night – name of Colonel Riverton, an' the stepmother of the young Riverton who's mixed up in this shootin' business on the *San Pedro*. You've seen it in the papers. Now I want to get a line on that woman. I want to know just who she was before she got herself married, who her family were, why she married old Riverton an' all about her. You've got to get all that for me by eleven o'clock tonight – understand? An' I want facts. I'll meet you tonight or telephone you at the Silver Bar between eleven an' twelve o'clock. If you've got what I want, you get twenty pounds tomorrow.'

Maninway said he thought he could do it.

Callaghan looked at his watch. It was five o'clock. He called through to the garage and told them to bring the car round with the hood down. Then he went up to his apartment and put on a thick overcoat and cap. He opened a wall safe behind a picture and took out ten ten-pound notes – part of his winnings over the Lonney fight.

When he got downstairs the car was waiting. He drove quietly out of London, threading through the traffic, his eyes on the road, his mind busy.

Fifteen miles outside London he pulled his cap down over his eyes and put his foot down on the gas. He let in the supercharger at fifty-five, listened to the drone of the engine as the car ate up the miles to Falleton.

His eyes never left the white ribbon of road that showed under the headlights. His head was down over the wheel, his fingers light and easy on it.

He was grinning.

The fellow who said that you never knew anything about women was dam' right thought Callaghan. The more they looked like saints the less they were likely to be like saints. It wasn't reasonable that a woman with a face and shape like Thorla Riverton could be able to keep out of trouble.

And he'd fallen for her act. He'd fallen for that stepmother stuff and stood there looking at her like a stuck pig while she did a big county act with him and tried to make him feel like something that the cat brought in, and but for the fact that Jimmy Wilpins couldn't go to sleep and had stuck his head out of the window just at the right moment she'd have got away with it.

Callaghan hung on the wheel and braked hard. As the headlights picked up an AA sign 'Dangerous Curves', he grinned.

'You're tellin' me,' said Callaghan.

CHAPTER SIX

Sunday

Horker comes across

It was cold and a thin rain was falling when Callaghan parked his car at the garage and walked round to his apartment. As he entered, Wilkie came out of his glass box.

'There was a telephone call for you, Mr Callaghan,' he said. 'It came through at 10.10 – about four minutes ago. It was from Mr Darkie. He said he'd like to have a word with you. And a Mrs Riverton called.'

Callaghan took off his wet cap, felt in his coat pocket for a cigarette. 'What did she want?' he asked.

'She wanted to see you,' said Wilkie. 'She left this note.'

He handed over the envelope. Callaghan went up to his apartment and took a hot shower. He put on a fresh suit, then stood looking at the envelope from Thorla Riverton. He tore it open. The note said:

I am terribly worried. I came up to town this evening to see Mr Gringall – the detective inspector who is in charge of the case. He seems to want to help as much as is possible.

He said that although Selby, Raukes & White were first-class lawyers, it might be better for my stepson if he were represented by a firm of solicitors more used to criminal proceedings. He said that I should be advised by you in this.

He told me that he had already seen you this afternoon, that you had produced a 'useful theory' – some theory of self-defence which might be of assistance to my stepson.

I have arranged to see Mr Selby tomorrow morning. I would like to talk to you first. Will you please telephone me when you get back? I am at the Chartres Hotel.

Thorla Riverton.

Callaghan began to grin. So she was coming off it. She was beginning to realize that it might be a good thing to be friendly.

He went over to the cupboard and drank three fingers of whisky neat. He lit a cigarette and telephoned Darkie.

Darkie's voice came wheezily over the line.

'I've got the strength of this Down Street business, Slim,' said Darkie. 'Young Riverton's place wasn't in Down Street. It was at the other end in Thurles Mews. There's a place there – No. 87b – a good-class rooming house. It's run by a feller called Horker – an ex-con. Riverton 'ad a room there.

'Now about this Privateer business, I stuck Mazeley in there like you said, but you take it from me, Gov'nor, there's sweet Fanny Adams doin' round there. This feller Henny The Boyo has got his mouth shut so bloody tight you couldn't prise it open with a bleedin' chisel. Any time anybody talks about Riverton or Azelda Dixon he just clamps down.'

'All right, Darkie,' said Callaghan. 'I'll tell you when I want you again.'

He hung up, put on a light overcoat and a black soft hat. He went downstairs. In the hallway he looked at his watch. It was ten-thirty. He stood for a moment in the entrance looking out at the rain. Then he walked back to the hall porter's box.

'Ring through to the Berkeley Square rank for a cab, Wilkie,' he said. 'When you've done that get through to the Chartres Hotel. Ask to speak to Mrs Riverton. Tell her that I've had her note. Tell her to telephone me tonight at twelve o'clock. I'll be back by then.'

When the cab came, Callaghan told the man to drive him to 87b Thurles Mews. Then he sat back in the corner of the cab thinking hard.

No. 87b was an old-fashioned three-storey narrow-fronted house towards the end of Thurles Mews at the top of Down Street. The place was in darkness except for the basement window through which a crack of light showed between the curtains.

Callaghan rang the bell and waited. Two or three minutes afterwards the door opened. Facing him in the dimly lit not badly furnished hallway was an oversized man. He looked like a bruiser. He had a cauliflower ear, shifty eyes. Callaghan thought he looked unpleasant.

'Well?' said the man.

Callaghan put his hands in his overcoat pockets.

'Good evenin',' he said pleasantly. 'My name's Callaghan. I'm makin' some enquiries about Wilfred Riverton. He had a room here. You're Horker, aren't you . . . an ex-con?'

The man nodded.

'That's right,' he said. 'My name's Horker an', as you say, I'm an ex-con, although what the hell that's got to do with you I don't know. I don't know anythin' about young Riverton. He lived here, that's all. I'm not answerin' any questions. So you know what you can do with your enquiries!'

He began to close the door. Callaghan put his foot out and kicked the door back. He stepped into the passage, closed the door behind him. He began to smile . . . ominously.

'So you're lookin' for a little trouble,' he said evenly. 'You want to be funny . . . hey?'

Horker said: 'Why not?'

Callaghan shrugged his shoulders.

'Oh well . . . ' he began.

He stepped backwards towards the door as if he intended leaving. Then, with a sudden movement, he brought his right hand out of his pocket and sent a vicious short-arm jab into Horker's stomach. Horker gasped, doubled up, fell with a crash against a hatstand. He lay there, gasping like a cod-fish, trying to straighten out.

Callaghan listened. No one in the house – if there was anybody in the place – seemed to take any notice of the noise.

Horker, his face twisted with pain, mouthing obscenities, began to get up. Callaghan bent down, put his left hand under Horker's chin, turned it round, smashed his right fist into the twisted face. Horker's head went back with a smack against the wainscoting. Callaghan went down on his knees. Quietly and systematically he began to slap Horker across the face . . . hard.

'So you're not talkin',' he said.

Horker said nothing. Callaghan put the thumb of his right hand on Horker's nose, pushed it flat against his face. Then, as he released the nose with his thumb, he brought his left fist over and smashed it flat again. Horker began to whimper.

Callaghan started slapping again. Two minutes afterwards Horker began to whine thinly and then decided to talk.

Callaghan stood in the centre of The Mug's bedroom. Between him and the doorway, with a blackened eye, with nose and cheeks puffed to nearly double their normal size, stood Horker.

Systematically Callaghan began to search the room. He covered every inch. He found nothing at all. He gave it up.

From his pocket he produced two cigarettes. He gave one to Horker.

Horker sat down. His eyes regarded Callaghan malevolently.

'You listen to me,' said Callaghan. 'I want to know something, and you can help me. This feller Riverton had been usin' dope. Somebody supplied it to him. You knew that? I reckon he used this room here as a place where he could sleep it off. Maybe he used to have a lady friend come here sometimes. Maybe she was the woman who supplied the dope. You know who she is. Her name's Azelda Dixon. I want to know where she lives.'

Horker ran his tongue over his swollen lips.

'She's got a flat in Sloane Street,' he said. 'No. 17 Court Mansions.'

He put the cigarette into his mouth.

'You think you're bloody smart,' he said, 'but if I was you I'd take it easy. You're not going to be too popular – you bastard—'

Callaghan grinned.

'That's a thing that never worries me,' he said. 'Now you tell me somethin' else, but before I ask the question I'd like to tell you a couple of things. You can play this business which way you like. My way or the other way. If you play it my way – all right, maybe there'll be a few pounds in it for you, an' you'll keep out of the hands of the police. If you don't, I'm goin' to get through to Scotland Yard an' tell Gringall – who's handlin' this case – that you were in with the Dixon woman in buyin' and sellin' this dope. Well that won't do you any good, will it? You wouldn't have a chance.'

'Well, what of it?' said Horker, 'and aren't you forgettin' something? If I play ball with you, I'm going to get a few quid and keep my nose clean. If I don't you're going to start talking to Scotland Yard. But there's a third thing. There's some other smart people might not like the idea of my talkin' so much to you.'

'That's easy,' said Callaghan. 'If you're gettin' scared pack your bag an' get out. Nobody would miss you.'

He blew a stream of cigarette smoke from one nostril.

'You take your mind back to yesterday night,' he said. 'What time did The Mug get here?'

'He was here at eight o'clock,' said Horker.

'All right,' said Callaghan, 'and after that somebody called for him in a car, didn't they? Somewhere about nine o'clock.'

'No,' said Horker. 'Nobody called for him. He went out. He asked me to get him a cab at twenty to nine.'

'How was he?' asked Callaghan. 'Was he hopped up?'

'No,' said Horker. 'He didn't look dopey to me. He was just cock-eyed.'

He got up from the bed and stretched himself, licking his dry lips.

'He told me to tell the driver to take him round to Court Mansions in Sloane Street, and he was in a hell of a hurry. He didn't even wait to put a collar on. He just turned up his overcoat collar and went as he was.'

'I see,' said Callaghan. 'So somethin' got him out in a hurry. Was there a phone call?'

Horker shook his head.

'He got a note,' he said. 'It was pushed through the doorway. His name was typewritten on the envelope. He got it when he came in, and that's the lot.'

'All right,' said Callaghan. 'Do you own this place?'

Horker shook his head.

'I just look after it,' he said. 'I'm a sort of sub-tenant.'

Callaghan grinned.

'Like hell you are,' he said. He walked to the door. 'You take a tip from me,' he said. 'You get out before they get at you.'

Horker grinned.

'You're tellin' me,' he said.

He felt tenderly over his face with careful fingers.

'I'm gettin' out,' he said. 'But I hope they get *you*. I hope they burn you alive . . . !'

Maninway was leaning up against the wall at the far end of the Silver Bar, wise-cracking with the barmaid. He was tall and slim and nicely turned out. His suit was well-cut and his shirt and collar were expensive. His hair was sleeked down, his eyes shifty and too close together.

When he saw Callaghan he said bye-bye to the barmaid and crossed over the room towards the detective. They sat down at a table against the wall. Callaghan ordered two double whiskies and sodas.

'Well . . . ?' he said.

Maninway straightened his tie.

'The twenty is as good as in my pocket,' he said airily. 'I know all about the lady. It wasn't a bit difficult.'

'All right,' said Callaghan. 'Start talkin'. I'm in a hurry.'

Maninway waited while the waiter put the drinks on the table. He took out a thin cigarette-case, offered a Turkish cigarette to Callaghan who refused it, took one himself, lit it, took a drink and began.

'Thorla Riverton is a honey,' he said. 'Everybody's agreed about that. She's thirty years old. She belongs to a nice old family who had a place in Northumberland named Southwick-Breon. She was one of those young women who are usually described as vital.

'She was engaged at twenty-two to a fellow called Mathieson. He was a very nice sort of person by what I can hear – an Army fellow. He was seconded to the Indian Army, and then got himself killed in one of those periodical show-downs that happen on the North-West Frontier. Apparently little Thorla was nuts about this Mathieson bird.

'Well, the news trickled home, and it hit her for six to the boundary. She went hay-wire. She'd always been a very steady sort of girl – popular with her family and all that, but when she heard that Mathieson had been killed rather unpleasantly – *after* he'd been wounded – she went off the deep end properly . . . you can imagine . . .'

Callaghan nodded.

'When she was twenty-four she came into some money and she proceeded to knock things about properly. She did a little dashing about and a lot of gambling. She was a one for gambling. I don't think that she let herself go where men were concerned, but she certainly knocked a hole into her money and got herself nicely tied up with a first-class bunch of moneylenders. I suppose she was certain that she could win if she went on long enough. I s'pose, really,' said Maninway, 'that she was indulgin' in that process commonly known as "trying to forget".

'Her old father practically bust himself putting the money thing straight and after that little Thorla took a pull at herself. I suppose she didn't really like the idea of hurtin' her family. When she was twenty-seven, old man Riverton came along, full of shekels an' lookin' for a pretty wife to act as a stay for his declinin' years. She married him. I rather think she was pushed into it by the family. Just after the marriage Riverton was taken ill. He's been ill ever since, but she's been what is known as a good wife. She's stayed put and behaved herself nicely and taken care of the old boy – at least that's what they say, although, I must say it's a bit hard to believe.'

'Why?' asked Callaghan.

Maninway shrugged.

'I don't know,' he said. 'But it's always been my experience that when a girl goes a bit wild when she's young an' unmarried, she usually wants to go a bit wild when she's a little older and married. But that's only my guess,' he concluded.

'It's as good as anybody's,' said Callaghan.

He finished his drink, took out his pocket-book and put two ten-pound notes on the table. Maninway picked them up with long, sensitive fingers and put them in his waistcoat pocket.

'Nice, easy work,' he said with a smile that showed his teeth.

Callaghan said:

'There'll be some more.' He lit a cigarette. 'Would you like to make another fifty?' he asked.

Maninway smiled.

'Try me,' he said.

'The main thing is that you keep your mouth shut,' said Callaghan. 'I don't trust you a lot, Maninway – you know that, an' I'd hate you to talk.'

'I'm no great believer in talking,' said Maninway casually. 'At least not to the wrong people. Besides I'm too clever to talk about *your* business.'

'Yes?' said Callaghan.

'Yes,' said Maninway, still smiling. 'I remember Percy Bellin. He did a job for you one time and also did a bit of talking about it afterwards. He got eight months a year later, and nobody could guess how the police got the evidence. *I guessed.*'

'Wise feller,' said Callaghan. He leaned over the table. 'There's a woman I know called Azelda Dixon,' he said. 'She's not a bad sort of woman. She's a bit scared at the moment, and she dopes a little. I think she was rather nice once.'

He stubbed out his cigarette.

'I want her kept amused one evenin',' he said. 'I want her stuck in some place talkin' just so that I know where she is and so that I know she won't be disturbing anybody for a bit. I'm goin' to get a friend of mine to tell her that a young feller who's unhappily married and who wants a divorce from his wife is lookin' for a professional co-respondent. I'm goin' to get my friend to tell her that there's a hundred in it for her, an' ask her if she'll meet the young feller and talk it over. That ought to take an hour or so.'

Maninway smiled happily.

'And I'm to be the unhappily married one, am I?' he said. 'And my job is to keep Azelda talkin' the matter over.'

'That's the idea,' said Callaghan. 'You think the story out – a nice long one. If I pull my end I'll tell you where you're to meet her. Have a good tale ready for her and tell it as if it was the truth – that ought to be easy – for you,' he said.

'I'm your man,' said Maninway. 'I'd tell anybody anything for fifty. Life around Mayfair is not so easy these days. You'll let me know?'

'I'll call you,' said Callaghan. 'Good night.'

Callaghan went into the Italian all-night café round the corner from Hay Hill. He ordered a cup of coffee and drank it slowly. Then he walked to the Green Park Tube Station and telephoned to Scotland Yard. He asked if Mr Gringall were there and if so would he speak to Mr Callaghan. Gringall came on the line.

'Hallo, Gringall,' he said. 'I'm sorry to worry you this time of night, but I'm a bit worried.'

'Too bad,' said Gringall. 'What's worrying you, Slim?'

'Mrs Riverton left a note at my place,' said Callaghan – he was picking his words carefully. 'She said that she'd been in to see you early this evenin'. She said that you'd told her that it might be a good thing if I put her on to a firm of lawyers who were more experienced in criminal practice than Selby, Raukes & White. I wondered what was in your mind. I rather thought that you took it that this case was in the bag, and I didn't want to do anything that would get me in wrong.'

'I see,' said Gringall.

There was a pause, then he went on:

'My talk with Mrs Riverton this evening was more or less unofficial – if there is such a thing. She's worried sick, naturally. Now that Colonel Riverton's dead she feels she's got to do her damnedest for young Riverton. That's understandable, isn't it?'

'Very,' said Callaghan.

He was fumbling with one hand for a cigarette.

'The point is that The Mug's taken a turn for the better,' Gringall continued. 'They operated this afternoon. They've got the bullet out of him and the surgeon thinks he's got an even chance. He's conscious but very weak. Now I was thinking that if you had a good lawyer who knew his stuff he might be able to help us *and* young Riverton. You know the law, and you know that we can't take any statement from a suspect that's likely to incriminate him. But it might easily be that young Riverton's prepared to talk – for his own good. He might have some reasonable sort of excuse for having put that slug into Jake Raffano – an excuse that a jury might consider reasonable, I mean. See what I'm getting at?'

Callaghan lit his cigarette. He was thinking that Gringall was a very clever police officer.

'I see . . . ' he said. 'Thanks for the tip, Gringall. If you're satisfied with the way things are goin', then I am. I just don't want to do anything that isn't in order.'

He was grinning.

Gringall said.

'I'm not satisfied, Slim. This case isn't so easy. I think it's in the bag that Raffano shot young Riverton. It's a stone certainty that young Riverton shot and killed Raffano, but there's more to it. There was somebody else on that boat and I want to find that somebody else. . . . '

'You don't say,' said Callaghan. There was note of surprise in his voice. 'So there was somebody else aboard. . . . '

'Of course there was,' Gringall's voice was casual. 'The fellow who telephoned through to the Yard with the news about the shooting. That fellow had been on the boat, hadn't he? My point is that young Riverton might know who that fellow was – that he might be prepared to tell his lawyer. Possibly that fellow might corroborate any favourable story that Riverton puts up, and there's a chance that a self-defence plea might get over with a jury. See . . . ?'

'I see,' said Callaghan. 'Thank you, Gringall. I'll have a talk with Mrs Riverton.'

'There's another thing,' said Gringall quietly. 'There was a safe let into the rear wall of the saloon. It was locked. I had it opened. It was empty and there were no fingerprints on it. Yet Raffano had a lot of money about him. My information is that he was carrying a lot of cash and that he'd drawn something like forty thousand from a bank that morning. I'd like to know where that money is. . . . '

'I bet you would,' said Callaghan. 'It would be dam' interesting.'

'All right,' said Gringall. 'Good night, Slim. Take care of yourself. I'll see you some time.'

Callaghan said good night and hung up. He walked back to Berkeley Square and went straight up to his apartment. He took off his overcoat and hat, took three fingers of neat whisky, went into the sitting-room and rang through on the house telephone to Wilkie. He looked at his watch. It was twelve-five. He asked if Mrs Riverton had telephoned. Wilkie said no.

Callaghan rang the Chartres Hotel on his bedroom telephone. The clerk said that Mrs Riverton wasn't in. At the same moment the house telephone jangled. Callaghan hung up and went back to his sitting-room. It was Wilkie, who said that Mrs Riverton was on the line. Callaghan took the call.

Her voice was very tired and a little unsteady.

'I'm a little late calling,' she said. 'You got my note, Mr Callaghan?'

'Yes,' he answered. 'Are you talking from the Chartres Hotel? I don't want anyone to overhear you.'

She said she was. Callaghan grinned.

'Hold on for a minute,' he said. 'There's someone at my apartment door.'

He walked quickly into the bedroom and got through to Wilkie on his private phone.

'Listen, Wilkie,' he said. 'I'm talkin' on one of your switchboard lines to Mrs Riverton. I'm goin' on talkin' to her. Directly I put this receiver down get through to the exchange on another line and check up where she's calling from. Understand?'

Wilkie said OK.

Callaghan went back to the sitting-room.

'It's all right, Madame,' he said. 'Now we can talk. An' there's quite a lot I want to say to you, but I don't want to say it on the telephone. I think you'd better come round here. Wilkie, the hall porter, will bring you up.'

There was a pause. Then she said:

'Very well . . . but I'm fearfully tired.'

'I'm sorry,' said Callaghan. 'I hate bein' tired too. I'll expect you in ten minutes. An' there's another thing,' he went on. 'When you come round bring your cheque book . . . you're goin' to need it.'

'What did you say?' she demanded. Her voice was odd.

81

'You heard,' said Callaghan. 'I told you to bring your cheque book. I'll expect you in ten minutes.'

He smacked the receiver back on the hook. He waited a moment, then took it off. Wilkie came on the line.

'Well?' said Callaghan.

'OK, Mr Callaghan,' he said. 'They checked that call. It came from the coffee bar in Bird Street just off Knightsbridge.'

'Nice work,' said Callaghan. He went back into his bedroom and drank some more whisky.

CHAPTER SEVEN

Sunday

Cross-examination for one

Callaghan was standing in front of the fire smoking. It was still raining. He was listening to the raindrops pattering on the window, thinking that you never knew anything about women, that if you did it didn't get you anywhere and you were usually wrong anyhow.

He straightened up as the lift came up, heard Wilkie open the apartment door.

Thorla Riverton stood in the doorway of the sitting-room. She was wearing a close fitting black dinner-gown underneath an open Persian lamb coat. Her face was very white, her eyes too bright. Callaghan looked at her, looked at the tiny satin shoes which showed under the edge of her gown. He found himself thinking that she had lovely feet, and wondering why the devil he should bother about that . . . now.

She came into the room. Callaghan motioned towards the big armchair with his head. She sat down. He offered her a cigarette, she refused it.

'I'm very tired,' she said, 'but I supposed that it was important that I should see you. I don't want to stay here longer than I can help.'

Callaghan said:

'You feel you want to get it over quickly. Well, I don't think that's goin' to be possible. I think you and I have got to talk about a lot of things. First of all, I'd like you to know that I know one or two things about you.'

He stopped and lit a cigarette. She watched him, her eyes steadily on him, unwavering.

'I don't want you to think,' said Callaghan, 'that I am interested in you just out of curiosity. I'm not. I've got another reason – I'll tell you that in a minute. In the meantime it is enough for you to know that I've more or less got an idea of your history. I know that you used to be pretty fond of gamblin', and I know that the whole set-up behind this killin' business on the *San Pedro* is a gamblin' set-up, so you'll understand that I'm lookin' on you now not merely as being my client in this case, but as somebody who I think has taken an active part in it.'

She moved a little.

'Exactly what do you mean by that, Mr Callaghan?' she said.

Callaghan grinned.

'I'll tell you,' he said. 'I went on the *San Pedro* about half-past twelve last night. I went aboard that boat because an operative of mine – Monty Kells – who'd been workin' in that district, found out where she was. I thought I'd like to get aboard because Jake would be packin' up to get out. I still think I was right. That's what he was doin'.

'I was on the telephone tonight to Gringall at Scotland Yard. He told me that Jake drew £40,000 out of the bank yesterday morning. Gringall seems to have an idea that that money, an' possibly some other money, was in the wall safe behind Raffano's desk in the saloon. Gringall had the safe opened. It was empty.

'Yesterday Kells telephoned through to me with a very interestin' bit of information. He called it a tit-bit an' maybe it was only a tit-bit to him because he didn't see the connection. Kells had found an old feller called Jimmy Wilpins who lived in a cottage at the end of the fork that led down to the landin' place at Falleton. This feller Wilpins couldn't sleep last night. He was lookin' out of the window at a quarter to twelve and he saw a woman land from the *San Pedro*. She was wearin' an ocelot cloak – he called it a tiger-skin cloak. That was *you*. . . . '

He was watching her. He saw her long jewelled fingers contract on the arms of the chair.

'I've got an idea what happened,' said Callaghan. 'You'd expected to go over to the Nursing Home at Swansdown Poulteney. You knew the Colonel was pretty ill and I bet the doctors had told you that they didn't think he could last much longer. But you didn't go over there. You didn't go over because something more important turned up – probably somebody telephoned you, and my guess is that that somebody was Jake Raffano.

'So you worked it out. You thought the thing for you to do was to get aboard the *San Pedro* as quickly as you could, get that interview over and cut across country to Swansdown. You hoped you'd make it in time, but you didn't. The Colonel was dead when you got there. Right?'

She said nothing.

'Now I don't suppose you want to talk to me very much,' Callaghan went on. 'You don't like me anyway, but even if you did you probably don't feel like makin' a confession as to why you were on that boat, although I've got a dam' good idea why you were there.'

She spoke. Her voice was very low, very tired, a little hoarse. She said:

'Well, why was I there?'

Callaghan grinned again.

'We'll come to that in a minute,' he said. 'In the meantime, I'd like to ask you a question or two. Now let me make myself quite plain as to why I'm askin' these questions. Nobody's goin' to suspect that you were on that boat. The feller who can give you away is Jimmy Wilpins. Well, I've taken care of him. I did some heavy drivin' earlier this evening an' I had a talk with Jimmy. He may be old but he still likes money, and you'd be surprised at what the sight of ten ten-pound notes did for him. He's takin' a little trip, gettin' out of Falleton for a few months, an' he's forgotten that he ever saw a woman in an ocelot cloak comin' off the *San Pedro*. So that's that.'

'Why did you do that?' she asked. Her voice was thin.

Callaghan threw his cigarette end into the fire.

'I'm not quite certain,' he said. He looked at her. 'I think the main reason is that I'm stuck on you. You look like a woman ought to look, you move an' speak in the way I think a woman ought to move an' speak. I suppose I didn't like the idea of you facin' a murder charge.'

She raised her eyebrows. Callaghan went on:

'You came off that boat at a quarter to twelve,' he said. 'Do you remember a waste-paper basket under the steel-legged table in the little saloon – the table that was beside the bar?'

She nodded.

'Nobody could help seein' into the waste-paper basket,' said Callaghan. 'There was some torn-up paper in it. It wasn't torn into small pieces either. It had been torn across rather as if whoever had thrown it into the waste-paper basket had wanted somebody to see what it was. Do you know what it was?'

She nodded again.

'It was an IOU for £22,000,' Callaghan went on, 'made out to Jake Raffano and signed by The Mug. I've got it in my desk drawer here. I'm goin' to burn it tonight. It's a dam' dangerous piece of evidence.'

'Is it?' she said. 'Why?'

'It constitutes a first-class motive for The Mug goin' down there an' killin' Raffano,' said Callaghan. 'Work it out. Raffano is packin' up to

85

get out. He wants to settle up his money affairs. He tells The Mug to come down an' see him an' straighten things out. He probably tells The Mug that he's got to raise that £22,000 somehow an' take up that IOU or else Jake is goin' to get dam' funny. Possibly he threatened to go an' see the Colonel about it.

'I think The Mug got desperate. I think he felt he'd got to raise that money somehow. Probably Raffano had got one or two things on him. I should think young Riverton tried everything he could and failed, an' then I should think as a last resource he rang you up an' told you that he was goin' down to the boat an' that he was goin' to see Raffano, that he was goin' to try an' get that IOU back. That's one good reason as to why you should have been on that boat, an' there's still another.'

'What is it?' she asked.

'Maybe it wasn't The Mug who told you he was goin' on that boat,' said Callaghan grimly. 'Maybe it was Azelda Dixon. Maybe you have been workin' with Raffano.'

'What do you mean?' she said softly . . . ominously.

'I'll tell you,' said Callaghan. 'First of all I think it's dam' odd that Raffano's boat should be down at Falleton which is about the nearest mooring place, for a boat that size, to Southing – where the Manor House is. See? You used to be hell of a gambler in the old days an' it's not easy to believe that after you married old Riverton you suddenly changed for the better. I bet you didn't give a damn about the old man. You married him because you'd got through your money an' used up a chunk of your father's in gettin' your gamblin' debts paid.

'Well, the old boy's been ill for some time, hasn't he? Maybe you knew he was goin' to die. You knew that The Mug would inherit the Riverton cash. Maybe you an' Jake had your own ideas about that. . . .'

She interrupted. She sat looking at him with extraordinarily bright eyes, not moving her head. She spoke as if she was reciting something.

'You awful liar,' she said. 'You beastly awful, terrible liar. . . . '

Callaghan looked at her sharply. He caught his lower lip between his teeth and continued to look at her for some moments, then he began to walk up and down the room in front of the fireplace. Most of the time he was watching her. He was thinking that she looked rather like a drooping lily that had been wired up.

'I'm interested in that IOU of The Mug's,' he went on. 'Very interested. Let's suppose for the sake of argument that we take it that

86

The Mug went down to the *San Pedro* for the purpose of gettin' back his IOU. Let's suppose that he got it back, an' let's forget for the moment that he was shot. Well, he wouldn't tear that IOU up and leave it in the waste-paper basket for somebody to find, would he? You bet he wouldn't. He would have taken it off with him.

'But he *was* shot, an' yet somebody tears up that IOU an' leaves it where somebody else is sure to find it. Well – that was done before The Mug was wounded, wasn't it?'

She moved suddenly. Callaghan saw her eyes, dark and burning, looking into his . . . searching his face. . . .

'Why do you say that?' she asked. 'Why do you say that someone tore up that IOU *before* Wilfred was wounded? How do you arrive at that conclusion?'

Callaghan shrugged. He went off on another track.

'All right,' he said. 'Let's try it your way. If somebody else was on that boat and tore up the IOU *after* The Mug was wounded, then the presumption is that they were on the boat and got that IOU off Jake or The Mug after the shootin'.'

He stopped his pacing to light another cigarette.

'That presupposes that whoever it was tore up the IOU just stood around, watched the gunfight between Jake an' The Mug an' then, when it was over an' Jake was dead an' The Mug unconscious, this somebody takes the IOU, tears it up an' throws it into the waste-paper basket where it will be found by the police, who will promptly come to the conclusion that this IOU was the cause of the shootin'.'

'Maybe,' said Callaghan pleasantly, 'that's your idea of the thing. Personally, I think you might be right, an' if you *are* right, it doesn't look so good for you, because everything that this somebody else did matches up pretty well with what you might have been doin' on that boat. See?'

She nodded.

'I see,' she said bitterly.

Callaghan looked at her keenly. She was almost limp with tiredness. She was keeping her head up on sheer will-power.

He stopped his pacing and went into the bedroom. He poured out four fingers of whisky into a glass and added soda water. He brought the drink to her and offered her a cigarette.

She took the drink and the cigarette.

Callaghan sat down in the armchair opposite. He said:

'Why did you say that you were telephonin' from the Chartres Hotel when you spoke to me? I had the call checked. You were speakin' from some place in Knightsbridge. What was the idea in that?'

'I won't answer your questions,' she said.

He shrugged.

'I don't care a damn, Madame, whether you answer 'em or not,' he said. 'I shall find out why. I'm what they call intrigued with you. I'd like to know where you've been since you left that note here this evenin'. What you've been doin' an' who you've been talkin' to. I'd like to know a lot of things.'

'I expect you would,' she said. A small cynical smile twisted her mouth. 'I expect you would,' she repeated. 'But these things do not come within your province, Mr Callaghan.'

He began to grin.

'You think you're sittin' pretty, don't you?' he said. 'I suppose you think you've got me bull-dozed like the other men you've met. Like old Riverton – an' he was a cute old bird too, you must have been dam' good to pull the wool over his eyes – an' possibly Jake Raffano, who thought he was goin' to get away with a packet of money an' only succeeded in winnin' himself a slug through the heart.'

He got up and took a cigarette from the box on the mantelpiece. He lit it slowly, stood with his back to the fire blowing smoke rings, his eyes on her face.

'I suppose you think that because I've squared old Jimmy Wilpins an' paid him to keep his mouth shut, that I've put myself alongside you an' that I've got myself in a spot that I can't get out of – sort of made myself an accessory "after the fact"? Well, maybe that's what I have done, but I've still got a kick left.'

She was lying back in the chair half-languorously.

'Have you, Mr Callaghan?' she said. 'How very interesting.'

'It's dam' interestin',' said Callaghan. 'I went aboard that boat last night at twelve-thirty. When I got aboard those two had been shot for some time . . . *exactly* how long I don't know, an' I don't suppose the doctors will either – at least not so's it'll do anybody any good.

'*You* were on that boat at half-past eleven anyway. You came off it at a quarter to twelve . . . that was the time that Wilpins saw you. All right, then, either the shootin' occurred before you got on to the boat, in which case you must have seen those two lyin' in the saloon, or else it occurred after you left the boat at a quarter to twelve. My guess is that it happened either before you got on to the boat or while you were on it.'

'Why?' she asked.

'Because Jake was gettin' nice an' stiff when I got down there,' he said. 'That feller had been dead for over an hour. I know that he wasn't shot between eleven forty-five when you left the boat an' twelve-thirty when I went on her. See . . . ?'

'Does it matter?' she said. 'Why, if you've been chivalrous enough' – she made no attempt to keep the sarcasm out of her voice – 'to take another of your sensational car journeys and bribe the man Wilpins to keep silence about having seen me, do all these points matter? Or are you merely trying to establish sufficient evidence against me so that it may be easy for you to blackmail me in the future?'

He grinned.

'That's a sweet one – comin' from you,' he said. 'It just makes me laugh, although before I'm through maybe you'll be right, an' maybe I shall do a little blackmailin'. Perhaps I'll start in tonight. But if you want to know why all these points matter, I'll tell you.

'First of all, don't you try an' believe that Gringall is satisfied with this job. He's not. He knows that somebody besides Raffano an' The Mug were on that boat. Maybe he thinks I know a bit more about this business than I've told him – an' he would be right! Gringall's no fool. He's as sharp as they make 'em. An' he's got a very good idea. He's passing us the buck.'

She wriggled back in her chair. She was restless, uncomfortable. She held the still burning cigarette in her left hand and the glass of whisky and soda in her right, but she wasn't worrying very much about either smoking or drinking.

'What do you mean?' she asked.

'Gringall can't take a statement from your stepson that would incriminate him,' said Callaghan. 'That's the law. He's suggested to me that I put you on to a good criminal lawyer an' that this lawyer should go down an' see Riverton an' get some sort of statement from him. Gringall's idea is that if The Mug comes across an' says just what happened on that boat, then possibly there might be a chance of our gettin' away with a self-defence plea on the lines that The Mug knew that Raffano was armed, that knowin' it he took a gun down there with him, an' that he only used it in self-defence *after* Raffano had fired the shot that wounded him. Gringall thinks that if this is what happened an' The Mug knows that there was somebody else on the boat then, we'll produce 'em to corroborate his story, after which Gringall can begin to do some *real* detective work because he'll have some new facts an' some new evidence to work on.'

She said: 'Perhaps Wilfred doesn't know that there was anyone else on the boat except himself and Jake Raffano . . . perhaps he doesn't know . . . ' her voice was dull and lifeless.

Callaghan grinned happily.

'Right,' he said. 'I'll bet my life he doesn't know. Because I'll bet that you went aboard after the shooting of Jake . . . '

She interrupted. She still spoke in a strange monotone.

'You are only trying to trap me,' she said. 'That's all . . . just trying to trap *me*!' Her voice almost shrilled at the end of the sentence.

'Don't talk nonsense,' said Callaghan. 'When you talk like that you make me tired – even if I do know why you're talkin' like that. I'm not botherin' about trappin' anybody. I told you I was goin' to handle this case in my own way, an' by God I'm goin' to do it, an' if you or anybody else tries to stop me, I'm goin' to get dam' funny . . . that's all.'

He walked over to the window, pulled aside the curtain, stood looking out at the teeming rain.

'I'm in this up to my neck,' he said. 'I've done it on Gringall by not tellin' him that I was on that boat last night. I've also made myself an accessory to a felony by bribin' old Wilpins to keep his mouth shut an' get out until this thing blows over. Well, I'm goin' to handle this my own way an' if you don't want to help to keep yourself out of a bunch of trouble you can do what you dam' well like, but what you *won't* do is to interfere with me . . . at least more than you usually do. . . . '

'What do you mean by that?' she asked. Her voice was under better control.

'You worry me all the time,' said Callaghan, dropping the curtain and going back to the fireplace. 'I'm too dam' interested in you. When I'm workin' on a case I like to keep my mind on it an' not concern myself with thinkin' about some woman, or how she puts her feet on the ground, or the nice way she talks or how she managed to get the kind of curves that she's got or . . . '

She smiled maliciously.

'Really, Mr Callaghan,' she said. 'Do you find curves dangerous. Is it possible that the great, the one and only Mr Callaghan is affected by mere curves . . . ?'

She began to laugh shrilly.

Callaghan said:

'I don't like you very much when you behave like that, when you talk in that odd voice and look as if you've lost somethin' of the quality that's about you. Don't you be a fool. I expect you're worried an' unhappy an' tired, an' maybe miserable, but there's no need for you to be doin' what you've been doin' tonight . . . *you* ought to know better. . . .'

She flushed. The flush started at her cheeks and spread down to her neck and shoulders.

Callaghan grinned. His eyes were on the flat evening-bag that lay on the chair beside her. In two steps he was at her side and the bag in his hand. She put up one hand in a futile gesture that was half-made, then gave a little shrug. She looked into the fire.

He opened the bag and found what he was looking for. Under all the oddments – the lace handkerchief, the little perfume spray, the loose money, the keys, the compact – he found it. The small glass bulb with the Japanese lettering on the paper capsule.

'Morphine,' he said thickly. 'I knew it when you couldn't drink that whisky . . . you bloody fool . . . ! An' I thought you had guts.'

He threw the bulb into the fire.

She put her head down between her hands. She began to sob . . . hoarsely.

Callaghan went into the bedroom. He rang a Mayfair number and waited, then:

'Is that you, Mumpey?' he said. 'This is Callaghan. Do you remember those anti-morphine ampoules – the calomelatrophine things you let me have last year . . . the ones we got for that Rocksell bird . . . OK. Send a couple round right away. Give 'em to Wilkie downstairs, put 'em in a plain box an' tell him to keep 'em until I ask for 'em. No . . . you don't need a strong dose . . . just a nice mild dose for a case that's been doin' a little morphine experimentin'. Thanks . . . good night.'

He went back into the sitting-room. She was still sitting with her head between her hands.

'All right,' said Callaghan. 'So you're beat. Now listen to a spot of sense. I'm gettin' this lawyer tomorrow an' he's smart enough. We're

91

goin' to get some sort of story out of young Riverton an' when we've got it we'll see what we can do with it. In the meantime you get back to the Manor House an' behave yourself like Mrs Thorla Riverton. I won't ask you what you've been doin' tonight or where you've been, because my guess is as good as anybody's.

'You go home and stay there. I'll get into touch with you. An' keep your head shut . . . don't talk to anybody. Understand?'

She nodded miserably.

'You're in a dam' tough spot,' said Callaghan. 'If Gringall so much as hears a whisper about you, an' checks up on you, he might begin to take a new angle on this case, an' he'd have all the motive in the world for thinkin' that way too.'

'Motive . . . ' the word was almost a whisper.

'That's the word,' said Callaghan. 'Motive . . . it's a word the police are very fond of.'

He lit a cigarette and drew the smoke down into his lungs.

'You knew old man Riverton was goin' to die,' he said. 'They'll say that you fixed it so that you were left as sole executor an' trustee to administer both his estate an' the money that was comin' to The Mug. They'll say that you an' Raffano got together and started The Mug on the drink an' dope business just so that the old boy wouldn't let him handle the money.

'All right. Well, the Colonel's dead, isn't he? That's that. An' there's a policeman sittin' in the hospital at Ballington waitin' for somethin' to happen to The Mug. Either he's goin' to die, in which case you'll have all the money an' be sittin' pretty or else he's goin' to get better, in which case – the way things look now – he's goin' to swing for killin' Jake, an' you still get the money. See? Does that look like motive or does it?'

She sat looking at him. She looked like death.

'This could be a honey of a case,' said Callaghan grimly. 'An' if I was Gringall, knowing what I know, I know how I'd think about it. The Mug went down to that boat to have a show-down with Raffano. He took a gun with him. He was goin' to have his IOU back and some of his money . . . an' I think I know what made him go down there to get those things. All right . . . Jake gets funny about it, an' The Mug pulls his gun. Jake goes for his own gun that is in the desk drawer, but The Mug fires first an' gets Jake through the heart.

'Well, there's somebody else on the boat, an' that somebody takes a hand in things. The Mug is doped silly, an' it's easy to put a bullet into him – whoever it was shot him left him for dead. Then this clever person puts their fingers round Jake's hand and pulls the trigger of his gun once – after they've got the gun pointing out of a porthole so that the bullet won't be found. Then they take the IOU and the cash out of the safe, usin' Jake's key an' wearin' gloves. They tear up the IOU an' leave it so that it's goin' to look as if that was the cause of the shootin'.'

He lit another cigarette.

'There's a possible reconstruction,' he said. 'An' it's a *very* possible one.'

'You're goin' back to the hotel now,' he went on. 'You'd better fix your face before you go. I've got some stuff comin' round here. I'll give it to you. It'll put that post-morphine feelin' right. You take one ampoule tonight in water an' another tomorrow mornin'. You'll have a head an' your throat'll feel lousy, but it'll get rid of that dope an' you'll be yourself.'

He went through the bedroom into the bathroom. He came back with an eau-de-Cologne spray, a face towel, and a small bottle of sal volatile. He gave them to her.

'You get busy on your face,' he said. 'You look like the wreck of the *Hesperus*.'

He went out of the apartment and rang for the lift. Wilkie came up with the small white box from the chemists. Callaghan took it from him, sent him down, went back to the sitting-room, opened her bag, put the ampoules inside.

She was standing in front of the mirror over the mantelpiece doing her face. He stood watching her. When she had finished she turned round.

'I don't quite know what to say to you,' she said.

He grinned.

'You don't have to say anything,' he said. 'Have you brought that cheque book?'

She nodded.

He produced a fountain pen.

'You write me out a cheque – an open cheque – payable to cash or Bearer for five thousand pounds,' he said casually.

She stiffened.

'So it is blackmail?' she said. Her voice was cutting.

He was still grinning.

'Anything you like, Madame,' he said. 'You write that cheque for five thousand . . . and like it . . . and if I want anything else I'll tell you.'

'What do you mean?' she said slowly. 'Anything else. . . . '

'I'll let you know,' said Callaghan.

He was grinning . . . wickedly.

She moved to the table. Took the cheque book out of the bag, wrote out the cheque. She got up and handed it to him. She held it as far away from her as she could.

He looked at it and put it in his pocket. He took up the house telephone.

'Get a cab, Wilkie,' he said. 'An' bring the lift up.'

He lit a cigarette and stood in front of the fireplace, watching her. She kept her eyes on the floor. They heard the lift arrive.

'Good night, Madame,' said Callaghan. 'Any time I want you for anythin' I'll let you know. Don't forget to take the first ampoule tonight.'

She walked out of the room. He heard the lift descend.

Callaghan went into the bedroom and walked over to the cupboard in the corner. He took out the whisky bottle and took a long drink from it. Then he went into the bathroom and began to rub eau-de-Cologne into his hair.

After a moment or two he started to swear, cursing somebody or something horribly.

CHAPTER EIGHT

Monday

Nice work

Meet Mr Valentine Gagel.

Mr Gagel was a lawyer with a definite sense of his own limitations. While other lawyers have, on occasion, been known to overstep the mark, no such accusation could be brought against Mr Gagel. He knew just where to stop.

His office, not a mile from Dover Street, was well-furnished, cosy and inclined to invite confidence. His clientele consisted in the main of a number of young ladies most of whom seemed to have spent their lives falling into unforeseen circumstances which placed them – temporarily – at the mercy of married gentlemen – usually over middle-age – who had 'taken advantage' of them and, in the process, entirely ruined a life which up till then had been officially spotless.

The cases seldom went to Court. Mr Gagel saw to that. The middle-aged gentlemen usually paid up and continued on their way poorer, if not wiser men. Then, after Mr Gagel had taken his cut, the young ladies went off to seek fresh prey who, under the influence of a little drink or two, might be induced to try *their* hands at the 'take advantage of' game.

Mr Valentine Gagel was middle-aged and thin, and smiling. He was always very well-dressed and wore pince-nez which gave him the appearance of a rather vicious owl. He knew the criminal law and practice backwards, and it has been said of him that one of his great virtues lay in knowing when to advise a client to plead guilty and not get the Court into a bad temper. There were no flies on Mr Gagel.

On the one occasion when he had come up against Callaghan he had not done so well. He had discovered that a rather unique brain lay under the exterior of the proprietor of Callaghan Investigations. But he bore no ill-will. On the contrary he paid Mr Callaghan the compliment of considering him the only individual who had ever pulled a fast one on Gagel, and this, coming from Valentine, was praise of the very highest order.

He sat back in his chair and regarded Callaghan across the polished mahogany desk benevolently.

'Well, Mr Callaghan,' he said, 'it seems to me to be an unfortunate but quite obvious case, and if your idea is right it will be to our advantage *of course* to endeavour to find out who the mysterious individual was who was on the *San Pedro* at the time that the shooting took place. There must be a number of mitigating circumstances in this case. We must find them and . . . '

Callaghan interrupted.

'I don't know that I'm very interested in findin' mitigatin' circumstances,' he said. 'When you go down to Ballington an' get this statement from young Riverton, I want you to remember that he's in a very weak state of health, that he's probably not quite certain of what he's sayin'.'

'I see,' said Mr Gagel. 'I see,' he repeated. He looked at the ceiling. 'I take it, Mr Callaghan,' he said, 'that this statement which I am to take from Wilfred Riverton is a "solicitor and client" statement – a confidential document on which counsel will advise us as to what lines the defence will take *in* the event of a criminal charge against my client, *if* I may call him that.'

'I think you can call him that, Gagel,' said Callaghan. 'But I don't know that we want to regard this statement as being a confidential document.'

'*Really!*' The lawyer pursed his lips. He looked surprised. 'The procedure seems a little out of the ordinary, don't you think?' he said.

'Maybe it is,' said Callaghan. 'But then this isn't an ordinary case. As you know, Gagel, the family is an important one – they've got money.'

'Quite,' said Gagel.

He relaxed, took a cigarette from a silver box on the desk and lit it. He looked smilingly at Callaghan.

'I suppose, Mr Callaghan,' he said, 'you haven't got any ideas yourself about the lines that this statement from Mr Riverton will take?'

Callaghan grinned amiably.

'Well, to tell you the truth,' he said, 'I have. I've got an idea that the statement will be on these lines . . . '

Mr Gagel lay back in his chair, closed his eyes. It seemed that he was remembering very carefully what Callaghan was saying.

'This feller Riverton's been gettin' around with a bad crowd,' said

Callaghan. 'It is the usual story – a lot of money an' no brains. Raffano arranges that Riverton meets one or two not-so-good women, does a considerable amount of drinkin' and then at the end, begins takin' a little dope. Riverton loses a lot of money. Well, naturally he doesn't like it, an' then he hears that Raffano is clearin' out. Young Riverton suddenly decides to have a show-down with Raffano . . . '

'Quite,' interrupted Gagel. 'Don't you think it would be very interesting for us to know just what provocation decided Riverton to have a show-down with Jake Raffano?'

'I don't know that I do,' said Callaghan. 'I'd rather Wilfred Riverton made up his mind on the spur of the moment – without any provocation – to go down an' see Jake rather than think about it.'

'I see,' said the lawyer. 'The idea is that the shooting of Raffano was premeditated?'

Callaghan grinned. 'Right,' he said.

Gagel nodded. His smile had gone.

'All right,' said Callaghan. 'So he decides to go down an' see Jake. He goes down . . . '

'Forgive me interrupting again, Mr Callaghan,' said Gagel, 'but wouldn't you like me to have the complete story? Am I not right in thinking that our client was under the influence of drugs when he went down to the *San Pedro*?'

'That's the idea,' said Callaghan.

'Well, if he was,' Gagel went on, 'how did he get there? If he was drunk or doped he couldn't very well drive a car, could he?'

'Right again,' said Callaghan.

'It's a point,' said Gagel.

'I think we'll leave it for the moment,' said Callaghan. 'All right, he gets down on the boat, he's got a gun in his pocket . . . because he believes that Raffano may be armed, because he thinks Raffano may try an' get tough.'

Gagel nodded his head.

'Here again I think I'd like to interrupt, Mr Callaghan,' he said. 'I take it that young Riverton has for some time been meeting Raffano, talking to him, being in his company – why should he suddenly believe that Raffano was going to shoot him? The point I'm getting at is who told Wilfred Riverton that Jake Raffano *might* shoot him?'

'As you say,' said Callaghan with a grin. 'But that's another point we won't worry about. You see, Gagel,' he went on, 'all the points you're raisin' are very sound points. You go on raisin' 'em. They're the points that the police officer in charge of this case might raise *if*—' Callaghan's grin became a little broader – 'somebody was lousy enough to let him have a look at the statement that you're goin' to take from young Riverton.'

'*I see*, Mr Callaghan,' said Gagel. 'So it's like *that*, is it?'

'It's just like that,' said Callaghan. He went on: 'All right, Riverton gets down there – we don't know how he got down there, but he got down there. He got on the boat – we don't know how he got on the boat, but he got on it. Well, he's on the boat, he goes down to the saloon an' he meets Raffano. He tells Raffano that he's heard he's clearin' out . . .'

Gagel interrupted again.

'You asked me to interrupt, Mr Callaghan,' he said. 'Wouldn't it be good to know who told him that Raffano was clearing out?'

'That doesn't matter,' said Callaghan. 'Riverton believed Raffano was clearin' out. He knew Raffano had got an IOU of his for £22,000. He wanted it back. He was afraid Raffano might call on the Colonel an' try an' collect before he went. He asked Raffano for the IOU an' I suppose Raffano laughed at him. Then young Riverton tried to get tough. He pulled a gun out of his pocket. He threatened Raffano.

'Raffano tried to stall. He wanted to get a little time. He probably told Riverton he'd give him the IOU. He opened the drawer of his desk, but he didn't take the IOU out. He pulled out a gun, but he wasn't quick enough. Riverton fired first an' just as the bullet hit Raffano he squeezed the trigger of his own gun an' shot Riverton. And there you are.'

'Quite,' said Gagel.

He stubbed out his cigarette and leaned towards Callaghan. He spoke softly.

'It isn't a *very* useful statement, is it, Mr Callaghan?' he said. 'You know what it means. . . .'

Callaghan grinned.

'Murder?' he said.

Gagel smiled.

'You're right. If I take this statement from Riverton, even if we don't show it to anybody, it's tantamount to a confession of murder – premeditated murder. It's tantamount to Riverton saying that he went down there for the purpose of getting that IOU, that if he couldn't get it one way he was going to get it another. He went armed. A jury would believe that he went there for the purpose of threatening Raffano with that gun and if necessary of shooting him, which in effect he did. If Riverton was threatening Raffano with a gun, Raffano was entitled to shoot in self-defence.'

Callaghan nodded.

'That's what I thought,' he said.

Gagel leaned back in his chair.

'Supposing, Mr Callaghan,' he said, 'that the statement I take from Wilfred Riverton when I see him this afternoon is not exactly on these lines?'

Callaghan got up. He put his hand into the breast pocket of his coat and produced a note case. He began to count out banknotes. He counted out ten £100 notes on to the corner of the lawyer's desk.

'That's your fee,' he said. 'An' it's your business to see that the statement that Riverton makes *is* on the lines I've indicated. If it is not . . . ' He paused. He smiled almost ominously at Gagel. '*You'll* be takin' the statement down,' he said. 'There'll be nobody else there, an' I should think it is more than possible that young Riverton will be much too weak to be able to read it through when you've written it down. See?'

Gagel put his hand out. His long thin fingers wrapped themselves round the banknotes. He put them in the drawer of his desk.

'I see, Mr Callaghan,' he said. 'And I have your assurance that the position with regard to Selby, Raukes & White going out of the defence is quite in order?'

'Absolutely,' said Callaghan. 'Mrs Riverton saw them this mornin' before she went back to Southing Manor. She told them that Detective Inspector Gringall, who's runnin' this case at the Yard, had advised her to get a good criminal lawyer. That he'd suggested that I might know the right man. Well—' he grinned innocently – 'I know *you*,' he said.

Gagel nodded.

'Naturally I'll do my best, Mr Callaghan,' he said. 'Of course when I take this statement this afternoon the police officer on duty at the hospital will be in another room. As you say, Wilfred Riverton must be very weak. Possibly he won't be quite certain as to what he says. In any event he won't remember.'

'I don't suppose he will,' said Callaghan. 'Well, I'd like to hear from you this afternoon.'

Gagel looked at his watch.

'I'm going down by car right away,' he said. 'I'll drop that statement in at your office late this afternoon myself. Good day, Mr Callaghan.'

'Good day,' said Callaghan.

He went out.

It was five o'clock. A high wind had sprung up. It whistled round the corner from Berkeley Square past Callaghan's office, and away towards Charles Street.

Effie Thompson brought in a cup of tea – the third since four o'clock. After she had put the cup down on his desk she stood for a moment, undecided, looking as if she were going to say something important. Then she took a look at his face and changed her mind. She went quietly out.

The telephone jangled. It was Kells coming through from Falleton. Callaghan visualized him, standing in the solitary telephone box down past the end of the little high street, a cigarette hanging out of his mouth, his hat over one eye.

'Hey, Slim,' said Kells. 'I'm ringin' through to confirm that date about tonight. Is it still OK?'

Callaghan said, yes, it was OK, that he'd be down somewhere about ten o'clock, that he'd meet Kells by the tree clump past the telephone box. He asked if there was anything doing at Falleton.

'Not a durn thing,' said Kells. 'Everything is nice an' quiet down here. They had some police guys aboard the boat doin' photography an' rushin' around, but they've gone.'

He paused for a moment, then:

'That old guy Jimmy Wilpins has scrammed, too,' he said. 'The old geezer who saw that dame come off the boat. Do I try an' get a line on him?'

'No,' said Callaghan. 'Leave him alone. I'm not interested. Has anybody been hanging round Greene's Place?'

'Not anybody,' Kells answered. 'I was around there an hour ago. The place is as quiet as a goddam graveyard, an' looks like one in this lousy weather. How's it goin', Slim?'

'It could be better an' it could be worse,' said Callaghan. 'All right,

Monty, you stay around an' keep your ears open. I'll be down at ten. There're some things I want to talk to you about an' we'll take a look round that Greene's Place. So long.'

'I'll be seein' you,' said Kells.

Callaghan hung up.

His office door opened. Effie Thompson stood in the doorway. 'Mr Gagel to see you,' she said.

She stood aside for Gagel as Callaghan nodded.

Gagel came into the room briskly. He looked a little tired, but he was smiling. He sat down in the chair that Callaghan indicated with a nod of his head.

Callaghan said: 'Did you get it?'

Gagel nodded.

'I've been thinking, Mr Callaghan,' he said. 'I've had quite a while to think things over. You don't expect me to conduct a defence for Riverton on the lines of this statement, do you?'

He produced a foolscap envelope from his breast pocket and laid it on his knee.

Callaghan pushed a silver cigarette box in the direction of the solicitor.

'I don't expect you to conduct *any* defence, Gagel,' he said. 'If you've got the statement the way I want it then your job's as good as done. You've earned a thousand dam' easily. An' what's the matter with the statement anyway?'

He leaned back in his chair and grinned at the lawyer.

Gagel shrugged his shoulders.

'It's a death warrant,' he said. 'There's not an extenuating circumstance. If anybody's going to work on that statement from a defence point of view they might as well plead guilty to murder right away and let 'em hang young Riverton and get it over with. If you were working for the prosecution I could understand. . . . '

Callaghan was silent for a moment, then:

'Does he admit to shootin' Raffano?'

'He admits everything you expected him to admit,' said Gagel. 'He practically says that he went down there to have a show-down with Raffano, that Raffano was damned irritating, and that he – Riverton – lost his temper and pulled out the gun, that directly Raffano saw the movement he went for the drawer of his desk. Riverton says he fired immediately and felt himself hit at almost the same moment. He admits he drew his pistol first – an admission that makes anything Raffano did self-defence.' Gagel shrugged his shoulders again. 'It's a hell of a statement,' he concluded.

Callaghan said:

'How much of that statement did you frame and how much did you get out of him?'

'Practically the lot came from him,' said Gagel. 'He was talking slowly and so I got it down on the lines you indicated, altering the context of a sentence here and there just enough to make the points stick. I didn't alter any material point in effect. I just strengthened them. Of course you know that I could have modified the statement – made it look a lot better for him, I mean – if I'd asked him some intelligent questions. The questions I ought to have asked.'

Callaghan looked at Gagel.

'Such as . . . ?' he queried.

'Such as why he went down there suddenly like that, such as how it was he got down there, such as how he knew Raffano was going to be aboard the *San Pedro*, such as how he got from the landing place on to the boat, and such as was there anybody else on the *San Pedro* besides Raffano.'

'An' you didn't ask him any of those questions?' asked Callaghan quietly.

Gagel said: 'You know damned well I didn't . . . you gave me explicit instructions not to. I've got to admit that I asked one question though. It sort of slipped out, if you know what I mean?'

Callaghan grinned.

'Professional habit, I s'pose,' he said. 'Yes . . . I know what you mean. What was the question?'

'I asked him if he went down to the boat on his own and if not, who was with him,' said Gagel. 'He told me to go to hell!'

'Nice boy,' said Callaghan. 'That's what they call bein' chivalrous!'

'All right,' he went on. 'Thank you, Gagel. I think you're finished on this job. An' I think you'll admit that the payment was generous. Are you satisfied?'

Gagel got up. 'I'm satisfied,' he said. 'Providing there's no come-back. If there's a come-back to this both you and I are going to be in damned bad.'

'There's not goin' to be any come-back,' said Callaghan. 'Well . . . good-evenin', Gagel.'

'Good-evening,' said Gagel.

He picked up his hat and went out. He left the foolscap envelope on the corner of Callaghan's desk.

A thin rain was falling when Callaghan parked the Jaguar on the grass patch behind the clump of trees that stood twenty yards from the telephone box outside Falleton.

He got out, looked at his watch, turned up his overcoat collar and lit a cigarette. It was seventeen minutes past ten. He walked along over the muddy grass verge towards the call-box. There was no one there. Callaghan cursed quietly to himself. It was unlike Kells to be late.

He leaned up against the outside of the call-box in the darkness, thinking about young Riverton's statement that reposed in the breast pocket of his coat. He began to smile. It would be funny if it came off.

He waited until half-past ten. The rain had stopped and the moon was coming up from behind the clouds. He walked back to the car, took a flash-lamp from under the seat, put it in his pocket and began to work his way round the outskirts of Falleton. He was looking for Greene's Place, cursing Kells for not having given him a better description of its whereabouts.

It was a quarter-past eleven when he found it. One side of the big iron gate that led into the carriage-drive was open. Callaghan began to walk up the gravel drive. It began to rain again.

In the sickly light from the moon he saw Greene's Place in front of him. It was a rambling Georgian house with park-land at the front, thickly wooded clumps at the side. There was no light about the place. The heavy entrace doors under the pillared portico were locked.

He walked round the side of the house to the back, and after a minute or two he found a small pantry window which looked like the one that Kells might have used to get through. He switched on his flash and found himself in a fair-sized room that might at one time have been used as a butler's pantry. He stepped out into a corridor that ran towards the front of the house.

There were rooms on either side, high-ceilinged, handsome rooms. They were well furnished and everything about them denoted that the place had recently been used.

In a room on the right of the entrance hall, a modern bar had been erected against one side of the wainscoted wall. Behind it shelves had been fixed. There were bottles, some of them nearly full. Callaghan got over the bar, found a bottle of Canadian bourbon and took a drink.

He went back into the hallway and whistled softly. Nothing happened. He stood for a moment or two thinking, and then began to walk up the wide staircase. He walked right up the stairs to the top storey of the house. He went through every room, flashing his lamp into the dark corners.

Twenty minutes afterwards he was back in the hall. He was wondering about Kells. He could find only one reason for his not being there. That was that somebody had got an inkling of what he was doing in Falleton, and Kells had thought it wiser to get out quickly, leaving it to Callaghan, who was unknown in the district, to search Greene's Place for himself. If so Kells had come to this decision fairly recently – since the time when he thought Callaghan would have started from London – otherwise he would have telephoned.

Callaghan walked along the corridor that led to the back of the house and turned through the door that led downwards to the servants' quarters. He walked through the kitchens, the store-rooms and the pantries. In the end room, that had obviously been used as a storage room for empty bottles, he saw a door in the corner that was ajar. He walked over, opened it. The radius of his flash-lamp showed him a flight of stone steps before him. There was no banister rail. The musty smell of an unswept cellar came up to him.

He began to walk down the stone steps, noticing as he did so that the dust on them was disturbed. Half-way down he flashed his lamp round the bottom of the stone steps. A few yards from the bottom stair, picked out by a circle of light, lay Kells. He was lying on his back with his right arm behind him, his body being twisted grotesquely over to the left. There was blood on the dusty floor and on Kells's left hand which lay flat beside him.

Callaghan went down the remaining stairs and stood looking at Kells. He was dead all right. Callaghan took his gloves from his overcoat and put them on. He unbuttoned Kells's waistcoat. The front of the shirt beneath was soaked with blood. Callaghan opened it. Kells had been shot underneath the heart, clean through the aorta artery.

Callaghan sighed. He buttoned up Kells's waistcoat. Then he took off his gloves and put them back in his pocket. He sat down on the bottom step and lit a cigarette. While he did so he was looking at Kells.

After a while he got up and began to walk round the cellar, flashing his light into corners. There were some barrels and a dozen empty packing cases stacked up against the walls. He went back to Kells. Standing behind the head of the corpse, Callaghan raised the right shoulder and straightened out the arm. As it came out from under the body he saw that there was something rolled up and clasped in the big hand of the late Canadian. Callaghan prised the fingers open. They were not yet quite stiff. The rolled up ball consisted of a pair of men's swimming trunks. Callaghan put the trunks in the right-hand pocket of his overcoat and sat down again on the step, drawing his cigarette smoke down into his lungs.

It looked pretty obvious that somebody had surprised Kells in the cellar. Somebody who had opened the door at the top and had begun to descend. Kells had walked over to the bottom of the stone steps to meet them. He'd had the swimming trunks in his hand.

Callaghan thought that whoever it was who had come down the stairs had suddenly switched on the light. Callaghan could see the switch key on the wall half-way down the stairs. Kells had put the hand holding the rolled-up swimming trunks behind him. Callaghan imagined the scene. The unknown standing half-way down the stairs and Monty Kells standing near the bottom with his right hand behind his back.

Then whoever it was had pulled a gun and shot Kells. And that was that.

Callaghan stubbed out his cigarette against the wall. He put the butt end into his left hand overcoat pocket. He stood for a moment looking down at Kells. Then he began to walk up the stone steps.

He went back into the room off the hallway. The room where the bar was. He was cursing very quietly, very thoroughly. He used every curse he had ever heard in any language.

He found the flap of the bar and went behind. He took the bottle of Canadian bourbon from the shelf, put the neck into his mouth and took a long drink. Then he put the bottle beside him, leaned his elbows on the bar and stood looking straight in front of him.

After a little while he put his hand in his pocket and took out the swimming trunks. He unrolled them, laid them out flat on the bar. They were good quality brown trunks with a fawn belt. He turned them inside out looking for a manufacturer's tab. Either there was none or it had been removed. But there was something else. Caught in the inside of the trunks was an oilskin tobacco pouch of good size, the sort of thing that a sailor might use.

He examined it carefully under the flash-lamp. Inside the pouch were one or two strands of tobacco.

Callaghan put the things back into his overcoat pocket and took another drink. Then, more from habit than anything else, he wiped the bottle over with his handkerchief and put it back on the shelf. Then he opened the flap in the bar and walked out into the hall, along the corridor, into the pantry at the end.

He got through the window and stood up against the rear wall of the house, looking over the lawn at the back, listening. He heard nothing at all except the rain falling on the dead leaves.

He walked round the side of the house, along the carriage-way, through the front gate. His head was bent and his hands were in his overcoat pockets.

He walked back to the car, started it up, turned off the grass patch and began to drive back to London. Outside Falleton, in spite of the slippery road, he let in the supercharger at fifty-eight.

At one time he touched eighty. On one bend he kept the car out of the ditch more by luck than anything else. Most of the time he was talking to himself.

'All right, Monty,' he muttered. 'All right. . . . You old son of a bitch . . . !'

Callaghan arrived at Doughty Street at a quarter-past two. He walked along until he came to Darkie's place. Then he started a tattoo on the iron door-knocker. After a while Darkie opened the door. He was wearing a blue pyjama jacket and a pair of trousers. The waist-belt of the trousers was too tight and his belly hung over the top. Callaghan thought his bare feet looked like nothing on earth.

'For crying out loud!' said Darkie. 'I thought there was a bleedin' fire or somethin'. What's the matter, guv'nor?'

He looked at Callaghan's face and stopped talking. He stood aside for Callaghan to enter, closed the door. They went into the little red-papered sitting-room.

Darkie went to the sideboard and produced a bottle of Johnny Walker and two glasses. He poured out the whisky. Callaghan lit a cigarette and threw the packet on the table.

'You listen to this, Darkie,' he said, 'and don't let's have any mistakes about it. It's about this Riverton business.'

Darkie nodded.

'I'm listenin',' he said.

'On Wednesday mornin',' Callaghan went on, 'a solicitor named Gagel is goin' to telephone to that skirt Azelda Dixon. She lives at 17 Court Mansions, in Sloane Street. He's goin' to tell her that he's got a bit of business for her. That he wants her to be a co-respondent in a divorce case, an' that he wants her to meet the husband an' get everything fixed.

'All right. Well, I've arranged that Maninway's to be the husband. Gagel will fix that Azelda meets Maninway at the Silver Bar Wednesday night about eleven-thirty, so that they can talk it over. She'll go all right because she'll be told that there'll be a hundred on account waitin' for her there. You got that?'

'I got it,' said Darkie. 'I'm ahead of you.'

'While she's there with Maninway – an' he'll arrange to keep her for an hour or so at least – I want the night porter out of the way at Court Mansions. That's your job. You've got all tomorrow to find out about him. Find out if he's got a family or a girl or something. You keep an eye on Court Mansions on Wednesday night an' directly you see Azelda clear out to keep that appointment with Maninway you pull something on that night porter to get him out of the way for half an hour or so. Ring through an' say that his girl's been pinched or that there's been an accident or somethin'. I leave that to you. Understand?'

'I got it,' said Darkie. 'I'll fix it. Is there anything wrong, Slim? You don't look so good to me. What's annoyin' you?'

'Nothing,' said Callaghan. 'Not a thing. Everything's marvellous.'

Darkie said nothing. He poured out some more whisky.

CHAPTER NINE

Tuesday

Nothing like love

Callaghan awoke at nine o'clock. He stretched, looked at the ceiling, began to think about Monty Kells. He grinned cynically. Was it dam' funny or was it that a man who had been in the Royal Canadian Police for five years, in the Chicago office of the Trans-Continental Detective Agency of America for seven years – with all that that implied – should be rubbed out in a cellar in rural England – and just because he hadn't got a gun! Callaghan remembered that but for him Monty would, in all probability, have been carrying a gun.

He got up, bathed, went down to the office. He threw a short smile at Effie Thompson as he walked through the outer office. He told her to get Juanita on the telephone.

Juanita was in good humour. Callaghan, sitting back in his chair, a cigarette hanging from the corner of his mouth, did some quick thinking while she was talking to him.

'Well, Slim,' she said, 'it looks as if you've got a nice case this time – everybody getting themselves killed all the time. What's goin' to happen?'

'I don't know,' said Callaghan. 'It's just one of those cases. It's got me beat.'

'You don't say!' said Juanita. 'I thought they didn't use private detectives on murders in this country?'

'They don't,' said Callaghan, ' . . . only unofficially. I've been retained by The Mug's family to try an' find what they call mitigatin' circumstances.'

He heard her laugh.

'Well, Slim,' she said, 'I reckon that if anybody could find mitigating circumstances it'd be you, and if you can't find 'em, you'll *make* 'em.'

'I wish I could,' said Callaghan. 'I don't think it looks so good for young Riverton.'

'How's he doin'?' asked Juanita. 'The papers said they didn't expect him to recover.'

'He's better,' said Callaghan. 'They've got the bullet out. Maybe he'll even get himself well enough to be hanged.'

There was a pause, then:

'Why did you call through?' asked Juanita. 'What're you trying to do – trying to make up to me again?'

Callaghan gave a deprecating chuckle.

'I'm not such a mug,' he said. 'Look, Juanita, you're doin' the right thing. You stick to Gill Charleston, he's the boy for you.'

'You're telling me,' said Juanita. 'Say, Slim, talkin' about Gill, I'd like to see you some time.'

'I want to see *you*,' said Callaghan. 'I want to talk to you like a father. That's why I rang up. I'm goin' to be busy today but I thought we might have a little drink together some time. What do you say?'

'Sure,' said Juanita. 'I'd love it. Look, why don't you come round about six o'clock and have a cocktail? Come round to the flat.'

'Yes,' said Callaghan, 'I'll be there. Make one of those gin snorters for me.'

'Gin snorters nothing!' said Juanita. 'What's the good of you making out you like hot cocktails? I'll get in a bottle of rye.'

'Thanks,' said Callaghan. 'Make it two while you're about it. I'll be seein' you, Juanita.'

He hung up. Then he went to the office door and told Effie to ring the garage to have the car sent round.

It was twelve o'clock when Callaghan stopped the Jaguar at the Manor House at Southing. He'd driven down slowly, turning over in his mind the possibly salient points of the interview. As he rang the bell, he was wondering what Thorla Riverton was going to look like this morning, just what she'd been thinking about, just what she'd been doing. . . .

He was shown into the room in which he'd seen her on the previous occasion. She was standing in front of the fireplace with one hand on it, her usual attitude. She was wearing a black angora frock with white ruffles at the neck and wrists. Callaghan, for no reason at all, found himself thinking that he liked ruffles.

Her eyes were tired, her face white and a little strained. It was obvious to Callaghan that she was herself once more. Definitely Mrs Riverton.

'I thought I'd better see you,' he said. 'I thought you'd want to know the way things are shapin'. I'm sorry to tell you that things don't look so good.'

She nodded.

'Please sit down, Mr Callaghan,' she said. 'Do you want a cigarette?'

'I'll smoke these, thank you,' said Callaghan, producing his case. 'But I'd like a drink.'

She rang the bell, ordered whisky to be brought. When it came she poured the whisky into a glass, held it up for him to see that the amount was right, added soda. She brought the glass over and put it on the table at his elbow. Then she went back to the fireplace.

'I wish I knew more about you,' she said. 'I think you're an extraordinary man. Half the time I find myself distrusting you, rather despising you. The other half of the time I have a vague and elusive idea that you might really be of help, that you might be a responsible person. . . .'

'I wouldn't worry if I were you, Madame,' said Callaghan. 'Before we're through with this job, we'll know pretty well all there is to know about each other, I think. Anyhow, I'm glad that your dislike isn't quite so active as it was.'

She shrugged her shoulders.

'It isn't very much use disliking *anybody* at *this* time, Mr Callaghan,' she said.

She looked at him.

'I've got a solicitor,' said Callaghan. 'He's pretty good. He's one of the best criminal men in London, and although he isn't in the absolutely first flight of criminal lawyers, maybe he'll be all the better for that. The smaller man always works harder, especially when he knows he's goin' to get well paid.

'I had a long talk with this feller yesterday,' said Callaghan. 'He saw your stepson at the hospital. Now you've got to realize, Mrs Riverton, that the most important thing in this case is your stepson's statement. The story he puts up in the first place is the one that he's goin' to be cross-examined on in the box, an' when a man's on trial on a murder charge I suppose the most important thing in the whole business is his cross-examination.'

'I understand that,' she said.

'All right,' said Callaghan. 'The lawyer – his name's Valentine Gagel – went down to Ballington yesterday an' listened to what

Wilfred had to say. As far as I can see there is not one extenuatin' circumstance in the case.' He paused. 'By the way, how is The Mug?' he asked.

'He's better this morning,' she said. 'They say he'll get better.'

Callaghan looked glum.

'Well, you mustn't be surprised if they charge him with murder within the next week or so,' he said. 'Because that's what'll happen, an' as far as I can see by the story that he's told Gagel you mustn't be surprised if they hang him.'

She sat down suddenly in the chair by the fireplace, her hands clasped in her lap. She looked straight at Callaghan.

'*That* mustn't happen,' she said. 'It *mustn't* happen.'

Callaghan said: 'Why are you so concerned? After all he's only your stepson an' from what I've heard an' seen of him he's a dam' bad hat. Why does it matter so much to you?'

She didn't reply for a little while. Then she said gravely:

'My husband thought a great deal of Wilfred. He thought he'd never really had a chance. He'd hoped for him – hoped he might turn into something really decent one day. He was a fine man, and even if I didn't love him a great deal I respected and admired him. In my heart I'd always thought that one of his reasons for marrying me – for getting me and my family out of the rather stupid mess I'd put them into – was because in his heart he thought I might be a good friend to Wilfred . . . a help. You understand?'

Callaghan nodded.

He threw his cigarette stub into the fire and lit another. He drank a little whisky.

'What will happen now, Mr Callaghan?' she asked.

'I'll tell you what is happenin' now at this moment,' said Callaghan. 'Gringall, who's in charge of this case, has got his boys out in Mayfair. They're checkin' up, findin' out about The Mug, findin' out about Raffano. Gringall isn't satisfied, because there are things about this case that he doesn't know. But he knows the main story all right. He knows there was a gunfight on that boat, an' the thing he wants to find out an' prove is who fired the first shot an' who did the threatenin'.'

He got up and walked over to the window. He stood for a moment looking out.

'Our criminal law is very fair in practice, Mrs Riverton,' he said. 'When a feller gets hanged in this country it's because he deserves it.

111

When the Court hear the story of the events leadin' up to this shootin', they'll decide on the facts as to whether The Mug ought to be hanged.'

She nodded. She looked very miserable.

'What did he say?' she asked.

Callaghan walked over to the fireplace. He stood with his back to the fire looking down at her. He produced from his breast pocket the statement taken by Gagel. He began to read it:

> Ballington Cottage Hospital.
> Monday, 19th November, 1938.

Original statement from Wilfred Eustace Riverton.

My name is Wilfred Eustace Riverton, and for some time past I have been residing in London. It does not matter where. During the last eight or nine months I have been behaving rather stupidly – drinking, gambling and getting about with a rather fast crowd.

One of the people at whose places I have done a great deal of gambling was a man called Jake Raffano, the man who was found in the saloon on the San Pedro where I was wounded. I understand that Raffano is dead. I shot him.

I have been informed by the Solicitor who is taking this statement, and who I understand is responsible for my defence to any charges which may be brought against me, that so far as he is concerned I may say as much or as little as I like. But he has informed me that for my own sake I would be advised to tell the exact truth, and in the process to produce any circumstances which could possibly condone or mitigate my actions on the San Pedro on the night of Saturday, the 17th November.

I'm afraid I do not feel inclined to say very much, except this: For some little time past I have been drinking heavily, and recently I have been using morphine, heroin and cocaine. I have been very worried because my finances were not good, and my father's solicitors had some time ago informed me that no further money would be forthcoming. I estimate that during the last eight months I have lost and spent somewhere in the region of £90,000.

Last Saturday afternoon, I went to the room where I have been living, and thinking things over it appeared to me that there was something very strange about my continuously losing. I got the idea that the games had not been straight. This idea was confirmed by the

112

fact that I had heard that my family were employing a private detective to investigate what was going on, and whilst I resented this it seemed an indication that my father's lawyers might suspect that I had been done down for the money.

I was not feeling very well, and I am afraid during the last two or three months my self-control has been getting less and less each day. I had heard that Raffano was going to clear out of England. This news infuriated me because I thought he might have given me a chance, at least, of winning some money back. I made up my mind to go and see him, and to have things out with him. He had an IOU of mine for £22,000, and I thought I would get this back from him, because I thought that there was a possibility that when he had left England he might send it to my father and try to extract the money, or possibly to my stepmother. I did not want this to happen as I knew that my father was already considering appointing my stepmother as trustee so that I should not have the handling of the additional money which would one day come to me. I did not want this to happen.

I had visited the San Pedro on many occasions before when gaming parties were in progress. I thought Raffano would be there. I left London on Saturday evening, taking with me an automatic pistol. I took it because I had made up my mind that if Raffano would not return the IOU and at least some money – enough to enable me to go on with for a bit – I would threaten to kill him.

I arrived at the landing stage at Falleton at about a quarter to eleven. I took one of the two boats that were tied up there and pulled out to the San Pedro. I tied the boat up and went on board. I went down through the small saloon into the main saloon.

Raffano was sitting at his desk counting some banknotes. Quite obviously he was preparing to go. He asked me what the devil I wanted. I told him that I wanted my IOU for £22,000 back, that I believed that most of his games aboard the San Pedro and in the different places in and around London at which we had played had been crooked. I said he had won enough money off me to be able to spare me £5,000 now that I was broke, and had got to have some money.

Raffano laughed at me and was very rude. He made some insulting remarks. I took the automatic pistol out of my pocket and told him that I intended to have that IOU and the money. He said: 'Well, if you're going to get tough about it I suppose the only thing I can do is to cash in.' He opened the drawer of his desk, I imagined, to take out the IOU, but when his hand appeared out of the drawer I saw he was holding an automatic pistol. As his hand came out of the drawer I fired. At the same moment his bullet hit me and I fell over backwards. I remember nothing else.

That is all I have to say.

Wilfred Riverton.

Callaghan folded up the statement and put it into his pocket. He took out his cigarette case and lit a cigarette. He walked back to his chair, finished his whisky.

'It's a hell of a statement, Mrs Riverton,' he said. 'There's not an extenuating circumstance. Any jury would say that Riverton went down to the *San Pedro*, armed, for the purpose of getting money and the IOU from Raffano. He says that he intended to threaten Raffano with the gun if he didn't come across. Can't you imagine what a judge's summing up would be like?'

She sat looking into the fire. Then, quite suddenly, she got up. She stood, her back to the fireplace, looking at Callaghan. Her eyes were very bright, very hard.

'I don't believe it,' she said. 'There's something odd – something wrong – about that statement. I'm certain it's true. I'm *certain* that Wilfred fired only in self-defence.'

Callaghan's smile was disarming.

'You ought to know,' he said. 'You were there!'

'That's another lie!' Her voice was icy. '*I was not there.*'

'All right,' said Callaghan easily. 'So you weren't there. That means you got there afterwards. . . . I always thought you did. An' if you got there afterwards, how the devil do *you* know what happened? You answer that one!'

'I intend to answer only what pleases me,' she said.

'All right,' said Callaghan. 'You do what you like. But I think you're bein' a fool. If you want to help Wilfred Riverton you're goin' a dam' funny way about it. I don't like your attitude. It's suspicious . . . dam' suspicious.'

He grinned at her provocatively. Her face was white with rage.

'I *loathe* you,' she said. 'Everything in that rather peculiar mind of yours is twisted. I suppose you've had to do with criminals and crooks so much that you can't believe that an ordinary decent person

114

naturally does their best to help justice to be done. . . . '

He laughed out loud.

'That's a good one from you,' he said. 'I suppose you imagine that you're doin' your best to see justice done. If you're bein' straight, why don't you open up and tell the truth. Why don't you say what happened – *as far as you know* – while you were aboard the *San Pedro*. Well, you needn't worry to be high hat an' tell me that you're not goin' to answer that because I know the answer. You're not talkin' because you can't talk. You're afraid to talk!'

'Possibly I'm afraid to talk to *you*, Mr Callaghan,' she said grimly. 'But it may be that my silence at the moment may be of more use than all your talk.'

'Maybe,' said Callaghan.

He was grinning.

'You're fearfully sure of yourself, aren't you?' she said. 'Fearfully certain of the clever Mr Callaghan. Haven't you realized that it might be to your own advantage to be careful. Possibly I may ask Selby, Raukes & White to demand an accounting for that five thousand pounds you got from me. Would you like me to do that, Mr Callaghan?'

'No,' said Callaghan. 'At the moment I can't say I would.'

He got up.

'I'll be on my way,' he said. 'But I think I ought to tell you that you needn't worry too much about that statement of Wilfred's. It's only a "solicitor and client" statement between him and Mr Gagel. Nobody else is goin' to see it, an' if The Mug decides that he wants to alter it after he's charged, well, nobody's goin' to stop him. Maybe there'll be some fresh evidence. Maybe you'll be able to produce some.'

His grin was maddening.

'You think yourself dam' lucky,' he said, 'that I'm rather for you. If I weren't I might make things very tough for you. You know that, don't you?'

'I don't know it.' She was almost hoarse with anger. 'I don't know it. I don't believe it. And what do I care if you consider yourself "for me" as you call it?' The contempt in her voice was superb. 'Do you think it interests me?'

'Not much,' said Callaghan cheerfully. 'I don't think it interests *me* a lot. I'm sort of impersonal about it – if you can understand that. I mean that I think you're an awfully nice person to look at an' that when you're in a bad temper I think you're marvellous. I'd pay a fiver any day just to get you into a bad temper an' watch you react. But I'm not suggestin' that I'd go any further with you than that. I'm very cautious sometimes – especially about women that I'm not sure of. You never know what they're goin' to do. Another thing is I think you're rather stupid sometimes an' if there's one thing I can't stand in a woman it's stupidity.'

He got up.

'I'll be goin',' he said. 'But I'd like to give you a tip straight from the horse's mouth. There are moments when even the silliest person realizes that he – or she – has *got* to trust somebody. It's a pity you don't realize that. But you don't. You just get dam' annoyed because I naturally annoy you, because I'm an annoyin' cuss to people like you. The joke is that you don't dislike me half as much as you like to make out.'

'Really,' she said. She began to smile. 'There are moments when you are positively naïve, Mr Callaghan. In a moment you'll be trying to persuade me that I'm rather fond of you!'

He stood by the door grinning back at her almost happily.

'I wouldn't even try to persuade you, Mrs Riverton,' he said. 'I leave it to you. I forget who the feller was who said that hate is akin to love. If you go on hatin' me hard enough you'll have a reaction one day. An' I hope I'll be there!'

The door had closed behind him before she had recovered the power of speech.

She sat down in the armchair. She began to cry. She was wondering why she was crying. The thought that it must be rage was somehow comforting.

Juanita, very attractive in a black negligée, was lounging on the big settee in front of the fire when Callaghan arrived.

'The drinks are on the sideboard, sleuth,' she said. 'Have you caught any murderers today?'

He said, no, he hadn't, that it was close season for murderers. He mixed himself bourbon and soda and ice, added a sprig of mint, took a cigarette and sat himself in the chair opposite her.

'How's it goin', Juanita?' he asked. 'Have you fixed it up yet?'

'What're you talkin' about, Slim?' she said, smiling. 'You're being mysterious.'

'Mysterious nothin',' said Callaghan. He grinned at her. 'You've been too quiet lately,' he said. 'You haven't been worryin' me so I sort of gathered that you an' Charleston were just like that. An' I hope he's goin' to do the right thing by you!'

Juanita stopped smiling. Her face took on a ponderous gravity that was almost funny.

'I'm gonna tell you something, you heel,' she said affectionately. 'An' for the love of Mike keep it under your hat. I'm gonna marry Gill Charleston an' you're practically responsible. You talked me into it . . . maybe just to get rid of me.'

He laughed.

'I won't tell a soul,' he said. 'I think it's great news. You two will get on together like a house afire. Anyhow, you were practically built for each other. Remind me to be godfather some time.'

He went to the sideboard and mixed himself a fresh drink.

'When's it comin' off, Juanita?' he asked.

'Pretty soon,' she said. 'Just as soon as Gill has finished up some business he's doin'. He's throwin' everything over here. We're going to the States to start a nice honest-to-goodness business an' make some real dough. But we're not tellin' anybody. We're just gonna do it nice an' quiet.'

Callaghan nodded.

'It's the best way,' he said. 'But you're goin' to tell me, aren't you? You've got to have some witnesses when you get married an' I'm goin' to take it as a personal affront if I'm not one of 'em, especially now that all this Riverton business is practically over.'

'Is it?' she said. 'What're they gonna do to that young hick, Riverton? That boy's been *misbehavin'*.'

Callaghan grinned.

'They'll hang him,' he said. 'He lost his temper an' shot Raffano. He admits it.' He felt in his pocket for Gagel's statement. 'Just between you an' me an' the doorpost,' he said, 'you read that.'

Juanita sat up. She began to read.

'Oh boy . . . ?' she said. 'Is this hot. It's like something out of True Crime Stories.'

She read through the statement, handed it back to Callaghan.

'So you're all washed up, Slim,' she said.

He nodded.

'I'm finishin' things off tomorrow,' he said, 'an' the day after –

Thursday – I'm goin' down to Southing Manor to tell 'em that I'm through with the case. There's nothin' else I can do. So after that when you want me for the weddin', let me know . . . besides, I want to buy you something, Juanita . . . something really nice . . . something with diamonds all over it!'

'I can take it, Slim,' she said. 'I'll tell you what. I'm seein' Gill tonight. I'll talk to him. I'll tell him you want to be in on the weddin' an' if he says OK, I'll call you an' let you know what we're goin' to do.'

'Nice work,' said Callaghan. He finished his drink and got up. 'I'll be goin', Juanita,' he said. 'I've got to take a look at the office. Let me know about things. You know I'll be rootin' for the pair of you all the time.'

'I know that, Slim,' said Juanita. 'I guess I'll always remember you too. . . .'

'You better had,' said Callaghan.

He bent over and kissed her on the tip of the nose.

'So long, honeybunch,' he said.

Callaghan went into the telephone box on the corner of Hay Hill and Berkeley Square. He dialled Gagel's number. Gagel came on the line.

'Well . . . ?' asked Callaghan.

'Everything is very nice, Mr Callaghan,' said Gagel. 'I rang through to Miss Azelda Dixon and told her that I needed her services in that little matter. I said that Mr Maninway would meet and discuss the whole thing with her tomorrow night and pay her an advance of £100 – at the Silver Bar. She seemed quite happy about it. She said she'd be there without fail.'

'How did she sound?' asked Callaghan. 'Was she cock-eyed?'

'No,' Gagel replied. 'I wouldn't say that exactly. A little thick perhaps, but cock-eyed . . . definitely no. I think she'll be there all right. I think she needs a little money.'

'All right,' said Callaghan. 'Thanks, Gagel.'

'Not at all,' said Gagel. 'I'm always ready and willing to do my best for a good client. Good day, Mr Callaghan.'

Callaghan took out his little book, found and rang Maninway's number.

'I've fixed that job with Azelda Dixon,' he said. 'You be at the Silver Bar at eleven tomorrow night and keep her there. Tell her that story we fixed and pay her the hundred. If you go round to the office in

118

the morning Effie Thompson will give you the money. Keep Azelda talkin' until after twelve. Understand?'

'Perfectly,' said Maninway. 'By the way . . . when do I draw my little retainer?'

'You get it when you've done your job,' said Callaghan.

'Thanks . . . you can consider it done!'

Callaghan hung up. He stood outside the telephone box and lit a cigarette. He hailed a cab and drove across the square to the office. He looked in for a moment, signed a letter or two, went up to his apartment. He gave himself three fingers of Canadian bourbon. Then he lay on the bed and began to think about Thorla Riverton. Women were hell. They always thought they knew such a hell of a lot, insisted on playing things *their* way, doing what *they* wanted.

If she hadn't been such a damned fool in the first place the job would have been easy. He could have played it a different way . . . handled it from an entirely different angle. As it was the only thing to do was to let things ride for a little and play it the hard way. And it might be very hard. If anything went wrong. . . .

He began to grin. It would be damned funny if anything went wrong. He'd have the whole damned lot of them on his neck. Gringall would be shouting about 'obstruction', 'interfering with the course of justice', etc., etc. Gagel would be shouting his head off, and Selby, Raukes & White would have a succession of fits.

He got up and lit a cigarette, began to walk about the room, undressing, throwing his clothes anywhere.

Of course he could have a show-down *now*. But if he started talking to anybody it would have to be to Gringall . . . and he couldn't prove anything. Policemen were always so damned pig-headed. They wanted *proof*.

His mind came back to Thorla Riverton. He found himself thinking that angora frocks were pretty good things for women with good figures. The ruffles had been good, too . . . she certainly knew how to wear clothes. . . .

He got into bed and switched off the light.

Women were a damned nuisance anyhow.

CHAPTER TEN

Wednesday

Mixed bag

It was eleven o'clock when Callaghan awoke. He got out of bed, stretched, looked out of the window. A pale, cold morning sunshine illuminated the houses on the opposite side of the street in a half-hearted manner. He thought vaguely that it would probably rain some time during the day, and then wondered what the hell he cared anyhow.

He threw off his pyjamas and began to walk about the bedroom, turning over odd points in his mind. Then he took a hot and cold shower, dressed himself carefully, went down to the office, drank a cup of coffee and told Effie Thompson to telephone Mr Selby of Selby, Raukes & White that Callaghan was on his way round.

Callaghan liked old Selby. He liked him because in his heart of hearts he had a weakness for tradition, and the firm of Selby, Raukes & White exuded tradition in lumps.

Seated inside the big office, a cigarette hanging out of the corner of his mouth, with the white-haired lawyer ready to listen, Callaghan started in on a carefully thought out plan of campaign.

'First of all, Mr Selby,' he said. 'I want you to know what I've been doin', an' I want to give you an idea as to why I've been doin' it. Maybe Mrs Riverton told you that I've put a solicitor named Gagel – Valentine Gagel – on to the job of takin' an original statement from Wilfred Riverton?'

Selby pursed his lips. He put his finger-tips together and looked at Callaghan seriously.

'Mrs Riverton telephoned me and told me that,' he said. 'I wondered just why you did that, Mr Callaghan. I don't know a great deal about Mr Gagel, but . . . '

'He was the man for the job,' said Callaghan promptly. 'I wanted the original statement from young Riverton taken in a certain way an' he was the feller to do it. He's done it. Now he's out. We shan't need him any more.'

The solicitor raised his eyebrows.

'Really?' he queried. 'What about the defence?'

Callaghan grinned.

'Don't let's look for any trouble before we come to it,' he said. 'There'll be lots of time to talk about gettin' a first-class criminal lawyer who knows his stuff when Gringall charges Riverton – which he's goin' to do pretty soon. He's got to. When that time comes I'll come an' talk to you about it an' we'll fix the right man together.'

'So you employed Gagel and took the statement for reasons of your own?' Selby queried.

Callaghan nodded.

'Right,' he said. 'The statement's lousy. Riverton admits that he took a gun down to the *San Pedro* for the purpose of gettin' an IOU out of Raffano, and for the purpose of gettin' back some of the money he'd lost. He admits pullin' the gun on Raffano. Then Raffano got a gun out of his desk drawer an' it looks as if they both fired at the same time. From the point of view of defence the statement's as much use as a sick headache. It's invitin' a verdict of guilty to a murder charge. But I wanted it an' I got it.'

Selby said: 'You didn't come round to tell me that, Mr Callaghan. What is it you really want?'

He was smiling. He knew Callaghan.

'Mr Selby,' he said, 'you know me pretty well, an' I know you. I think we trust each other. Do you remember the Paynter case?'

'I remember it,' said Selby. 'It was a unique case, and you handled it in a unique manner. I thought you'd slip up badly . . . but you didn't.'

'Right,' said Callaghan. 'I didn't. I don't like slippin' up. That's why I want to put my cards down on the table.'

He lit a cigarette.

'I don't think that Mrs Riverton likes me a lot,' he said. 'She doesn't trust me a hell of a lot, an' I don't know any particular reason why she should. Maybe I've rubbed her up the wrong way.'

Selby smiled again.

'I rather thought you had,' he said. 'Perhaps you haven't been very tactful with her. However . . . '

'Quite,' said Callaghan. 'What she thinks or what she doesn't think, doesn't matter a dam' so long as this job's goin' the way I want it to go. An' it's goin' all right. Gringall will have enough stuff in a day or so for him to make his charge. I want young Riverton charged with murder an' I want it to be known that he's goin' to be charged, an' I want to know one or two things from you.'

'And you don't want me to ask too many questions – is that it?' said Selby.

'Right,' answered Callaghan. 'Now the first thing is this: What money is there available in the estate at the moment? When I say money I mean *big* money. Supposin' I was to come along to you an' ask you for a really big sum – somewhere in the region of twenty thousand pounds? Supposin' I could show you that by havin' that sum of money I could straighten this job out? Supposin' I satisfied you that it was the only way? Could you find it . . . quickly?'

Selby looked serious.

'There's very little available money,' he said. 'We haven't even begun to probate Colonel Riverton's will yet. Of course, the estate is very big and Mrs Riverton will be an extremely wealthy woman in any event, but there isn't anything like twenty thousand pounds in cash in our Riverton Estate account at the moment, and in any case . . . '

'In any case what?' said Callaghan.

Selby sat back in his chair.

'I don't quite understand what you're getting at about this money. You haven't by any chance made the same sort of request to Mrs Riverton, have you?'

Callaghan sent a stream of smoke out of one nostril, slowly. He paused for a moment, then:

'Did she say I had?' he asked.

Selby shook his head.

'No,' he said, 'she didn't.' He looked at Callaghan curiously. 'She asked us if we had twenty thousand pounds available for her immediate use,' he said slowly. 'She telephoned through yesterday, in the early afternoon from the Manor House at Southing. I understood from her that you'd been to see her.'

Callaghan got up. He was smiling.

'That's all right,' he said. 'That's what I wanted to know. Well, Mr Selby, I'll be on my way.'

Selby said:

'You'll keep in touch with us? Have you any idea what's going to happen?'

Callaghan shook his head.

'I don't know anything except maybe *one* thing,' he said pleasantly, 'but directly I do know something, if it's right for me to tell you, I'll tell you. I want to get these Yard boys movin'. I want 'em to get their case nice an' solid an' complete against young Riverton.'

The solicitor said:

'Would you care to tell me – it's between *us*, of course – why you're so keen for the police to move against Wilfred Riverton?'

'I don't mind tellin' you,' said Callaghan. 'Listen. . . . ' He leaned across the desk and spoke softly. 'If they get to the point of bringin' a murder charge, an' suddenly decide to drop it, they'll drop the whole dam' thing. They won't bring any lesser charge . . . see?'

'Quite,' said Selby. 'An' you've got something up your sleeve that may cause them to drop the murder charge?'

Callaghan grinned.

'Like hell I have,' he said. '*I know that Wilfred Riverton didn't shoot Raffano. All I'm worryin' about is how I'm goin' to prove it without startin' some more trouble!* Good day, Mr Selby.'

Selby watched the door close behind Callaghan. His mouth was wide open.

'Good God!' he said.

Effie Thompson brought Callaghan's cup of tea into his office at four o'clock exactly. He had his feet on the desk and the ashtray was filled with cigarette stubs. She put the cup down on the corner of the desk.

Callaghan said:

'Effie, who's outside in the staff-room? Is anybody there?'

'Nikolas is there,' she answered. 'He's finished that cinema case.'

'Send him in,' said Callaghan. 'Has anybody phoned?'

'No,' said Effie. 'Were you expecting a call? Did you mean Kells? He hasn't been through.'

'No,' said Callaghan. 'I didn't mean Kells. He won't be comin' through any more.'

Effie raised her eyebrows.

'So he's not working for you any more,' she said.

'That's right,' said Callaghan rather grimly. 'He's not workin' for me any more. I wonder if you'll miss him pinchin' your behind, Effie . . . '

She said: 'Did you sack him for that?'

'No,' he answered. 'I wouldn't do a thing like that. I feel like pinchin' it myself sometimes . . . but I lack the necessary courage.'

He smiled at her.

She looked at him through half-closed eyes.

'Like hell, you do,' she murmured, as she went out.

Nikolas came in. Callaghan threw him a cigarette. Nikolas caught it and lit it. Callaghan said:

'It's five-past four. If you go round to the Yellow Lamp now, you'll find the proprietor in. His name's Perruqui. He gets there about this time to do the accounts. You bring him round here in a cab. I want to talk to him.'

'I s'pose he'll come?' asked Nikolas.

Callaghan looked at him with one eyebrow raised.

'If he gets funny about comin' round,' he said, 'you tell him that, if necessary, I'll go round to that dam' club of his an' take him by the scruff of the neck an' kick him every inch of the way round here. Tell him I mean business. He'll come all right.'

'I see,' said Nikolas.

He went out grinning.

Perruqui sat in the big arm-chair by the side of the fire in Callaghan's office. He looked affronted and unhappy . . . almost tearful. His expression showed a deep sense of indignity and hurt.

Callaghan, busily engaged in stirring his third cup of tea, regarded the Italian with equanimity.

'So Nikolas had to be a bit tough with you to get you round here,' he said. 'You didn't like comin' round, did you? You didn't like comin' round because you're a decent, honest, law-abidin' citizen who keeps his nose clean an' keeps the law so carefully that the DDI at Vine Street bursts into tears every time he hears your name mentioned . . . you louse!'

Perruqui sat up.

'Meester Callaghan,' he said. 'I lika you. I have all the time lika you. Why should I be insult lika thees? I wanna know!'

Callaghan grinned.

'You'll know all right,' he said. 'I'll tell you.' He lit a fresh cigarette from the stub of the old one. 'Last Friday night I came round to your place an' had a little talk with you,' he said. 'I had a little talk with you about where young Riverton was gettin' drugs from. You gave me a tip off about Henny The Boyo. All right, directly I'd gone, you got through on the telephone or sent somebody round pretty quick to tip off Azelda Dixon. She tried to beat me in gettin' round to see Henny at the Privateer Bar. Well, she didn't make it. When I went downstairs there she was just comin' out of his room. I knew she'd been in there to see him to tell him to keep his mouth shut an' say nothin'.'

He blew a perfect smoke ring and watched it sail across the room.

'So I didn't even worry to talk to Henny,' Callaghan went on. 'I just contented myself with havin' a word or two with Azelda. Then I sat down an' waited for ten minutes to give her time to do a little phonin' an' get in touch with the tough guy that Henny had tipped her off about. The guy who was waitin' for me at the end of the passage, the feller who was goin' to carve me up with the razor blades he'd got fixed on his glove.'

He paused and looked at Perruqui.

'Of course you don't know anything about all that, do you, Perruqui?'

'I don' know a goddam theeng,' said Perruqui. 'I don' know nozzing . . . '

He wriggled a little in his chair.

'You tell me what I want to know or I'm goin' to fix you,' said Callaghan. 'An' when I say fix you I mean it. I'll make things so dam' tough for you that you'll wish you hadn't been born. I've got enough on you an' that lousy night haunt of yours to stick you inside for about five years. Well, how do you feel about it?'

Perruqui spread his hands.

'I don' know why you treat me like thees,' he muttered. 'I've always been a good fren' to you, Meester Callaghan . . . any leetle theeng you wanna know . . . '

'All right,' said Callaghan. 'You take it easy an' relax. Now you tell me if I'm right an' don't make any mistakes.'

He got up and stood over Perruqui, looking down on him.

'First of all, some of the Yard boys have been around talkin' to you, haven't they?' he asked. 'Gringall's boys. They've been askin' questions about young Riverton, haven't they? They've asked you about his takin' dope an' where he got it from, an' you've told 'em you don't know. Right?'

Perruqui nodded dumbly.

'An' the next thing they wanted to know,' Callaghan went on, 'was whether you'd seen young Riverton around your place with Jake Raffano. They wanted to know what you knew about young Riverton an' Jake Raffano. They knew that The Mug had used your place plenty. They knew that you were a guy who used to make a bit on the side by introducin' people to gamin' places around the West End an' Mayfair districts. They asked you whether you knew anything about The Mug playin' at Raffano's places, an' you told 'em that everybody knew that The Mug was losin' money like hell to Raffano, but that you didn't know where the play used to go on. Right?'

Perruqui nodded again.

'They asked you whether The Mug had ever had any rows with Raffano. They asked you whether you'd ever heard of him threatenin' to kill Raffano and you said you *had* . . . didn't you?'

'Yes,' said Perruqui. 'Eet was the trut'. I had. I 'ear Meester Riverton say that two t'ree time. . . . '

'You're a liar,' said Callaghan. 'You never heard him threaten Raffano. You never got the chance. All right. Well, what else did they want to know?'

Perruqui shrugged his shoulders.

'They ask me a lot of dam' fool questions,' he said. 'They ask eef I know where Riverton was living. I say no, I don' know. They ask me eef I know the women he ees getting about with. I tell 'em I don' know. Then they take a statement from me. They take a statement about the time I say I 'ear Riverton make a t'reat against Raffano.'

Callaghan grunted.

'Was there anybody else there except you when he made it?' he asked, grinning.

'No,' said Perruqui. ''E was talking to heem in my office by heemself.'

'I see,' said Callaghan. 'An' I bet you were able to give 'em the names of some other people who had heard The Mug threatenin' Raffano, weren't you?'

'Yes,' said Perruqui. 'I tol' 'em two t'ree people had heard heem.'

Callaghan lit another cigarette.

'All right, Perruqui,' he said. 'You get out an' you take a tip from me. You go back to that club of yours, get into your office and stick there. You try some telephonin' to your friends about this little conversation we've just had an' see what I'll do to you. By the time I've finished with you they'll be able to pick up the pieces in a dust-pan.'

Perruqui got up.

'Me . . . I'm not gonna do a goddam theeng, Meester Callaghan,' he said. 'I onlee do what I gotta do . . . I don' wanna get myself

meex up in thees. I don' wanna get anybodies inta any troubles at all
. . .'

Callaghan laughed.

'That's a good one,' he said. 'You listen to me, you dam' fool.' He
produced the Riverton statement from his pocket and tapped it.
'We're supposed to be tryin' to defend The Mug,' he said. 'Our only
chance is to persuade a jury that he shot Raffano in self-defence. He
admits he shot him . . . he's dam' fool enough to say here that he fired
first. Well, what a hell of a hope we've got if you an' everybody else
round at that dam' club of yours is tellin' the police that Riverton had
been threatenin' Raffano for days. Can't you see that, you double-
barrelled fool?'

Perruqui shrugged.

'I see now . . . Meester Callaghan,' he said. 'Eef I'd known you
didn't want it said I wouldn'ta said one goddam word. . . . '

'All right,' said Callaghan. 'The harm's done. You get out and keep
your mouth shut from now on . . . understand?'

Perruqui said he understood. He went out quietly.

Callaghan looked at the Riverton statement. On the front of the
folded document Gagel had written: 'Strictly Confidential'. Callaghan
grinned. Then he began to tear the statement into small pieces. He
threw them into the fire.

A sleeting rain was beating in Callaghan's face as he stood pressed
against the wall at the end of the Mews opposite Court Mansions. Soon
after eleven o'clock, the hall porter came down the steps and whistled
for a taxicab. Two or three minutes later, Azelda Dixon, well wrapped
in a fur coat, came out, got into the cab, and drove off. Callaghan
breathed a sigh of relief and lit a cigarette, his eyes still on the doorway
on the opposite side of the street.

Ten minutes passed, then a cab drove up. Fred Mazely got out.
Callaghan wondered what scheme Darkie was pulling to get the hall
porter out of the way. Mazely went into Court Mansions, leaving the
cab at the door. He came out five minutes later with the hall porter.
They both got into the cab, which drove off.

Callaghan turned up his overcoat collar and walked quickly across
the road. He entered Court Mansions, walked up to the first floor along
the corridor until he found No. 17. He took a bunch of keys out of his
pocket and tried them one after the other until he found the right one.

He stepped into the Dixon flat, closing the door softly behind him. He found the light switch. He was in a small square hall. There was a door opposite him and one on each side of him. He tried the one on the right.

As he opened it an odour of warm stale perfume greeted his nostrils, the kind of smell that emanates from a room where the windows are hardly ever opened. Callaghan stepped inside and switched on the light. It was Azelda's bedroom – the sort of bedroom that Azelda *would* have. The bed – the expensive silk cover lay untidily on the floor – looked as if it hadn't been made for days. Drawers were half-open with articles of feminine lingerie hanging out. The dressing-table was chaotic. On a tallboy on the left of the bed were a bottle of brandy half-full, two empty gin bottles and some dirty glasses.

Callaghan saw that the curtains were drawn, began to search. He started on the right-hand side of the room and worked systematically round, opening every drawer, turning out every box, even looking under the cover on the dressing-table. He found nothing. He turned out the light, went into the sitting-room. It was half-past eleven. He worked quickly through the sitting-room but with no results.

He tried the doorway on the left of the hall. Behind it was a short passage. At the end of the passage was the kitchen and on the left another door leading to a bathroom. On the right-hand side of the passage was a third door. Callaghan opened it.

It was a small windowless room ventilated by an air-shaft let into one of the walls. It looked like a spare sitting-room. It was crowded with furniture and knick-knacks. Open cardboard boxes containing dresses were thrown about the floor. In one corner was a woman's dress stand with a half-finished costume hanging on it. In another corner of the room a pile of clothes had been thrown down higgledy-piggledy. Sticking through the top of the pile was the top frond of a rubber plant.

Callaghan began to throw all the clothes into the middle of the room. He searched through everything. Nothing missed his eyes and his fingers. Underneath the pile of dresses and odd garments which surrounded the rubber plant in the corner was a cardboard box filled with an odd miscellany of articles – electric light bulbs, old advertisements, empty cigarette boxes, letters demanding payment of accounts.

Callaghan grinned. Azelda was running true to type. He had seen flats like hers before. He took the box into the middle of the room and began to work through it. He was hoping. He knew that Azelda's type of woman – the type whose brain is never really clear and who is either suffering from a hangover from dope or doing a little drinking after one is well over – seldom has sufficient concentration to be tidy or to burn or destroy anything. He worked quickly but carefully, opening every piece of paper in the box. Down almost at the bottom of the box he found it – a screwed-up ball of paper.

He opened it and read it. The paper laid out flat showed itself to be a quarto sheet of cheap typing paper. The words on it were typewritten. Callaghan began to grin. He read:

Somewhere around Mayfair.

To Wilfred Riverton, Esq.,
   'Grand Master of the Worshipful Order of Mugs.

Dear Bloody Fool,
   Aren't you the complete, the utter mug? It almost hurts to see you being separated from your dough. Didn't anybody ever tell you that Raffano hasn't ever played a straight game in his life? Don't you know that every party, every game you've been in on has been crooked? That all the little spielers around town, where some of your lady friends have taken you, were just set-ups for a mug like you? Why don't you get some sense, or do you like being twisted? If you don't, why don't you go after your dough – before it goes to America with Jake?

A Friend.

Callaghan took the letter under the electric light. He read it through again carefully, noticing one or two faults due to bad mechanism in the typewriter. It had been a very old typewriter, he thought.

He looked at his wrist-watch. It was five-past twelve. He folded the letter, put it into his waistcoat pocket. Then he replaced the box in the corner of the room, threw back the mass of oddments that he'd taken out of it, began to throw the old dresses and garments around it and on top of it round the base of the rubber plant.

Then he saw something. The rubber plant was in an earthenware pot, three-quarters filled with earth. The top of one side of the earth in the pot seemed a little looser than that on the other which was hard and dry from non-watering. Callaghan knelt down and began to scrape earth out of the pot with his gloved hands. A couple of inches down he found something hard. He was almost laughing as he pulled it out. It was a .32 Spanish automatic – an Esmeralda.

Callaghan put the gun into his pocket, and continued turning over the earth in the pot. Almost at the bottom he found a cardboard box. On it, printed in Spanish, were the words '50 Rounds Esmeralda'.

Callaghan took the box out and opened it. Inside, closely packed, were forty rounds of .32 ammunition, and in the empty space from which the other ten rounds had been removed were ten leaden slugs. Callaghan put the box into his pocket, replaced the earth, threw back the remainder of the clothes over it, switched off the light.

He went back to the untidy bedroom, walked round the bed, pulled the cork out of the brandy bottle and smelt it. It was brandy. Callaghan wiped the neck of the bottle carefully with his handkerchief, put the bottle into his mouth and took a long swig. He replaced the bottle on the tallboy, walked to the front door of the flat, opened it a little, listened. He heard nothing. He slipped quietly out, walked quickly down the stairs, out of Court Mansions into Sloane Street.

It was cold and the slanting rain stung his face. Callaghan looked almost happy. He walked quickly to Knightsbridge tube station and went into a telephone box. He rang through to the Silver Bar and asked to speak to Gallusta – the barman in the upstairs bar. He waited while they fetched the man.

'Hallo, Gallusta,' said Callaghan. 'This is Mr Callaghan. Mr Maninway's in your bar, isn't he, with a lady?'

Gallusta said he was.

'How's the lady?' asked Callaghan.

Gallusta said she was a little tight but only pleasantly so.

'All right,' said Callaghan. 'You go upstairs an' bring Mr Maninway down to the telephone. Tell him a lady wants to speak to him. Don't mention my name.'

After a minute Maninway came on the line.

'Listen, Maninway,' said Callaghan. 'This is Callaghan speakin'. I understand that Azelda's a little tight.'

'Just nicely,' said Maninway. 'She's being quite pleasant.'

'All right,' said Callaghan. 'Well, you see that she has a few more drinks an' you can mix 'em if you like. It's a quarter-past twelve now. You keep her up there in that bar until twelve-thirty-five. Then suggest that you're goin' to take her home. When you get outside, look around for a taxicab parked close by with the driver readin' a newspaper. Put her in that cab. One of my boys will be inside. Just shut the door an' go home. He'll look after her. You can call in for your money in the mornin'.'

'Right,' said Maninway. 'I suppose you know what you're doing.'

'Any time I don't I'll come to you for advice. Until then keep your dam' remarks to yourself,' said Callaghan.

'My mistake,' said Maninway. 'I beg your pardon.'

'Granted as soon as asked,' said Callaghan. 'Good night.'

He waited a minute or two and then rang through to Darkie.

'Listen, Darkie,' he said. 'Get Fred Mazely to go round quickly an' get that cab of Horridge's. He'd better borrow Horridge's cap, too. He's to drive right away to the Silver Bar. You go with him. Get Fred to park the cab just down the road an' read a newspaper.

'At twelve thirty-five Maninway'll come out of the Silver Bar with a woman. He'll put her into your cab. She'll be pretty high. If she tries to do any shoutin' put your hand over her mouth. When she's quietened down a bit tell her that you've had instructions to take her down to your place until tomorrow night. Tell her that there's a bit of trouble flyin' about over the Riverton business an' that your boss thinks she'll be better out of the way for a bit. If she wants to know who your boss is, tell her not to be silly an' that *she* ought to know that questions like that don't get answered.

'Take her down to Doughty Street an' give her all the liquor she wants. She's fond of gin. But don't let her stir out until twelve o'clock tomorrow night. Then tell her she can go home, that everything's all right. You got all that?'

'I got it,' said Darkie. 'Is she likely to start bawlin' for the blue-inks?'

'Not on your life,' said Callaghan. 'She doesn't like policemen at any time. At the moment she hates 'em. I don't suppose you'll have much trouble. Tell Fred to get a move on.'

'OK,' said Darkie. 'So long, guv'nor. Pleasant dreams.'

Callaghan hung up. He went out into Knightsbridge and began to walk towards Piccadilly. The rain had stopped.

He stopped to light a cigarette, then he continued strolling in the direction of Berkeley Square.

He was quite satisfied. It had been a very nice day.

CHAPTER ELEVEN

Thursday

Interview with reservations

Callaghan sat up in bed, drank coffee and ate toast and marmalade off a tray. The fact that the Chinese clock on the mantelpiece had chimed twelve o'clock disturbed him not at all. He was thinking about Azelda Dixon.

Azelda was, he thought, an intriguing type. He imagined that she had been rather a nice sort of woman at one time. Probably life had been a little tough on her and she had hit back in the only way she knew. He thought it a pity that the Azeldas of life 'couldn't take it' and must forever be trying to score off the fates that treated them – from their point of view – too harshly for endurance.

Callaghan, a piece of toast poised half-way between the tray and his mouth, wondered just how much she really knew, just how much she was merely a 'stooge'. He thought it was probably a fifty-fifty job. He did not think that Azelda was a brave woman, but she might produce a little desperation if and when love was concerned. After all, she was getting on, and if a man is kind to a woman who is getting on it doesn't matter how fatuous or tough or silly he is, the woman will always endow him with qualities he hasn't got, will produce for him a remnant of courage born of desperation.

He thought that it was probably like that with Azelda. Of course she was a bad hat, but being a bad hat was, after all, a matter of comparison. No one ever thought themselves *really* bad. Callaghan, finishing his coffee, found it in his heart to be a trifle sorry for Azelda – especially having regard to what he thought was coming to her.

He took a shower and began to dress. Half-way through he telephoned through to Darkie.

'Good mornin', Darkie,' he said cheerfully. 'How's your visitor?'

Darkie grunted.

'You didn't 'arf give me a bleedin' 'andful this time, Slim,' he said. 'She's a fair knockout an' as rorty as 'ell. Of course I've sort of made 'er see that it ain't any good 'er goin' orf the deep-end, but you ought to 'ave 'eard 'er last night. Blimey . . . ! I've never 'eard such a flow. She's quietened down a bit this mornin' an' my ole girl's 'ad a talk with 'er an' sort of smoothed 'er over a bit.'

'I suppose she wanted to know all about it?' asked Callaghan.

'She did . . . not arf she didn't!' said Darkie. 'But I was very mysterious about everythink. I said that it was for 'er own good an' that the big feller 'ad sent word to me that she was to be picked up an' kept out of 'arm's way until tonight. I told 'er she could go 'ome tonight. I sort of made out that the coppers were stickin' their long noses in all round the place askin' questions an' that if they couldn't get 'old of 'er they *couldn't* ask 'er anything she didn't want to answer. That seemed to satisfy 'er an' she piped down.'

'All right,' said Callaghan. 'Let her go at twelve o'clock tonight, an' get Horridge to drive her back to Court Mansions in his cab. Tell him to get her back there about twenty past twelve, because maybe I'll want to see her about then. So-long, Darkie.'

He finished dressing and went down to the office. He read the papers, smoked a cigarette. Then, at a quarter to one, he telephoned through to Scotland Yard. He asked for Mr Gringall.

Gringall came on the line.

'Hallo, Slim,' he said. 'How are things with you?'

Callaghan said, 'To tell you the truth, Gringall, I'm a bit worried. . . . '

'I don't believe it,' said Gringall. 'My belief is that you'd sleep through murder, arson and pillage with a smile on your face. If anything's really worrying you it must be something gigantic.'

'It is really,' said Callaghan. 'It's this dam' Riverton case.'

'Well,' said Gringall. He spoke a little more slowly. 'I don't think *you've* got anything to worry about. I don't think there's anything you can do. I don't think there's anything for anybody to do. It's in the bag.'

Callaghan's voice was glum.

'I'm afraid it is,' he said. 'Still, I'd like to have a word with you about it, if you could spare the time. I'd like to ask your advice.'

'Oh, yes . . . !' Gringall's voice took on a tone of slightly amused suspicion. 'So it's advice, eh? I'm always a bit scared when you want to ask for advice. It usually means that you've got something funny up your sleeve. Are you coming round here?'

'I'd like to,' Callaghan replied. 'I'd like to come round about three if that's all right with you.'

Gringall said that would be fine so far as he was concerned.

Callaghan rang the bell for Effie Thompson. When she came in he took out his note-case and extracted twenty ten-pound notes.

'When you go out to lunch I want you to buy me a bit of jewellery, Effie,' he said. 'Something really nice and expensive with diamonds in it. You'd better get it in Bond Street. You can spend all this.'

He laid the twenty ten-pound notes on his desk. She picked them up.

'I suppose it's for a woman?' she queried.

He noticed that her eyes were very green, and her figure especially trim.

'Yes, Effie,' he said. 'It's for a very nice woman. I thought something like a true lover's knot in diamonds on a platinum backing would look good.'

'Nothing could be better,' she said.

As she was on her way to the door, Callaghan said:

'Congratulations on the new belt, Effie. It's a great success.'

She turned.

'I know you notice most things,' she said, smiling, 'but I didn't think your observation took in *everything*. You're quite right, though. . . . I bought myself a new belt yesterday at a sale. I'm glad you like it,' she added primly.

Callaghan grinned.

'I'm glad you're glad, Effie,' he said.

'Thank you, Mr Callaghan,' she said. He saw the mischief in her eyes. 'I didn't think you were interested in *my* figure.'

'You'd be surprised,' said Callaghan as she closed the door.

Gringall was looking out of the window, smoking a short pipe with obvious pleasure, when Fields came in. He said:

'D'you get anything else?'

'A bit more on the same lines, sir,' answered Fields. 'I put two detective officers in at the Privateer Bar last night. I borrowed them from "K" Division so that they wouldn't be recognized. There was a certain amount of talk going on about Riverton. Quite one or two of the boys there seemed to know about him.'

'Did they?' said Gringall, still looking out of the window. 'That's funny.'

The Detective Sergeant looked surprised.

'Funny . . . why?' he asked.

'I'll bet any money that young Riverton never used the Privateer,' he said. 'Why should he? It wasn't his sort of place and the people who use it are not his sort of people.'

Fields hung up his hat and sat down at his desk.

'I wouldn't like to be too sure of that, Mr Gringall,' he said. 'If there's a tie-up, it's from the dope angle. Henny The Boyo has been peddling on and off for years. We've had him twice for it. Once in '24 and again in '35. He's been a bit more careful during the last year or two, that's all.'

Gringall nodded. He walked to his own desk and sat down. He began to draw fruit on the blotter for a moment or two, then gave it up for the more congenial task of cleaning out his pipe with a hairpin extracted from a packet – stolen from Mrs Gringall – that he kept in a drawer.

After a while he said:

'Well, what did they get?'

'The idea was that Henny knew that Riverton was fed up to the back teeth with Raffano,' Fields answered. 'Apparently the Dixon woman – the woman they call "Swing-it" – used to go round there sometimes and talk to Henny. She used to get excited quite often. She was the woman who was getting about with Riverton.'

'What's she got to say?' asked Gringall. 'Have you seen her?'

'I'd got her down for today,' said Fields. 'She lives at a place called Court Mansions in Sloane Street – quite a nice place. It's fairly expensive. I'd left her for a bit because you remember you said we were to be careful about her. There's nothing known against her and she's supposed to have an income of her own. She's a very excitable type. . . . '

'All those night-club women are excitable types,' said Gringall. 'If they weren't they wouldn't go on doing it. Well, when are you going to see her?'

'I went round there this morning,' said Fields. 'She wasn't in. She went out last night and she hasn't come back. The hall porter thinks she might be on a jag. He says she often stays away for a day or so.'

Gringall nodded.

'All right,' he said. 'You find out if she's back tomorrow. Give her until tomorrow afternoon, and then telephone through and see if she's back. If she is I'll go round and see her myself. If she isn't I

135

think I'd like to know where she is. We'll have to find out. I want to talk to that lady.'

'Very good, sir,' said Fields. 'Is there anything else you want done?'

'Yes, there is,' Gringall replied. 'I want to know what young Riverton was doing on Saturday afternoon and evening *before* he went down to Falleton. Haven't you found out where he was living? What's all the mystery about his address?'

Fields looked puzzled.

'It is a bit of a mystery,' he said. 'He's done a certain amount of moving about. First of all he had a flat in Welbeck Street – quite a nice sort of place. He got out of that four months ago and sold the furniture. It was good furniture too. I s'pose he was hard up. Then he took some furnished rooms in Mortimer Street. He paid three guineas a week for them, but he was only there about five weeks. Then he had a room out at St John's Wood – Acacia Road – a rooming house kept by two old ladies. He was there two weeks. He never seems to have had any correspondence and he didn't leave any forwarding address when he left. Then he went and lived in a room in Victoria Street. He was there quite a time – eight weeks. But I can't find where he went to after that. It does seem a bit odd. . . . '

'It'll be damned odd for you if you don't find out,' said Gringall. 'I want to know. And I want to know what he was doing on Saturday afternoon and early evening. It's important – and I want to know how he got down to Falleton. Have you seen the railway people down there?'

'Yes, but I've drawn a blank,' Fields replied. 'He could have gone down by train to Ballington, or Swansdown Poulteney, or any of the places around there, and taken a bus over to Falleton. There are good bus services down there. None of the railway people remember seeing him or anybody like him. He might have gone down by Green Line bus. Or he might have gone down by car.'

'All very interesting,' said Gringall. 'And he might have gone down there by balloon – or walked. Supposing somebody gets out and does a little leg work and finds out just how he *did* get down there.'

He resumed his artistic efforts on the blotter. He drew a cucumber, examined the result with his head on one side, rubbed it out and began to draw it again.

'Callaghan's coming in at three o'clock,' he said. 'I don't want you to be here when he comes. He says he wants to ask some advice from me.'

He looked at Fields. Fields grinned.

'With a bit of luck I'll get hold of something,' said Gringall. 'I know Callaghan's technique in asking advice.'

Fields got up.

'I'll go and see the ballistics merchant if you like,' he said. 'They've got the report done on the bullet that came out of Wilfred Riverton.'

'That's an idea,' said Gringall. 'Come back in an hour.'

Fields went out. Gringall began to put the finishing touches on an illustration of a prize pumpkin.

It was ten past three when Callaghan was shown into Gringall's room. The Detective Inspector, looking up with his usual non-committal smile, noticed that Callaghan was not looking so pleased about something. The fact did not excite him. He knew Callaghan's abilities as an actor.

He opened a drawer and produced a box of Player's cigarettes. He nodded towards a chair and pushed the cigarettes towards Callaghan.

'Nice suit, Slim,' he said cheerfully.

'Yes,' said Callaghan. 'I'm lookin' a bit dressy today, I know. I wish I felt like it.'

'What's wrong?' asked Gringall. 'Mind you,' he went on, 'you know you don't *have* to talk about the Riverton business. You and I are on opposite sides of the fence, but you're much too old a hand for me to have to tell you that you've only got to say what you want me to hear. I'm not *asking* for anything.'

Callaghan nodded. He took one of the cigarettes and lit it. He leaned back in the arm-chair and looked at Gringall.

'I know all about that,' he said. 'But I don't want to get myself into a jam, and I certainly don't want to get in bad with you boys round here.'

He began to blow smoke out of one nostril, and watched the effect.

'Look, Gringall,' he said. 'I'm goin' to put my cards on the table. Here's the fix I'm in. I want to tell you something that may help you quite a bit, but I don't want to start openin' my mouth if the time's not right for it. D'you see . . . ?'

Gringall began to grin. Callaghan was at his old tricks again. He said:

'D'you remember when we had that bit of a row here, in this very

137

room, about the Meraulton case, the time when you threatened to go to the Commissioner about the lousy deal I was giving you . . . ?'

Callaghan grinned. They grinned at each other.

'Oh . . . that,' said Callaghan. 'That was just a bit of technique . . . that's all that was.'

'Quite so,' murmured Gringall. 'And how do I know that this isn't a bit of technique too?'

Callaghan shrugged his shoulders.

'If you answer me one question,' he said, 'I'll talk. An' then you'll see that there's dam' little technique about my comin' round here this afternoon.'

'All right,' said Gringall. 'What's the question?'

Callaghan blew a smoke ring.

'When are you goin' to charge Wilfred Riverton?' he asked.

Gringall raised his eyebrows.

'You've got your nerve,' he said pleasantly. 'I might as well ask you to tell me what young Riverton told Gagel – that solicitor you've got in on the job – when he went down to Ballington the other day.'

'That's all right,' said Callaghan. 'I don't mind tellin' you that.'

'What!' said Gringall. 'Are you telling me you're going to disclose your client's original statement and practically hand me the line the defence is going to take on a plate?'

'Why not?' said Callaghan glumly. He leaned towards Gringall. 'What the hell's the use of playin' with this situation?' he asked, spreading his hands. 'It's in the bag, an' you know it. You know dam' well that if there'd been any sort of *real* defence I wouldn't have gone to Valentine Gagel. You *know* that, don't you?'

Gringall permitted himself to nod.

'I must say I sort of surmised something like that,' he said. 'So you're telling me that, in fact, there's no defence. That means to say that Gagel's going to find a hell of a lot of mitigating circumstances, dire provocation, near-temporary insanity through dope and drink, and anything else he can lay his or anybody else's hands on.'

Callaghan said sadly, 'I wish I could even say that.'

Gringall looked amazed.

'My God!' he said. 'You're not telling me you're going to let him plead guilty, are you?'

Callaghan hesitated.

'No,' he said, 'I wouldn't go so far as to say exactly *that*, but . . . '

138

He shrugged his shoulders expressively. 'When are *you* going to talk to him, Gringall?' he asked. 'Come on . . . let's get this feinting for an openin' over. Let's get down to hard tacks, for the love of Mike!'

'All right,' said Gringall. 'There isn't any real reason why you shouldn't know now. The papers'll all have it tomorrow night anyhow.'

He began to refill his pipe.

'I'm going down to Ballington tomorrow,' he said. 'Our surgeon says he's all right to talk now, that without any slip-ups he's going to make a good recovery. His constitution was good enough to stand the drink and stuff he's been sucking in as well as Raffano's bullet. *All right*. . . . He can say as much or as little as he likes. I'm not going to ask him to say a word. I'm going to charge him in spite of the fact that I didn't want to do it until I'd found something out.'

He looked at Callaghan.

'What did you want to find out, Gringall,' said Callaghan, 'that you haven't been able to find out?'

'I wanted to get that fellow who was on the boat,' said Gringall. 'The cove who telephoned through to the Yard and told us about the shooting. That cove must have phoned through from the call-box on the grass verge that's about a hundred an' fifty yards from the top end of the Falleton main road. And it's quite obvious to you why I wanted that man. He was on the boat. He either got there after the shooting or else he was there when it happened. If this fellow is an ordinary decent citizen I don't see any reason why he shouldn't have given his name and come forward and told us the whole story. The fact that he's behaved in the way he has makes me think he might have been on the *San Pedro* when the shooting took place and is keeping out of the way for reasons best known to himself.'

He paused to relight his pipe.

'The Commissioner wanted me to pick up that fellow – *if* I could – because he didn't want the defence to get hold of him and suddenly produce him with some cock-and-bull story at a later stage . . . some story about self-defence or something, that was going to gum up our case. Well, I haven't been able to do it.'

'An' you've come to the conclusion that it doesn't matter?'

'Right. I'd like to have this man on our side if possible, but it doesn't matter *too* much because our experts here can prove that the bullet that killed Raffano was fired out of Riverton's gun, and we know now that the bullet that they took out of Riverton was fired by Raffano. In other words, these two had a shooting match. They were trying to kill each other. Well, I've got a lot of evidence that young Riverton has been going around saying what he was going to do to Raffano if he got the chance. I've no doubt that Raffano knew that. He was all ready for Riverton. Raffano had a damned bad record in the States. He's used to handling a gun, so he just waited for the Riverton idiot to show up. Riverton's *not* used to a gun. He was probably half-tight and he gave Raffano time to get his bullet off at practically the same time. There's the story and I don't see how anybody can pick a hole in it.'

'I'm dam' sure they can't,' said Callaghan. He sighed. 'Young Riverton even agrees with it *himself*!'

He looked at Gringall. Gringall said:

'Well . . . I've put *my* cards on the table.'

Callaghan stubbed out his cigarette slowly. Then he took another one from Gringall's box and lit it.

'Look here, Gringall,' he said. 'I'm going to do the right thing by you an' tell you about that feller who was on the *San Pedro* – the feller who telephoned through here to the Yard about the shootin'. Of course there wasn't any *real* reason why I shouldn't have let you know about it before, because he's no good to you. He doesn't know a thing. He got there after it was all over.'

'You don't say,' said Gringall, raising his eyebrows. 'Well, who was he?'

'It was me,' said Callaghan.

He grinned innocently at Gringall.

'Well, I'll be damned,' said Gringall. 'What in the name of all that's holy were you doing down there?'

Callaghan blew a smoke ring and watched it.

'It's all very simple,' he said. 'Last Friday mornin', the Riverton family began to get on my tail over the investigation I was doin' for 'em. I thought I'd better get a move on.

'On Friday night I went over to Joe Martinella's place. There was a fight on over there between Lonney an' some black. I heard that Raffano had put the fight in the bag, that he'd fixed it for the black to win – I suppose he'd been layin' big odds against Lonney. Well, I messed things up for him. I had a talk with Lonney an' I made it worth his while to win the fight. He won it.'

Gringall whistled.

'I bet Raffano didn't like *that*,' he said.

'I bet he didn't,' said Callaghan. 'All right, when the fight was over I had a little bit of trouble with two or three of Raffano's boys, some of the smart alecs who've been workin' for him over here. I let 'em know I was goin' along to the Parlour Club. I knew Raffano would show up. I knew he'd be dam' curious to know why I thought I could mess him up by straightenin' up that fight. And I knew that he'd also think that before I'd do a thing like that I'd have to have something pretty good on him, something that would put me on top in any trouble that was likely to occur.'

'And had you got anything on him?' Gringall asked.

Callaghan shrugged.

'Not a thing,' he said, 'not really. But a little bluff never hurts.'

'You're telling me,' said Gringall. '*You* ought to know that.'

Callaghan went on:

'I was keen on findin' out just where Raffano had been takin' The Mug for all this money,' he said. 'I'd had a tip-off that he'd got a boat somewhere in the country. I knew one or two things about Raffano. I knew that in the old days he used to run a gamblin' boat around the Californian coast until the Federal boys got a bit too hot for him. I thought it was on the cards that he'd bring the boat somewhere over here, that he'd have her moored some place where it was fairly easy for people to get down from town and also fairly easy for him to make a quick getaway if he wanted to.

'Then I began to wonder just how he'd originally got in touch with The Mug, and thinking about that brought me to something else. I found a return half of a railway ticket from Malindon in some woman's handbag, and I began to think that Raffano's boat might be somewhere around the Falleton district.'

'Nice deduction,' said Gringall. 'By the way, what was the name of the woman in whose handbag you found the return half railway ticket, or is that a great secret not to be divulged by Messrs Callaghan Investigations?'

'I don't think it's a great secret,' said Callaghan, 'not *now*. The woman's name was Azelda Dixon. She's got a nickname. They call her "Swing-It".'

Gringall nodded.

'I thought that was going to be the name,' he said.

Callaghan said humorously:

'It just shows you, doesn't it? It just shows you that you police boys are a dam' sight smarter than a lot of people would like to believe.'

Gringall made an exaggerated bow over the top of his desk.

'Go on, Slim,' he said.

'I sent an operative down to Falleton early Saturday morning,' said Callaghan. 'His instructions were to get around that neighbourhood and see if he could find the boat. Well, he found it. He found the *San Pedro*. He came through to me an' told me. I had an idea that Jake would be clearin' out. I thought it might be rather amusin' to get down there, find him on the boat, pull a fast one on him. . . . '

'Such as?' queried Gringall.

'Such as bluffin' him that the Riverton family were goin' to institute criminal proceedin's against him, an' if he got sufficiently scared, try to get some of The Mug's money back.'

'Nice technique,' said Gringall. 'You private detectives get around, don't you?'

'You'd be surprised,' said Callaghan. 'All right. Well, I got down there at half-past twelve. I went down to the landin' stage. There was a boat tied up there. I pulled out to the *San Pedro*. When I got there I found another dinghy tied up at the bottom of the accommodation ladder. I had the idea in my head afterwards that that was the dinghy that young Riverton had used to pull out to the *San Pedro*.

'I went aboard the boat, but I couldn't hear anything. I went downstairs an' started lookin' around. I spent two or three minutes in the small saloon – the one this end of the passage that led to the bigger saloon, the place where the gamin' went on. I just hung about there an' took a look round. I couldn't see a thing.

'Then I noticed through the half-open door behind the velvet curtain at the other end of the passage that there was a light on in the big saloon. I went in. I found 'em. Jake was as dead as a doornail and The Mug was breathin' his head off. It was obvious he had been shot through the lung.'

'Very interesting,' said Gringall. 'What did you do then?'

'I stuck around for a minute or two an' smoked a cigarette,' Callaghan replied. 'It was pretty obvious what had happened. Then I went off the boat, pulled back to the landing stage. I knew I'd got to do something about it. My first idea was to drop in on the Ballington police on my way home an' tell 'em, but I thought why should I do a thing like that, why not put the big boys at the Yard in on the job right away?' He grinned at Gringall. 'So I drove to that telephone box – the one you were talkin' about – and put the call through. I didn't say who I was, because, quite candidly, I didn't think the time was ripe for gettin' myself rung in as a police witness. I thought I'd like to see how things were movin' first.'

Gringall knocked out his cold pipe. He began to refill it.

'Well, that's a help, Slim,' he said. 'Although it doesn't affect the situation one way or the other. Naturally, I'm glad to know who it was on that boat, because it means the defence can't pull any surprise act on us.'

'Quite,' said Callaghan. 'So you'll be goin' right ahead?'

'That's right,' said Gringall, 'some time tomorrow.'

Callaghan got up. He picked up his hat and walked to the door.

'Of course, Gringall,' he said, 'if you want a statement from me, I'm perfectly prepared to give one. My evidence is impersonal – it's neither for one side or the other. I just found 'em, that's all I know.'

Gringall nodded.

'It's all right, Slim,' he said. 'I don't think we're going to need you.'

Callaghan had his hand on the door-knob when he spoke again.

'There is just a little thing, Gringall,' he said. 'You've got to admit I've played the game with you, comin' down here an' tellin' you all about this stuff. Of course I wouldn't have done it if I'd thought I'd be lettin' my clients down, but you know me, I always try to do the right thing.'

'Like hell you do,' said Gringall. 'I know the motto of Callaghan Investigations.'

'You don't say,' said Callaghan. 'What is it?'

'I've always understood your motto was: "We get there somehow and who the hell cares how." And I can't quite make that go with this new law-abiding-wanting-to-do-everybody-a-good-turn attitude on your part. But still I always think the best of people when I can.'

'Me, too,' said Callaghan. 'I'm sort of interested in your career, Gringall, an' between you an' me an' the gate-post, I think it's time they made you a Chief Detective Inspector, because, besides being a very good police officer, I've always looked on you as being rather a friend of mine.'

'Go on, Slim,' said Gringall. 'You're making me nervous. . . . '

'The thing is,' said Callaghan, 'about your goin' down to Ballington tomorrow to charge young Riverton. If it wouldn't make any difference to you I'd be awfully glad if you could leave it till Saturday mornin'. . . . ' He put up his hand to stop the question that he saw in Gringall's eyes. 'I'll tell you why I'm askin' this,' said Callaghan. 'I'm just thinkin' about Mrs Riverton. She's a hell of a nice woman, an' she's havin' a very tough time. What with the death of the Colonel an' then young Riverton gettin' himself into this jam things haven't been too easy for her.'

He walked back into the office and stood looking down at Gringall.

'I'm going to see her tomorrow,' he said. 'I'm signin' off this job. I'm through. There's nothing else I can do an' I know it. But I'd like to warn her that you're goin' to charge The Mug, sort of get her used to the idea, an' I'd like it to come from me, see . . . ?'

'I see,' said Gringall. 'You go down there and sign off the job, having got every bit of available information you could out of me, and then you get taken on again working for the defence lawyer – the real defence lawyer. You're not going to be such a fool as to use Gagel.'

'You're tellin' me,' said Callaghan. 'Well, Gringall, what about it?'

Gringall leaned back in his chair.

'It doesn't make any odds,' he said. 'Young Riverton might just as well be in Ballington Cottage Hospital as in gaol. He's just as safe there. All right, I'm going to be busy tomorrow anyway. I'll charge him on Saturday morning.'

Callaghan's face beamed with gratitude.

'Thanks, Gringall,' he said. 'I always knew you were a pal.'

He closed the door quietly behind him.

Fields came back at ten minutes past four. He had the ballistics expert's report in his hand. He gave it to Gringall.

'Any luck with Callaghan, sir?' he asked.

Gringall smiled.

'He wanted to find out when I was going to charge Riverton. And I'd like to know why he considered it so important. I think Callaghan's got something up his sleeve. I think he's going to pull something in a little while. I know that bird.'

Fields began to grin.

'Did you tell him?' he asked.

Gringall said, 'I told him that I was going to charge Riverton tomorrow – which is a dam' lie, as you know. I didn't intend to charge him until next week. The doctor said he wanted a few more days to rest up and pull himself together. Well, when I told Callaghan that I was going to do the job tomorrow he put on a big act about wanting to prepare Mrs Riverton – just as if she hasn't been preparing herself for it for days. He asked me to lay off charging Riverton until Saturday – as a favour. I told him I would.'

'I wonder what that means?' asked Fields.

'He's going to pull something,' said Gringall. 'I feel it in my bones, and he's going to pull it between now and Saturday morning. *I* know Callaghan.'

'D'you think he's got something up his sleeve – a surprise witness or something?' Fields queried.

Gringall walked over to the window and looked out.

'He's got some stunt on,' he said. 'I remember him in the Meraulton case. He nearly got himself killed over that job. He took the chance because he was stuck on Cynthis Meraulton. He worked himself to pieces over that case and put himself on his feet doing it.'

He took out his pipe and began to fill it.

'Cynthis Meraulton was a beauty – one of those cold-looking girls who can be so attractive,' he went on. 'Mrs Riverton, the stepmother in this business, is a beauty too. She's the type that Callaghan goes for. Maybe he thinks that he's got a chance of pulling a hot chestnut out of the fire at the last moment and getting himself in good with her. *I* wouldn't be surprised.'

'He's got a hell of a hope, sir,' said Fields.

Gringall turned round.

'I wouldn't be too sure,' he said. 'I know Callaghan. He's a wily bird and he has the one virtue that a private detective has *got* to have.'

'What's that?' asked Fields.

Gringall lit his pipe.

'He knows the psychological moment to take a chance. He picks his time and takes one big chance. That's his technique and it's been very successful. Do you remember the Palquette job . . . the job when the principal Crown witness disappeared and we couldn't find him for days – until it was too late. Well, the reason we couldn't find him was that Callaghan got him certified as a lunatic and stuck into a private mental home.'

He grinned at the memory.

'That bird's got brains,' he said. 'And guts. And that's a hell of a combination, Fields. I'm telling *you*!'

CHAPTER TWELVE

Thursday

Enter Henny – exit Henny

Callaghan got up from his desk and went over to the window. He stood looking at the reflection of the street lamps on the wet asphalt. He looked at his wrist-watch. It was six o'clock.

He went back to his desk, lit a cigarette. He rang for Effie. When she came in Callaghan said quite casually:

'Somebody shot Kells.'

He blew a smoke ring and put his forefinger through it as it sailed over the desk.

'My God!' said Effie.

She stood looking at Callaghan, her face deathly white.

Callaghan went on: 'I expect it'll be in the papers some time tomorrow – either tomorrow afternoon or in the evenin' editions. Directly you see it in the papers you telephone through to Gringall at Scotland Yard. I expect that by that time the Ballington Police'll have moved the body to the local mortuary. You tell Gringall that I'd be obliged if he'd let the undertakers have it as soon as possible. You got that?'

She nodded.

'Kells hadn't got any people,' Callaghan went on, 'at least any who matter a hell of a lot. There's a father somewhere in the States. You'd better get through to an undertaker after you've spoken to Gringall. Tell 'em we want a decent coffin for Kells with a proper plate on it with his name on and everything. Then you can send a notice to a couple of American newspapers and a couple of Canadian papers – *The Montreal Star* to be one of 'em. Just say: "*In Memoriam. Montague Kells, one-time Sergeant in the Royal Canadian Mounted Police, five years senior operative Trans-Continental Detective Agency of America, and latterly first assistant to Rupert Patrick Callaghan of Callaghan Investigations, London, England, died of a wound received in course of an investigation on the night of Monday, the 19th November. Nearest relative should apply through a solicitor to Callaghan Investigations, Charles Street, Berkeley Square, London, England, for further information and a gratuity due to the deceased.*" '

Effie nodded.

'It's terrible,' she said. 'He was as nice as anything, really . . . I'm sorry I grumbled about his little ways.'

Callaghan grinned.

'Monty's all right,' he said. 'Wherever he's gone, he'll start something good, I'll bet!'

'Do you know who did it?' she asked.

Callaghan nodded.

'That's all right,' he said. 'I'll look after that.'

She went out. Listening, Callaghan heard her trying not to cry while she typed out the *In Memoriam* notice.

He took up the telephone and dialled the number of the Yellow Lamp. After a minute Perruqui came on the line.

'Hallo, Perruqui,' said Callaghan cheerfully. 'Are you still behavin' yourself?'

Perruqui mumbled: 'Don't you ride me, Meester Callaghan. You laya off me. I got plenty troubles.'

'You don't say,' said Callaghan. 'What's happened now?'

'Juanita,' said Perruqui. 'She'sa walked out on me. She'sa give me no notice. She'sa fineesh tonight. What the hell. . . . Now I gotta no star!'

'Too bad,' said Callaghan. 'Well . . . that's all right. You'll get another.'

He hung up, lit a fresh cigarette.

He went into the outer office. Effie was dabbing her eyes with an infinitesimal handkerchief.

'What are you cryin' about?' asked Callaghan.

She looked up.

'I wasn't crying,' she said.

He grinned.

'All right, Effie, if you weren't crying you go an' see a doctor, you've got something wrong with your eyes. I'm goin' to bed,' he went on. 'Before you go, you get on to Nikolas an' Findon. Tell 'em to stick around here in the staff-room tomorrow. I might need 'em. Then you can write a personal note – I'll sign it in the morning – to Moore Peake at the Trans-Continental Agency in Chicago. Tell him that Kells got himself killed over here, that I'm lookin' for a new first assistant. Tell him if he likes to come over here an' start in, I'll give him £500 a year an' a cut. Tell him it's a nice job.'

She nodded slowly. She waited till she heard the lift go up, then she pushed her typewriter to one side, put her elbows on the desk and had a really good cry.

It was ten o'clock when Callaghan woke up. He listened to the Chinese clock as it chimed the hour. He felt rested, almost agreeable. He got up, drew back the curtains from the windows, looked out into the wet street, then began to walk about the bedroom in the half-darkness.

After a bit he switched on the light, went to the telephone and dialled Juanita's number.

'Hallo, bride,' he said. 'Where's that husband-to-be of yours? Is he in circulation tonight? I thought maybe I'd drop round and drink a little whisky with you both.'

'Nothin' doin', Slim,' said Juanita. 'Gill and I are hitting the high spots tonight. We're gonna do a show an' dance.'

'Very nice too,' he said. 'Well, I've got a little thing for you – a brooch covered with diamonds. It looks just like one you'd have picked for yourself. When would you like to have it?'

'Are you *swell*!' said Juanita delightedly. 'Thanks a million, Slim. Look . . . I've an idea. Gill's got to go off tomorrow evening to fix some business. He won't be back until late. What about givin' me a little dinner and we can have a talk. It'll be the last one for some time too . . . we're blowin' on Saturday morning.'

'You don't say,' said Callaghan. 'Where are you goin', Juanita?' His voice held just the right note of regret.

'Well . . . if I tell you, not a word,' she said. 'We're leaving Croydon by air at five o'clock on Saturday. Gill's chartered a private plane. We're gonna be married in Paris. Don't let *anybody* know I told you. I told Gill I wouldn't tell a soul.'

'I won't,' said Callaghan. 'I'll drop around and pick you up for dinner tomorrow night. Well . . . so long, honey.'

'So long, Slim,' said Juanita. 'I'll expect you tomorrow about eightish. An' I'm dyin' to get my fingers on that brooch!'

Callaghan was smiling as he hung up the receiver. He went into the bathroom and took a shower, dressed himself in a dark grey suit, put on an overcoat, drank three fingers of rye whisky neat and took the lift down to the office floor. He unlocked the door, went into his own room, switched on the light, opened the bottom right-hand drawer of his desk. He took out a Luger pistol, examined the ammunition clip, snapped it into place, put on the safety catch and put the gun into the inside breast pocket of his overcoat.

He locked the offices and took the lift down to the ground floor. He picked up a cab outside in Charles Street and told the driver to take him to the Privateer Bar in Soho.

Then he leaned back in the cab, pulled down the folding seat in front, put his feet up on it, lit a cigarette and relaxed.

He was smiling. He looked quite happy.

Callaghan walked down the stairs to the basement room in the Privateer Bar. There were three or four habitués sitting grouped round a table at the stairs end of the room. At the other end the tired young man was sitting at the piano, a cigarette hanging limply from his lips, playing a soft swing number – 'I Can't Get Around Without You!' – with a certain sympathetic technique that appealed to Callaghan immensely.

He walked straight past the little platform on which the piano stood and up the short flight of wooden stairs beyond. He pushed open the door and walked softly along the short passage. At the end was a slightly open door. Through the crack a slice of light came into the dark passage.

Callaghan kicked the door open and went in.

The room was small and dimly lit, dirty, untidy. Dust was everywhere. On the other side of the room, sitting at a roll-top desk with his back to the door, was Henny The Boyo. He swung round as Callaghan came in.

'Hallo, Henny,' said Callaghan pleasantly.

He looked at Henny's half-closed eyes, at his trembling fingers.

He said: 'So you've been hittin' the hop again! What a lousy dope you are, Henny!'

Henny The Boyo caught the fingers of his left hand in those of his right. Callaghan could see his knuckles whiten under the grip of the talon-like fingers.

'Listen, Callaghan,' he said hoarsely. 'You get out of here. You get to hell out of here. I've got some right boys who'll take care of you if you don't. I'm not afraid of you, Callaghan. You get to hell out of here. . . . '

He began to mutter horribly to himself.

Callaghan took two steps towards Henny. He raised his hand slowly and smacked Henny hard across the face. Henny began to whimper. Then suddenly he lashed out with his right foot. Callaghan, caught unawares, went over like a ninepin. Henny, with an oath, went for the blackjack in one of the pigeon-holes in the desk.

Callaghan didn't bother t8 get up. He pushed himself forward on the floor with his hands, raised his foot and kicked out almost in one movement. The kick caught Henny just behind the knee. He howled, dropped back into the chair.

Callaghan got up slowly and began to brush the back of his coat with his gloved hand. Then he fetched a chair from the other corner, dusted it off with his handkerchief, drew it up opposite Henny and sat down.

'This is serious, Henny,' he said quietly. 'You've *got* to listen. It's no dam' good havin' hysterics or gettin' excited *now*. It's too late. . . . '

'What the hell do you want?' Henny asked petulantly. He looked anywhere except at Callaghan. 'What're you after me for, you damned snitch?'

'Don't make me laugh,' said Callaghan. 'An' don't be rude. I've been pretty good to you, Henny. I've laid off you for a long time. Why, dammit, the last time I was round here I sat down an' waited outside so that Azelda could go off and telephone that thug of yours to wait for me an' try an' carve me up . . . not that it did him any good!'

A thin stream of saliva began to run from one corner of Henny The Boyo's mouth. The muscles of his face began to work spasmodically. He looked like a gargoyle with spasms.

Callaghan said: 'Take it easy, Henny, an' relax. You're through here. The best thing you can do is to listen to me an' get out while the goin's good. If you don't you'll be pulled in tomorrow, an' it won't be on a peddlin' charge either . . . not this time . . . it'll be accessory to murder. . . . Did you hear that . . . *accessory to murder*. . . . '

'You're a damned liar, Callaghan . . . a damned lousy liar. . . . You're bluffing. Nobody's got anything on me!'

Callaghan grinned. He got up.

'I want to borrow the typewriter for a minute, Henny,' he said. 'D'you mind if I practise a little typing?'

He moved over to the other table – the one with the machine on it. He picked up a piece of blank quarto typing paper. Henny came up behind him, caught him by the arm weakly, mouthing something. . . .

Callaghan spun round and hit him with his open hand. Henny went down with a bang. Callaghan reached down for him, yanked him up with one hand, sat him back on his chair. Henny put his head down on the desk and began to cry . . . horribly.

Callaghan put the sheet of notepaper in the machine and began to type with one finger of each hand. The clicking of the typewriter keys seemed to affect Henny strangely. He stopped whimpering, sat up and watched Callaghan.

Callaghan finished his typing. He pulled the sheet of paper out of the machine and began to read what he had written.

'It's a dam' funny thing,' he said. 'I s'pose it's just one of those coincidences you read about in books. I found a letter last night. I found it round at Azelda Dixon's place. She's been fool enough not to burn it. It was written on this machine. She typed it in this office some time last Saturday morning or afternoon . . . knowin' Azelda, I'd say it was the afternoon. Would you like to hear what that note said?'

He felt in his waistcoat pocket and produced the folded letter that he had found in Azelda's room. He read it over to Henny. Henny sat staring straight in front of him, his hands clasped, the fingers twitching.

'Somebody shot Monty Kells,' said Callaghan. 'I found him down at the house called Greene's Place near Falleton. Somebody had given it to him through the pump. They made a certainty of him. Now, Henny, would you like to hear what I've just typed on your typewriter? I'll read it to you. You sit back an' relax an' listen carefully – for your own sake.'

He began to read:

To Detective Inspector Gringall, CID,
  New Scotland Yard,
    Whitehall, SW1

Dear Sir,
  My name is Azelda Dixon and I live at 17 Court Mansions, Sloane Street. I have to inform you that Montague Kells, an operative employed by Callaghan Investigations, was shot dead on Monday night at the house called Greene's Place, which is situated just behind Falleton Common. I know who killed Kells. I wish to make a statement in this and other matters relating to this murder. I am typing this letter on a machine at Henny The Boyo's Privateer Bar in

Soho. I wish to point out that the discrepancies in the lettering due to the age of the machine will be found to be duplicated in another typewritten letter which was sent to Wilfred Riverton on Saturday last. The letter which caused him to go to Falleton to see Jake Raffano. This letter is, at the moment, in the possession of Callaghan Investigations who will probably produce it in due course.

Azelda Dixon.

Callaghan folded the note, picked up an envelope from the typing table, addressed it to Detective Inspector Gringall at New Scotland Yard, put the note inside, but did not seal down the envelope. He put it into his breast pocket.

'How'd you like that, Henny?' said Callaghan. 'I don't think things are goin' to be too bright for you. . . . What do *you* think?'

Henny got up. He opened a drawer of his desk and took out a white paper screw – a bindle. He unwrapped it and shook the cocaine on to the back of his hand. He held the back of his hand under his nose and sniffed up the cocaine. He sat down in the chair. Callaghan, lighting a cigarette, watched him begin to relax.

Two or three minutes passed. Then Henny said:

'What the hell is it you want, Callaghan?'

'Nothin' much,' said Callaghan slowly. 'Just stop me if I'm wrong an' tell me afterwards if I'm right. . . . Last Friday night I crossed up Raffano over a fight at Joe Martinella's place. I saw Raffano afterwards at the Parlour Club. I had a show-down with him. He made up his mind to get out while the goin' was good.'

He drew smoke down into his lungs, blew it out through one nostril.

'Afterwards I went to the Yellow Lamp an' put on an act with Monty Kells,' he continued. 'I wanted to get at the stuff inside Azelda Dixon's handbag. Afterwards I saw Perruqui. I asked him where she was gettin' dope from. He got frightened and talked. He told me it was you. I said I was comin' round here to see you. Soon after I left Perruqui's place he telephoned through to you, didn't he? He told you that he was sendin' Azelda round here an' that you were to take your instructions from her? Well, she got round here ahead of me. She told you that I was makin' a dam' nuisance of myself and that it might be a good thing for me if somebody took a slash at me with a razor an' put me out of circulation for a bit. She told you that you needn't worry about any trouble afterwards because anybody who was interested would be certain that Raffano had tipped off one of his boys to carve me up, because I'd crossed him up over the fight. Is that right?'

Henny nodded his head. He was not feeling like talking. Callaghan went on:

'On Saturday mornin' or afternoon . . . probably afternoon . . . Azelda Dixon came round here an' typed that letter I read to you on the typewriter here. Did you know what was in it?'

'No, I didn't,' said Henny. 'I didn't know a thing about it. She just wrote it an' sealed it up. I'll swear to that.'

'An' you delivered it, didn't you?' said Callaghan. 'You took it round to Riverton's place off Down Street an' pushed it through the letter box late in the afternoon. Right?'

Henny The Boyo nodded his head once more. He looked very frightened.

Callaghan got up.

'Aren't you the complete mug?' he asked. 'Just a stooge who's goin' to get it in the neck an' who never even made a bean out of it. You're so full of cocaine that your brain's gone dead on you.'

Henny got up suddenly.

'I'm gettin' out,' he said shrilly. 'I'm gettin' out of this dam' dump. I'm blowin'. They've got nothin' on me, but I'm goin' to blow.' He seized the blackjack, waved it threateningly. 'You try an' stop me . . . you try,' he mouthed, desperately trying to work up some courage by the sound of his own voice.

Callaghan grinned.

'I wouldn't try an' stop you for worlds,' he said. 'You run away, Henny . . . I think you're bein' wise for once in your life . . . an' if I were you I'd run a long way because the blue-inks'll catch up with you if you don't. You know Gringall . . . he's a very consistent feller.'

Henny put the blackjack in his trouser pocket. He began to close the roll-top desk. In his twisted mind pursuit had already begun.

Callaghan lit a fresh cigarette.

'Good night, Henny,' he said. 'I'll come an' feed you a bun through the bars one day. But you'll miss those bindles in the place where they're goin' to send you!'

He walked out of the office, down the short flight of steps into

153

the basement room. The exhausted young man was still playing the piano softly. One or two odd looking coffee drinkers looked up curiously at Callaghan as he went out.

It was twelve-thirty when Callaghan turned into Court Mansions and walked quickly and quietly up the stairs to the first floor. He rang the bell of No. 17, nobody took any notice. Callaghan put his finger on the bell-push and kept it there.

After a few moments the door opened just a little way. He put his foot into the crack through which Azelda was peering and pushed the door back against her. He stepped into the hall.

'You . . . ' said Azelda. She used a very rude word.

Callaghan said: 'Take it easy, Azelda, I want to talk to you an' it's no good gettin' excited or ringin' for the hall porter or talkin' to me about sendin' for a policeman. Maybe I'll send for one myself before the night's out.'

She stood with her back against the bedroom door.

'What do *you* want?' she said. 'What is it? I've got nothing to say to you.'

'Don't you believe it,' said Callaghan. 'You've got an awful lot to say to me. You're goin' to do more talkin' to me than you've ever done before.'

'Am I?' she said, smiling cynically. 'You think you're very clever, don't you, Mr Callaghan? But *I* don't think you're so hot. And I'm not talking to you.'

Callaghan said: 'Listen, Azelda, why don't you give up. You know everything has to come to an end one day. This is the end of *your* day I'm afraid, an' it's been a pretty busy one . . . one way and another.'

He took off his hat and undid his overcoat. She stood quite still, backed against the wall, staring at him. She was frightened of Callaghan . . . she knew that in her heart.

'I hope you liked your little visit to my friend, Darkie,' said Callaghan. 'I had you picked up last night an' that business that Maninway talked to you about at the Silver Bar was just a lot of rubbish . . . a plant. While he kept you there I went over this flat – you ought to get somebody to tidy up a bit, Azelda – an' I found what I wanted to find. I found the note you typed to The Mug last Saturday an' I found that Esmeralda automatic an' the slugs in the rubber plant pot under the mould where you hid 'em. Well . . . ?'

154

Azelda was breathing heavily. Under the thin silk kimono Callaghan could see her breast heaving.

'Let's go into that nice sittin'-room of yours,' said Callaghan. 'Maybe you can find me a drink. I want to talk to you, Azelda. I want to give you a little friendly advice—' His voice was almost kindly. 'You're in bad but you can make things a bit easier for yourself.'

'I'm not talking to *you* now or any time,' said Azelda slowly. 'I've got nothing to be afraid of.'

'Rats,' said Callaghan. 'You've got a hell of a lot to be afraid of an' you know it. The trouble with you women is that you will go on kiddin' yourselves. You're egoists, that's what it is. You never take a look at yourselves in the mirror and face facts. You never see the crow's-feet beginnin' to come round your eyes, or that tired look that's so dam' difficult to get rid of. You never realize that, like everythin' else, the sort of love you go in for comes to an end . . . '

Azelda began to laugh. It didn't sound a very convincing laugh.

'You won't admit that you haven't got what it takes any more,' said Callaghan evenly. 'An' so when some good-lookin' feller comes along an' tells you how easy this an' that is goin' to be, an' how you're goin' to be in the money when the job's done, you believe him. You don't stop to think that a double-crosser is always a double-crosser an' that if it's good enough for him to get you in on a stunt to twist somebody else, the odds are that he'll twist you before you're through. If you had had some sense an' watched points for yourself, instead of bein' blinded by thinkin' that you were in love an' that *he* was in love with you, you might have saved yourself a lot of trouble . . . trouble that's comin' to you, Azelda.'

'I'm not afraid of you,' said Azelda, rather weakly. 'I've got nothing to be afraid of.'

Callaghan took out his cigarette case. He selected a cigarette and lit it. His eyes never left hers.

'Haven't you?' he said with a grin. 'I think you have . . . that's all.' His voice became *quite* pleasant.

'I'm sorry to come here so late,' he said. 'But I told Darkie to get you back here about twelve so that I could see you for a bit. I'm goin' to be busy tomorrow an' I've got to see Gill Charleston an' Juanita off on Saturday mornin' early . . . '

'*What!*' said Azelda. Her voice was like a rasp.

Callaghan's face took on a look of complete and utter amazement.

'Didn't you know,' he said. 'Didn't you know that Gill an' Juanita are flyin' off on Saturday mornin' to Paris. They're goin' to be married there. I bought Juanita a hell of a nice true lover's-knot brooch an' . . .'

'My God,' said Azelda. 'You liar . . . I don't believe it . . . you *liar*!'

Callaghan said: 'So you're goin' on kiddin' yourself. Why don't you get a little sense, Azelda. Who did you think you were to be able to hold a man like that one. I've told you the truth. They're goin' off on Saturday mornin'. He's keepin' it quiet but Juanita let me in on it in confidence. She told me because she hoped that it might make *me* feel a bit jealous, that I'd been a fool not to hang on to her for myself.'

Azelda said: 'I thought she was stuck on *you*. I thought. . . '

'That's just what he wanted you to think,' said Callaghan softly. 'Think it out for yourself. You've just been another stooge . . . '

He began to grin.

'What about that little drink, Azelda,' he said. 'An' a nice quiet talk.'

He put his hand into his pocket and brought out the note that he had typed round at Henny The Boyo's place. He took it out of the envelope.

'You remember Kells,' he said. 'That feller of mine that put that act up with me . . . the night we had that row at the Yellow Lamp?'

She nodded. She could not trust herself to speak.

'Kells was gettin' around at Falleton, doin' a little investigatin',' Callaghan went on. 'He got into that place of Raffano's – Greene's Place – an' somebody shot him. The joke was that when they shot him, Monty had got the swimming trunks in his hand. He was clever, when he saw that there wasn't any way out an' that he was goin' to get himself shot he held his hand with the trunks rolled up in it behind him. He fell back on 'em.'

He paused for a moment.

'I thought you might guess who that somebody was,' he continued. 'In fact, I've taken the liberty of typin' a note signed with your name to Gringall at Scotland Yard, tellin' him that you knew that Kells had been shot . . . sayin' that you knew who had done it. I'm goin' to send that note to Gringall tomorrow.'

He stubbed out his cigarette against the iron ring of the umbrella stand.

'You can make it a lot easier for yourself, Azelda,' he said. 'You're licked an' you know it. I'm not pullin' anything on you. I'm not bluffin'. I'm telling' you that Juanita an' Charleston are gettin' married in Paris an' that they're goin' on Saturday . . . take a look at this!'

He produced from his hip pocket the leather jeweller's case, flipped it open. Inside, nestling against the white velvet she saw the diamond true lover's knot.

'That's my present to Juanita,' said Callaghan. 'Nice piece, isn't it?'

Azelda turned round and put her hands up against the wall. She began to sob. Callaghan lit a fresh cigarette and leaned against the wall watching her. After a little while she turned round. Her eyes were red and dry. She looked like a devil.

'All right,' she said. 'I'm talking.'

Callaghan sighed.

She led the way towards the sitting-room. As she opened the door he said:

'I left some brandy in that bottle next to your bed last night. I think you need a little drink.'

She turned and began to walk unsteadily towards the bedroom. Callaghan called after her:

'Wash the glasses, Azelda. I hate the taste of lipstick with brandy.'

CHAPTER THIRTEEN

Friday

The lady has brains

Callaghan ate luncheon at Hatchett's in Piccadilly, arrived back to the office at two-thirty. Five minutes after his arrival Selby of Selby, Raukes & White came through on the telephone.

'Mr Callaghan,' said the lawyer, 'I'd be glad if you could come round and see me. Something's happened – in *re* Riverton, I mean – something important.'

'You don't say,' said Callaghan airily. 'Something interestin'?'

'Very interesting,' said Selby. 'I don't think I want to talk about it on the telephone. Can you come round?'

'I'll be with you in ten minutes,' said Callaghan.

He walked to the lift quickly. He did not even wait to put his hat on. A cab got him to the office of Selby, Raukes & White in seven minutes. He walked straight into Selby's room.

'So there's big news flyin' about,' he said.

Selby nodded.

'Yes, Mr Callaghan,' he said. 'But I can tell you so much and no more. My client's instructions are quite definite.'

'I see,' said Callaghan. 'So Mrs Riverton's been gettin' annoyed again!'

'Well . . . ' said Selby. He leaned back in his chair. 'You know,' he said, 'possibly we've misjudged Mrs Riverton. Perhaps she has more brains than we gave her credit for. I've been down to see her this morning. Briefly, she has found herself, during the last few days, in a position of the most extreme difficulty. You can imagine my surprise, Mr Callaghan, when she informed me this morning that she herself had been on the *San Pedro* the night that the shooting occurred, and that you were aware of the fact. She told me that she could now definitely state that within the next twenty-four hours she will actually produce evidence conclusively proving that Wilfred Riverton shot Raffano in self-defence.'

Callaghan nodded. He began to grin.

'I would like you to know,' Selby went on, 'that I broke no confidence of yours. The last time I saw you in this office you amazed me by telling me that Wilfred Riverton had *not* shot Raffano.

Candidly I found it very difficult to believe that, but I was not so concerned with that as with the possibilities of your being able to make the prosecution believe it.'

Selby paused for a moment. Callaghan said:

'Go on . . . I'm listenin'.'

'Needless to say,' continued Selby, 'I said nothing to Mrs Riverton of what you had told me, first of all because I did not want to raise any false hopes in her breast, and secondly because I didn't think that you – even *you*—' Selby smiled as he made the compliment – 'could be right this time.'

'I see,' said Callaghan.

'I've been a lawyer for a long time, Mr Callaghan,' said Selby, 'and I think I can say that never in the whole course of my experience have I ever encountered a case in which the evidence is so strong against an accused as it is – on the face of it – in this case against Wilfred Riverton. Thinking it over – especially having regard to what Mrs Riverton now says – it occurred to me that although you might sincerely believe in your ability to produce a new theory, we ought to be very certain of that before we proceed on lines which, if broken down by the prosecution, would serve merely to annoy a judge and jury.'

Callaghed nodded.

'You mean,' he said, 'that you think there's a possibility that I might be fakin' the new defence, that I might be tryin' to pull a fast one and that if it didn't come off it would do more harm than good. Well . . . you're entitled to your opinion.'

'Yes,' said Selby. 'I mean that unless your evidence is *absolutely indisputable* we should be wise to leave the matter to Mrs Riverton.'

Callaghan inhaled deeply.

'I get it,' he said. 'Your idea is that of the two evils we choose the lesser. Having heard Mrs Riverton's story, you think there is a good chance of provin' self-defence. You think that if we can prove that Riverton fired in self-defence he'll get away with it. You've heard Mrs Riverton's story an' you think there's more chance of provin' that than in succeedin' in my idea, which is that Riverton didn't shoot Raffano at all.'

Selby nodded.

'That is my opinion,' he said.

'And did you send for me to tell me that,' Callaghan asked, 'or was there something else?'

159

He grinned mischievously at the lawyer. Selby looked uncomfortable.

'Mrs Riverton informed me,' he said, 'that on last Sunday night, she handed you an open cheque for £5,000. She felt at the time that she should do so, that if she had fallen out with you – having regard to the state of her own negotiation at that moment – you could have created a very difficult situation for her, a situation which might have nullified the evidence which she has now been able to secure.'

Callaghan nodded.

'And so you gave her the £20,000?' he said.

Selby looked surprised.

'How did you know that?' he asked.

'Not only did you give her the £20,000,' Callaghan went on, 'but she also told you that I was to be laid off, that I was to make an accounting to you for what I'd done with that £5,000, and that after she'd pulled this dramatic stunt she's got on, you were to go out and make things as tough for me as possible. In other words I was goin' to pay that money back *or else* . . . Is that right?'

Selby looked even more uncomfortable.

'Well, it was something on those lines,' he admitted.

Callaghan smiled.

'Look, Mr Selby,' he said, 'you and I know each other pretty well. You've had your instructions from Mrs Riverton. She's told you that everything's got to be kept a great secret from me, all this new stuff of hers I mean, just in case the wicked Mr Callaghan, who blackmailed her out of £5,000, starts jumpin' around an' makin' some more trouble. Now I'm goin' to make a few guesses. This is what she told you. . . . '

Callaghan settled back in his chair. He was enjoying himself.

'Last Saturday night,' he said, 'when Mrs Riverton was preparin' to go round to the Nursing Home at Swansdown Poulteney as she'd arranged, somebody telephoned her. That somebody told her that Wilfred Riverton was goin' aboard the *San Pedro* to have an interview with Jake, that there was likely to be a lot of trouble flyin' about. Her informant also told her that he thought that trouble could be obviated an' he'd tell her how. He told her he wanted to see her, an' the best thing she could do would be to meet him. He told her where. Possibly she didn't like the idea of that, but he produced a threat, a threat that was so strong that she preferred to keep that appointment rather than go over to the Nursing Home. She thought it was the lesser of two evils. Well . . . ?'

'It's most extraordinary!' said Selby. 'How did you know all that?'

'That's what they call logical deduction,' said Callaghan humorously. He got up. 'You're in a difficult position, Mr Selby,' he said. 'I realize that you're trying' to do your best for everybody. Don't you worry about me. As for that £5,000, don't you worry about that either. I'm not worryin' about it. We'll put an account in. Callaghan Investigations always tells its clients how it spends their money . . . if necessary.'

'In the meantime . . . ' said Selby.

'In the meantime nothing,' interrupted Callaghan. 'If you're tryin' to tell me to lay off this case, you try again!'

He lit another cigarette.

'I'll send that account round on Monday mornin',' he said. His expression was cynically contrite. 'I wouldn't like you to have to take proceedin's against Callaghan Investigations to get that money back. Just think of the harm it would do my firm.'

He walked over to the door.

'An' when you get into touch with Thorla Riverton again,' he continued wickedly, 'you tell her that I'm dam' glad to know that you've discovered that she's got brains!'

He opened the door.

'My God!' he said caustically. 'The lady with brains. Hear me laugh . . . !'

The door slammed viciously behind him.

The Chinese clock chimed seven times. Callaghan, sitting in the big chair in front of his bedroom fireplace, his feet on the mantelpiece, eased himself up as Effie Thompson telephoned from the office downstairs.

'Findon and Nikolas are still here,' she said. 'Are they to stay?'

'Findon can go,' said Callaghan. 'Tell Nikolas to stay there. I'm comin' down . . . now.'

'There's a letter for you,' Effie went on, 'from Southing. It's marked "*personal*".'

'How nice,' said Callaghan, as he hung up the receiver.

He went into the sitting-room and unlocked the bureau in the corner. He took out the .32 Esmeralda automatic and the ten slugs that he had found in the rubber plant pot at Azelda's. He put them

161

into his coat pocket. He put his overcoat over his arm, his hat on one side of his head. He went down to the office.

On his desk lay the letter from Southing. He opened it, looked at the signature – 'Thorla Riverton'. He began to read:

Dear Mr Callaghan,

Tomorrow morning Mr Selby of Selby, Raukes & White is coming here to Southing to see me. I propose to give him certain instructions. One of these instructions is that from now on you and your organization will have nothing further to do with the case respecting my stepson.

There are several reasons for my decision. You have pointed out to me on more than one occasion that I seem to dislike you, and I would not wish you to consider that this was the reason for terminating your connection with this business. I neither like nor dislike you. From a personal point of view I am not in the remotest degree interested in you.

It was on the advice of Mr Gringall – the police officer – and in spite of my own inclinations, that I allowed you to have anything to do with the selection of a lawyer to represent Wilfred Riverton. I understand that the man Gagel selected by you is a person of peculiar professional reputation and certainly not fitted to act in this matter.

On the occasion when I saw you at your apartment – a time when I was terribly worried and not quite myself – you were able, for the moment, to intimidate me into giving you a cheque for five thousand pounds which you have cashed. I gave you this cheque because, at that time, I wanted no one to know that I had been on the San Pedro on the night of the shootings. I had my own reasons for wishing this fact to be kept secret. I consider that your attitude on that occasion was that of a blackmailer and I have made up my mind and am instructing Mr Selby to the effect that you will account for every penny of that money, and that failing the return of the balance over the sum of £100 per week – the sum due to you under the agreement made with my late husband – he will take the most rigorous proceedings against you for the return of that balance.

From the moment when my husband first became seriously ill and began to leave his affairs in my hands I believed that you were merely hanging out the investigation which my husband had asked you to undertake in order to continue to draw your retainer. It is my sincere belief that if you had proceeded honestly and sincerely with your

162

investigations in the first place the situation culminating in that fearful business last Saturday night on the San Pedro would never have taken place.

And I now know that you have, on more than one occasion, stated that it was your intention to draw out your so-called "investigations", that at an interview between you and the man Raffano who was shot, in self-defence, on the San Pedro by my stepson, you actually stated that this was the case.

These are the reasons for the instructions I am giving Mr Selby, who will see that they are carried out immediately.

Thorla Riverton.

Callaghan sat back in his chair. He began to laugh. Effie Thompson, at her desk in the outer office, pricked up her ears. She had never heard Callaghan laugh so loudly. Then his bell rang. She went in.

'Bring in your typewriter an' put it on my desk,' ordered Callaghan. 'An' I want a little cardboard box and a quarto manilla envelope – a stout one – an' some sealing-wax.' He looked at his watch. 'It's ten past seven,' he said. 'You tell Nikolas that he can go out an' get himself a drink an' come back here at a quarter to eight, an' you can go home.'

'Very well,' said Effie. 'Is there anything else?'

'Yes,' said Callaghan. 'There is. I don't want to be worried tomorrow mornin'. Just leave me alone an' don't bother me. I'm goin' to be late tonight. I shall want to sleep late.'

'Very well,' Effie repeated.

She had reached the door when he said:

'About Kells . . . telephone through to Gringall like I told you, at eleven o'clock tonight. You can do it from your place.'

Callaghan put a sheet of 'Callaghan Investigations' notepaper in the typewriter and began to type with two fingers:

Dear Gringall,

I'm afraid you're going to be a bit fed up with me because I've got to admit that I've been holding out on you like hell. But I've been in a spot. I daren't talk to you before now, and even now I'm holding up this letter so that you don't get it until after ten o'clock, because I've still got one or two things to do.

But I'm going to make it up to you all right. You're going to have a lovely pinch and if you don't get that Chief Detective Inspectorship after this then the Chief Commissioner ought to be poleaxed. Of course you don't have to tell him that Callaghan Investigations really did the work!

I know that you haven't really had a dog's chance from the start on this job. First of all because the frame-up against Wilfred Riverton was so beautifully planned that I might almost have worked it out myself. I just had to let things ride. My putting in Gagel to get that phoney statement out of Riverton was another stunt I had to do. Riverton actually made the statement to Gagel. The poor mug believed, and is still believing at the moment, that he shot Raffano.

You remember when you came round to my office last Sunday afternoon, you were talking about Riverton having shot Jake. You said it was a nice shot on the part of The Mug to have got Raffano through the heart at twelve yards. Having regard to the fact that when The Mug went down there he was full of dope the shot must have been marvellous. So marvellous that it didn't even happen!

All right. Here we go: Inside the envelope carrying this letter are three things:

1. A typewritten letter signed 'A Friend' that was delivered by Henny The Boyo to Riverton at his room off Down Street last Saturday afternoon or early evening. This letter says that Raffano had been taking The Mug for a long time. That Raffano's games were crooked. This was the letter that made Riverton rush off and – after he'd seen Azelda Dixon at Court Mansions – go down to Falleton to have a show-down with Raffano. He took a gun with him all right but he never used it. He couldn't have used it. We shan't ever find that gun unless you like to get a diver to work in Falleton Big Water where the San Pedro was moored, but I'll bet you twenty to one that a diver would find that gun underneath the San Pedro. It was dropped out through a porthole.

2. A second typewritten letter signed by Azelda Dixon. I typed this out myself on the typewriter in Henny The Boyo's office at The Privateer Bar in Soho. You will notice that the typing discrepancies – the out of place 'F's and 'E's and 'D's and 'A's in both letters – are the same. So that tells us that the letter to The Mug was typed round at Henny's place. It was typed by Azelda Dixon.

The second letter tells you that Azelda knows who it was shot Kells down at Greene's Place. I found him down there some days ago. He'd come across a bit of evidence but somebody blew in and got him before he had a chance. Effie Thompson, my secretary, is telephoning you tonight about our getting the body.

Azelda saw the letter signed by her. I had a long talk with her last night. She's waiting in for you at Court Mansions. If you send a car round for her tonight, when you get this letter, and pick her up, she'll make a full statement which will give you most of the details. I hope that you'll give her the best break you can. Of course she's an accessory to murder, but you know she's been doping for quite a while and anyhow she's turning King's Evidence. I'm a little bit sorry for Azelda.

Her statement will put you in possession of what you boys usually call the 'salient' facts of the case, but it will stop short of letting you know just when and where you can pick up her boy friend. That's the thing that concerns me at the moment. If I could let you know definitely I would, but I can't. However, if you'll be sitting at that desk of yours at eleven o'clock tonight, or thereabouts (and I bet you'll be drawing fruit on the blotter!) I'll come through and give you the final details. I've got an idea about them now but there's just a possibility that somebody's pulled a fast one on me and that the information I've got is not quite correct.

If I don't come through to you by twelve midnight . . . you ring my operative Nikolas at Speedwell 45632 at five past twelve and he'll tell you where you can come and look for me. Maybe you'll have still another corpse on your hands . . . but I don't think so.

3.   *The third thing enclosed is a cardboard box with some unused cartridge slugs inside. If you get your ballistics fellow to check up on these you will find that they are ammunition for the same type of gun that killed Kells – an Esmeralda Spanish .32 automatic – and if you like to get the slug out of Kells – which you will anyhow do – you will find that it came out of a gun that will, I am sure, be in your possession before very long.*

Well, au revoir, Gringall, till soon,

S. Callaghan.

Callaghan read the letter through, folded it, addressed the manilla envelope to Gringall, at New Scotland Yard, and put the letter in. Then he took the Esmeralda automatic out of his pocket, and took out the clip. There were only nine cartridges inside the clip. Callaghan grinned, replaced the clip and put the gun back into the breast pocket of his coat.

He put the cardboard box with the slugs in it in the envelope with the two typewritten letters, licked the flap, sealed it down with the wax. He called to Nikolas who had returned and was hanging about in the outer office.

Nikolas came in. Callaghan gave him the envelope.

'Listen, Nik,' he said. 'You hang on to this until ten minutes to ten. Don't leave this office until then. At ten minutes to ten you go out an' grab a cab from the Berkeley Square rank. Go down to Scotland Yard an' give this to Detective Inspector Gringall. Don't give it to anybody else. If they say he's not there tell 'em to get him. Tell 'em it's from me an' that he's wanting it. Then you go home. Stick around at home until ten past twelve. If Gringall rings you up between twelve and twelve ten an' asks you where I am, you say that I'm down at the Manor House at Southing. Don't tell anybody else but Gringall an' don't tell him at any other time except between twelve an' ten past – an' only if he rings you personally. You got that?'

Nikolas said he'd got it.

'All right,' said Callaghan. 'I'm going round now to a flat. The telephone number's Mayfair 78326. I'll be round there at eight o'clock . . . the name's Senora Juanita. You telephone through there at eight-twenty and ask to speak to me. When I talk back to you just don't take any notice. See?'

Nikolas said that would be OK. He went back to the staff-room to play solitaire and take a little drink.

Callaghan looked at his watch. It was twenty minutes to eight. He put on his overcoat and hat, took the Luger out of the bottom drawer of his desk, examined the clip, slipped it into his right hand overcoat pocket.

He went out, walked quickly round to the garage, started up the Jaguar, drove towards Juanita's flat.

Callaghan stopped the car two blocks from Juanita's building. He walked towards it on the other side of the road. Outside the building a car was parked. Callaghan stood in a convenient doorway and

166

waited. After a few minutes Gill Charleston came out, got into the car, drove off.

Callaghan lit a cigarette. He waited for five minutes, crossed the road, entered the building and went up to Juanita's place.

She opened the door. Her eyes were sparkling. Juanita was excited.

'Hallo, Slim,' she said. 'Did you see Gill?'

Callaghan nodded.

'I ran into him outside . . . ' He lied easily. 'I said all the right things.'

She led the way into the sitting-room. The place was bestrewn with new frocks, coats and skirts, hats. . . . Callaghan said:

'All this has cost somebody some money!'

He put his hand into his hip pocket and produced the diamond and platinum brooch. He opened the case, held it out towards her. Juanita squealed with delight.

'Wow!' she exclaimed. 'What a honey. . . . Oh boy! Are you swell!'

She pinned the clip on to her frock, stood admiring herself before the mirror.

Callaghan, helping himself to a drink from the sideboard, said:

'If you ever get really fed up with me, Juanita . . . you know . . . sort of disliking my memory or anything like that, just take a look at that brooch. It'll make you feel better!'

She laughed. Then, quite suddenly, she became serious.

'You're a helluva funny guy,' she said. 'I used to think I was nuts about you . . . maybe I still am. What do you know about that!'

He grinned.

'Don't you believe it,' he said. 'I'm a very unreliable cuss where women are concerned.'

'Maybe,' said Juanita, 'but even unreliability can be OK. Sometimes. I s'pose I'm *really* very fond of Gill. . . . '

Callaghan took a quick glance at his watch. It was twelve minutes past eight. He decided to take a chance:

'Gill told me outside about the alteration in your plans.'

'Well, for crying out loud,' said Juanita. 'What do you know about that guy! He told me that I wasn't to tell anybody – not even you. I only knew myself half an hour ago that we were goin' off from Croydon at two this morning instead of five. Gill says he's got to be in Paris first thing in the morning an' he's keen to do a little night flying. I don't see why we couldn't have waited and gone tomorrow later. Still . . . it'll be fun.'

Callaghan said yes. The telephone rang. She went over and answered it.

'Somebody for you, Slim,' she said. 'Urgent.'

Callaghan took up the telephone.

'Hallo . . . ' he said. 'Yes . . . Yes . . . No, dam' it, I won't do it. I'm just goin' out to dinner with a lady. What . . . Oh, all right then. . . . '

He hung up, turned to her a picture of misery.

'Look, honey,' he said. 'Now don't start ridin' me. *I* can't help it. I've got to go off for half an hour. It's urgent . . . some big business has just come in. I'll come back for you then.'

'My God,' she said. 'Are you awful or are you. Every time I have a date with you something happens. If you don't come back in half an hour I'll murder you the next time I see you.'

'I'll be seeing you,' said Callaghan.

He picked up his hat and coat, kissed her on the tip of the nose.

'No, Slim,' she said softly. 'Not like that. It's the last time. Make it a real one.'

He made it a real one.

Callaghan walked back to the Jaguar. He sat in the driving seat for a few minutes thinking. Then he started the car and drove off. He was quite relaxed, almost happy.

The evening traffic was heavy in the West End. He took his time. He began to whistle quietly.

Outside London he put his foot down on the gas. The car shot forward. The speedometer needle hovered between fifty and sixty.

He let in the supercharger. He started to hum an old Chinese laundry song:

> '*For value received I promise to pay*
> *Two or three dollars in two or three day,*
> *If man no come an' money no bring,*
> *Who the hell cares . . . it's all the same thing!*'

Callaghan got out a cigarette with one hand, lit it with an electric lighter on the dashboard. The night was cold and dry and the tourer top was down.

The wind roared past as the Jaguar ate up the road.

CHAPTER FOURTEEN

Friday

Conversation between friends

It was a quarter to eleven when Callaghan arrived at Southing. He slowed the car down and stopped it fifty yards from the iron gates that led to the carriage drive of the Manor House. He looked about him for a convenient clump of trees off the road, found one, drove the car over the grass verge, parked it behind the trees and walked slowly along the narrow road, keeping in the shadows.

A wind had sprung up. The sky was cloudy with an occasional pale moon showing through. Callaghan, his hands in his overcoat pockets, arrived at the iron gates, found one of them open.

He walked quickly through the gate, passed by the lodge just inside and, keeping on the grass at the side of the drive, began to walk towards the house.

The drive was a long one. Half-way towards the house he could see a red light showing a foot or two off the ground, on the left hand side of the drive. He gave a sigh of relief. He increased his pace and came up with the light. It was the rear light on Charleston's car.

Callaghan opened the nearside door, slipped into the passenger seat and began to search with his fingers in the cubby holes in the dashboard. He found nothing. He turned his attention to the pocket in the offside driver's door. His fingers encountered a miscellany of articles, a duster, a road map, a tin of defrosting paste – all the odd things that a car driver collects and seldom uses.

He moved over to the driver's seat, put his hand into the breast pocket of his lounge jacket, brought out the Esmeralda automatic that he had found in Azelda's flat. He took all the articles out of the door pocket and pushed the automatic pistol down to the bottom, replacing the other things on top of the gun. He got out of the car.

He moved off the drive into the shadow of the trees that stood in profusion between the drive and the estate wall fifty yards away. Behind a tree he lit a cigarette, shielding the flame of his lighter with his hands. He stood there smoking happily.

The minutes passed. Callaghan stood quite still, looking into the darkness, blowing smoke rings that he could not even see. It was half an hour later that he heard a noise.

He turned in the direction of the Manor House entrance. He saw the double doors open and two figures stand for a moment framed in the square of light. Then the door shut.

As the sound of feet on the gravel drive grew louder, Callaghan began to move towards Charleston's car. He stood behind it and waited while Charleston slipped into the driver's seat and started the engine, then he moved forward and spoke through the open window to Charleston.

'Hallo, pal . . . ' said Callaghan.

Charleston flipped on the dashboard light. He turned his head and saw Callaghan, saw the barrel of the Luger automatic in Callaghan's hand levelled through the window.

'Why, it's Slim!' he said easily. 'What's the idea? Practising for a stick-up or something?'

He was smiling.

Callaghan said: 'Turn the car round and drive off the carriage drive on to the grass verge. Put your head and rear lights off but leave the dashboard light on. Don't try any funny business because if you do I'll put a bullet through you. See?'

'I see,' said Charleston.

He began to turn the car. Callaghan moved with it, keeping in line with the window. When Charleston had brought the car on to the grass verge into the shadows with the lights turned off, Callaghan said:

'Open the door and get out. Sit down on the step so that the dashboard light's behind you.'

Charleston did as he was told. Then he said softly:

'What's the idea, Slim? Have you gone nuts or something?'

'Not quite,' said Callaghan. 'For the love of Mike, Gill, don't try to put up any acts. I'm wise to you. I've been wise to you all along. This is the show-down.'

Charleston grinned.

'Can I smoke?' he asked. 'Is that allowed?'

'Why not?' said Callaghan. 'I'll give you a cigarette.'

He felt in his pocket with his free hand, produced two cigarettes and a lighter. He handed one to Charleston, put the other in his own mouth. He snapped the lighter into flame, lit the cigarettes.

'It was nearly very nice work, Gill,' he said. 'But it wasn't quite smart enough.'

Charleston shrugged his shoulders.

'You're a clever fellow,' he said. 'I thought I'd even pulled it on *you*. I ought to have got out days ago. I was a mug.' He shrugged his shoulders again. 'Where do we go from here?' he asked.

Callaghan looked at Charleston. Behind the casual eyes he could almost see Gill's quick brain working. He did not answer the question.

'You're right,' he said. 'You ought to have got out. Then you'd have stood a chance. You might have got away with it. But I was wise to you last Friday night, that's why I put Juanita on to you so that you'd stay an' try an' get her as well. You're greedy, aren't you, Gill . . . you wanted to grab off Juanita as well as that extra money. If you'd have been satisfied with the forty thousand odd you took off Jake after you shot him; if you'd been clever enough to have got out an' taken *Azelda* with you — you could always have ditched her afterwards — you'd have got away with the whole bag of tricks an' young Riverton would have swung on the end of a rope. But you had to have everything. You even had to try to make Thorla Riverton too. It was a pity that the morphine you slipped her didn't work better. What did you tell her it was — something for a headache?'

Charleston said: 'Have a heart . . . I didn't try to make her. But I knew she was going along to see you. She'd told me she was. I thought it might be a good thing if she wasn't thinking too clearly. Well, it was a good thing — for you. You took her for five thousand pounds. She told me tonight. She says she's given you the order of the boot from this job too. It's damned funny, isn't it? Women can be mugs. . . . '

'You'd be surprised,' said Callaghan. 'I suppose she told you about my havin' that five thousand to explain why she'd only got twenty thousand pounds instead of twenty-two thousand pounds. Is that right?'

'That's right,' said Charleston.

In the dim light of the dashboard bulb, Callaghan could see his eyes alter. He knew that Charleston was thinking out the big idea. The thought amused him.

Charleston said: 'Were you wise last Friday night . . . when you saw me at Joe Martinella's place?'

'What do you think?' said Callaghan sarcastically. 'Do you think that Callaghan Investigations are so dam' dumb that I didn't know then that you an' Raffano had been partners over here. What did you think we'd been doin' for weeks? Well, you wanted to think we didn't know anything so you thought it. An' when I came up to you at the fight an' told you that I was up against a brick wall and couldn't get a move on, you got a big idea. It wasn't a bad idea either. You knew Jake Raffano was goin' to blow. You knew that he was goin' to take the cash with him and do you down for your cut because he knew *you* couldn't squeal.

'So you told me that it was Raffano who had been takin' The Mug for all that money. You told me about that fight bein' in the bag just because you knew that I'd get Lonney to win it, so's to bring Jake up against me quick an' I'd scare him off. You knew dam' well that Jake would make a quick getaway next day. I reckon the *San Pedro* would have been gone by Sunday mornin' if you hadn't shot Jake.'

Charleston said: 'Aren't you the little Sherlock Holmes?'

Callaghan went on, speaking quite evenly:

'You made a couple of dam' silly mistakes. Maybe you'd like to hear what they were. First of all you telephoned through to The Mug on Friday night after I'd left Martinella's place an' told him that I was on his tail, that his stepmother was riding me to get a move on. The dam' fool came an' waited for me outside my place an' started to shout his head off in Berkeley Square. He told me to mind my own business an' suggested that his stepmother could mind hers too. Well, there was only one person could have told him that . . . there was only one person who knew. That was you . . . see?'

'I see,' said Charleston. 'It's damned funny how a man can make a little mistake. You're a clever bastard, Slim.'

He went on smoking. Callaghan knew that Charleston was trying to find out just how much he knew . . . wondering if there was still a chance. Well . . . why not let him think he still had a chance. Why not give him another kick out of life . . . let him think he'd got away with it all, and then just as he was congratulating himself on the fact . . . *Why not!*

Callaghan grinned inwardly. He was enjoying himself. It was like a cat playing with a mouse. Quite suddenly, and for no particular reason, he remembered Monty Kells lying at the foot of the cellar steps. . . . Callaghan thought it would be damned funny to let Charleston think that he had got away with that too. . . .

He said: 'You made another dam' silly mistake. After I went round to see Perruqui, an' did a little threatenin' to find out where Azelda Dixon had been gettin' the dope that you had got her to feed to The Mug, I came out of his office an' met you in the entrance of the Yellow Lamp. You were just goin' home. Remember? Well, directly I'd gone Perruqui came rushin' out an' told you about it, asked you what the hell was to be done. *You* told him to telephone through to Azelda to rush round to Henny The Boyo's an' tell him to keep his mouth shut, an' it was you who hired that thug to wait for me an' carve me up afterwards. If it had come off you thought I'd think Raffano was behind it.

'I always thought Azelda was workin' for you. You were the feller who started her on dope an' it was you who got her to start young Riverton on it. When Perruqui an' Henny went out of their way to tell me that she was workin' for Raffano I *knew* she was workin' for you. Everything had to be blamed on Raffano because you knew he was blowin' an' you knew that with him out of the way an' suspected of everything, you were goin' to be all right. How's that?'

'Not so bad,' said Charleston. 'You're doing fine, Slim.'

'I'll do better in a minute,' said Callaghan. 'You got your big idea on Friday night. You went round to see Azelda after she'd been to see Henny The Boyo. She told you what had happened an' how she'd met me round there. You'd got that poor piece nutty about you an' I reckon she'd have done murder for you . . . which is what she helped to do.

'You put a hell of a scheme up to her. She was to go round to Henny's on Saturday an' write an anonymous note to young Riverton tellin' him that the Raffano games had all been crooked. You knew that he would go dashin' around with that note to Azelda's. You knew he'd go there because she was the only pal he had. He was stuck on her because she was kind to him. All right. When he got there she was to tell him that it was easy, that all he had to do was to go down to Falleton, get aboard the *San Pedro* and have a show-down with Jake. She was to tell him that Jake was yellow when it came to the push, an' that if he took a gun down there an' threatened Jake, Jake would give him back the IOU for the £22,000, and some cash to be goin' on with.

'An' she was to give him a couple of shots of dope so that he'd be haywire an' think he could get away with it. She was also to hand him the gun to do the threatenin' with an' take him down there herself in her car because you knew dam' well he wasn't fit to drive two yards.

'But what that poor fathead didn't know was that you had fixed with Azelda for her to give him a gun that was loaded with ten blank cartridges. She took the slugs out of the shells before he came round. You weren't goin' to trust that poor dope-soaked idiot to go rushin' around the *San Pedro* shootin' off a gun. You knew he couldn't hit a haystack anyway *an' you wanted Jake killed.*

'On Saturday afternoon or early evenin' you sent a message to Jake, on the *San Pedro*. You told him that The Mug was comin' down to get him, that he was carryin' a gun an' that anyway he wasn't used to a gun an' it would be a dam' good thing if he was bumped . . . that he might get desperate an' start talkin'. Jake was waitin' for him all ready for the fray. What you didn't tell Jake was that you were goin' to be aboard the *San Pedro* too!'

Charleston flipped the ash from his cigarette. 'You know, Slim,' he said, 'you're *good*. You're too good to be a private detective rushing around the place, using your brains and getting kicked for it. You ought to be in the big money. If you had some real capital you could do a lot for yourself.'

'I know,' said Callaghan, 'I've been thinkin' that myself for a long time.' He laughed a little. 'Let's get on with the story,' he said.

'You fixed it with Azelda that she was to get The Mug down there at ten-thirty sharp. She was to wait until she'd seen Riverton pull the dinghy out to the *San Pedro*. Then she was to drive to Greene's Place and pick you up. You were waitin' for her all ready with a pair of swimmin' trunks on under your shirt. She drove you to the telephone box off the end of Falleton High Street an' you proceeded to pull your big idea. You telephoned through to Thorla Riverton who was gettin' ready to go over to the Nursing Home at Swansdown Poulteney. You told her that Jake Raffano had an IOU for £22,000 from her stepson an' that unless something was done about it, he was goin' to take it over to the Colonel at the Nursing Home and ask for payment. You knew dam' well she'd do anything to stop *that*. You fixed for her to meet you on the *San Pedro* at eleven-thirty. You told her to pull out in the remainin' dinghy that was tied up at the landin' stage, that you'd meet her aboard and come to some arrangement. She didn't like it but what could she do. Well . . . how am I doin'?'

'Go on, Slim,' said Charleston. 'It's a nice story anyhow.'

He threw his cigarette stub away.

'So Thorla Riverton said she'd be there. You told her that if she'd bring an IOU *payable to you an' signed by her*, you'd tear up The Mug's IOU an' give her time to pay the other one. You said that you didn't mind *her* IOU because you knew that would be all right. You said that was the only way to stop Raffano goin' over to the Nursing Home an' raisin' hell.

'Then Azelda drove you down to that clump of trees near to the landin' stage. You got out of your clothes an' swam out to the *San Pedro*. Azelda turned the car round, an' waited for you to show up, dress, an' go back to town with her – just like a pair of sweethearts.

'You know what happened on the *San Pedro*. When you got there an' crept down to the main saloon Raffano an' The Mug were havin' the row of their lives. You probably watched it through the crack in the door at the end of the passage that leads from the little saloon. Then The Mug, doin' what he's been told to do by Azelda, pulls out his gun an' starts wavin' it about. Raffano goes for his own gun an' The Mug fires – that poor idiot thinks he really fired at Raffano. In fact he fired a blank cartridge. Raffano let him have it. He shot him through the lung an' The Mug went down unconscious.

'Before Jake could even move you stepped through the door. You'd brought an Esmeralda automatic pistol out with you. You carried it in a sailor's rubber tobacco pouch under the waistbelt of your swimmin' suit. You shot Raffano clean through the heart before he knew what was happenin'.

'Then it was easy. You grabbed the gun out of Riverton's hand, wiped your finger-prints off the butt of the Esmeralda and stuck it into his hand. You knew the police would find that the bullet out of that gun killed Jake an' that the bullet out of Jake's gun had got Riverton. You thought Riverton was goin' to die. So did I when I went down there an' saw him.

'All right, then you dropped the gun he'd had, the one loaded with blanks, out of a porthole. Then you went along the passage into the little saloon – the one with the bar – an' put on a dressin'-gown. It was still damp when I got on the boat an' found it. Then you went back to the main saloon, cleared out the safe – you got the key out of Raffano's pocket, got The Mug's IOU to Raffano for £22,000, went into the little saloon, shuttin' the door of the main one carefully behind you, an' stuck around and had a drink while you waited for Thorla Riverton.

'When she came you took the IOU she'd brought with her, an' tore up the other one. You dropped it in the waste-paper basket under the table in the little saloon. You thought that when the police saw it they'd know it was the cause of the trouble between Raffano an' Riverton. Well, that was a hell of a mistake on your part. First of all they never saw it, because I got hold of it first, and secondly, it told me a lot . . . '

'Meaning what?' said Charleston. His voice was grim.

'Meanin' this,' Callaghan went on. 'If you'd thought for a minute you'd have realized that if Raffano an' Riverton were havin' a row about that IOU, Raffano wouldn't have torn it up before Riverton arrived, would he? Well, Riverton couldn't have torn it up when he did arrive because that was what the shootin' was supposed to be about. If Riverton an' Raffano shot each other at practically the same time how the hell could either of them have torn it up, walked out of the saloon, through the passage into the little saloon, an' put the pieces in the waste-paper basket? Well . . . ?'

Charleston said in an odd voice: 'Elementary, my dear Watson.'

Callaghan felt in his pocket for another cigarette and lit it, watching Charleston through the flame of the lighter. He still held the Luger on him.

'So I knew that somebody else had been on the *San Pedro*,' Callaghan went on in his quietest voice. 'When I found out that Thorla Riverton had been aboard I thought for a little while that she might have lost her temper an' done a little shootin' herself. I don't know that I'd have blamed her a lot. But she didn't.

'Well . . . then the fat was in the fire. The police get busy an' Riverton doesn't die. The next thing you hear – an' you heard it from Thorla Riverton the night she came round to see you just before she came round to my apartment, the night you were bein' such a good friend to her an' gave her that dope so that she didn't know who was who or what was what – is that Riverton is probably to be charged with murder an' that everybody, includin' Mrs Riverton, believes that he *did* murder Raffano.' Callaghan began to grin. 'Why,' he said half-humorously, 'that poor mug even believes *now* that he shot Jake.

'I knew Thorla Riverton was around at your place. She was supposed to be ringin' me from the Chartres Hotel, but I was able to check the call. She was telephonin' from an all-night coffee bar in Knightsbridge, an' you'd pulled a very clever one on her, I must

176

admit. You told her that the shootin' took place on the *San Pedro after* she'd gone. That Riverton had arrived soon after she'd left, with Raffano. That they'd had a hell of a row an' shot each other. *But you told her that Raffano had pulled his gun first, that Riverton had fired in self-defence,* an' you told her that if she'd cash in with the £20,000 you'd go down to Scotland Yard an' tell 'em the whole story an' get Riverton off. But you said that you'd got to have the money first, an' that if she told anybody about it before you had the money, you'd keep your mouth shut an' let Riverton hang. So what could she say? She had to say yes again. Nice work, Gill. . . . '

Charleston said: 'Oh, well . . . Have you got any more cigarettes, Slim?'

'No,' said Callaghan, 'not for *you*. I've got about five more an' I need 'em for myself. It was too bad you had to shoot Kells, Gill.'

'You don't say,' said Charleston a little hoarsely. 'So I shot Kells, did I?'

'You bet you did,' said Callaghan. 'You *had* to. It was pretty tough on Monty that you suddenly remembered the swimming trunks with the rubber pouch tacked inside that you'd left behind at Greene's Place when you dressed after you'd swum back from the *San Pedro*. You went back to get 'em. You couldn't find 'em because Monty had already found 'em. He was carryin' 'em screwed up in his hand, searchin' around in the cellar, when you heard him an' came down with a gun an' shot him . . . the gun bein' the sister gun to the one you shot Jake with, a .32 Esmeralda Spanish automatic. I found it in the rubber plant pot at Azelda's place, where you'd hidden it. I found the slugs she'd taken out of the cartridges too. . . . '

'Hell!' said Charleston. He paused, then he said: 'By God, you're a tough proposition, Slim.'

Callaghan said nothing. There was a long silence, then Charleston said:

'Can we do a deal, Slim?'

Callaghan grinned.

'What the hell do you think I'm doin' lurkin' about here in the undergrowth if not for the purpose of doin' a deal?' he said pleasantly. 'How much did you take off the *San Pedro*?'

'About £27,000,' said Charleston with a gulp. 'But a lot of that was in cheques . . . and they won't be any good.'

His face had brightened considerably.

Callaghan said: 'I'll take the £20,000 you just got from Thorla Riverton. Hand it over.'

Charleston felt in his breast pocket. He produced an envelope.

'Take out the notes an' count 'em for me under the dashboard light,' said Callaghan.

Charleston did it.

Callaghan put out his hand and took the banknotes.

'Now you can get out,' he said. 'An' you can thank your lucky stars that I'm ready an' willin' to do a deal. Now get out an' be damned to you!'

Charleston slid into the driving seat. He was smiling. He said:

'You're a pal, Slim. I've always known you were a good guy at heart. There's nobody got a dam' thing on me except you. It's a deal. You get twenty thousand and the odd five thousand you took the Riverton woman for, an' I get the rest. Well . . . so-long, Slim. I'll be seeing you one of these fine days.'

He switched on the headlights, started the engine. The car droned down the drive, through the open gate, along the road.

Callaghan stood looking after it. He was grinning like a devil. He stood there for quite a time, muttering to himself, still grinning. Then he began to walk quickly down the drive.

He went through the iron gates, walked back to his car, started the engine, turned the car and drove off. He turned off the main road, took a side secondary road that he knew would take him past Greene's Place. In twenty minutes' time he passed the house. Every window was lit and there were four cars standing in the driveway. Gringall had moved quickly.

Callaghan drove back towards Falleton, stopped at the telephone box on the grass verge at the end of the High Street. He dialled the Scotland Yard number. He gave his name.

A minute later Gringall came on the line.

'Hallo, Slim,' he said. 'I think you private detectives are marvellous. Thanks for the letter and the enclosures.'

'I'm speakin' from Falleton,' said Callaghan. 'I've just passed Greene's Place. I saw the lights on an' the cars outside. . . . '

'I've put the county police on to it,' said Gringall. 'I've told 'em about Kells. They'll hand the body over to your undertaker directly our own surgeon's made an autopsy.'

'All right, Gringall,' said Callaghan. 'Now you listen to me. I can tell you how you get Charleston. He's on his way back to town now. He thinks he's goin' to get away with it. He's goin' to pick up a girl named Juanita in Mayfair, an' he's takin' a private plane for France from Croydon. He chartered it a day or so ago. You get him. I don't like that feller.'

'I'll get him all right,' said Gringall.

'There's just one thing,' said Callaghan. 'That girl Juanita is a nice piece. She doesn't know a dam' thing about all this. She's as innocent as a babe unborn. I had to throw her at Charleston to get a certain amount of information an' to keep him hangin' around until the right time came. Let her go directly you've pinched him, Gringall. She'll be pretty fed up anyway. She thinks she's goin' to marry him.'

'All right,' said Gringall. 'I'll do my best, but I wouldn't like to be you when she finds out. She'll want to tear you in bits.'

Callaghan said: 'Did Azelda talk?'

'The whole book,' said Gringall. 'She's shopped him properly – and herself too.'

Callaghan said: ' "Hell hath no fury . . . " Anyhow you know the rest, Gringall. By the way,' he went on, 'I think I can tell you where you'll find the second Esmeralda – the gun that Charleston shot Kells with. I've got an idea it's in the right-hand door pocket in Charleston's car.'

'Right,' said Gringall. 'And, Callaghan, if you like to give me the number of Charleston's car – if you know it – we'll never let him get to Croydon. We'll pick him up outside London. That would save the Juanita woman some trouble. I'll send a man round to explain to her. What's her address?'

'Nice work,' said Callaghan. He gave the car number, and the address.

'You might drop in some time tomorrow,' said Gringall. 'I want to present you with the freedom of the City of London, a thick ear, a whisky and soda – all that unofficially, of course. Officially I want to hand you a stern warning about holding up evidence in criminal cases, obstruction, etc. But I've an idea that I've done that before once or twice.'

'Right,' said Callaghan. 'An' I bet you'll be doin' it again some time. Good night, Gringall.'

'Good night, Callaghan,' Gringall replied, 'and – unofficially – thank you.'

'Not at all,' said Callaghan. 'Not at all, my dear Watson. . . . '

He hung up.

He got back into the car, turned it, headed for Southing. As he approached Greene's Place he began to smile. He was thinking of Charleston bent over the wheel, making London as fast as the car would go, congratulating himself. . . .

Callaghan's smile broadened into a laugh. It faded as the picture faded to that of a bleak prison yard . . . the scaffold . . . the hangman. . . .

He put his foot on the accelerator. Greene's Place flashed past. The lights were still on.

Callaghan put his hand out of the window, waved it.

'OK, Monty,' he said. 'It's all right . . . !'

The car droned towards Southing. The headlights picked up the AA sign on the secondary road . . . 'Dangerous Curves'. . . .

'Dangerous nothin',' said Callaghan, and let in the supercharger.

CHAPTER FIFTEEN

Friday

You'd be surprised

Callaghan slowed the car down to thirty as he ran into the narrow road that branched off the Falleton-London road, towards Southing. He felt about in his overcoat pocket for a cigarette and his lighter. He lit the cigarette and inhaled deeply.

The car was running sweetly. He listened with appreciation to the steady hum of the engine which, at that moment, missed and sputtered as an air bubble in the petrol caused a temporary lock in the feed. He grinned. Life was like that – a more or less steady hum until something turned up like the Riverton case and then the fireworks started.

But it had been a nice week. . . . He reviewed the days one by one and, at the end, recollected that there was still going to be a little trouble with Juanita.

A *little* trouble! He smiled ruefully as he imagined Juanita's language at their next meeting. The fact that, in any event, Callaghan had stopped her at the very last moment marrying a double murderer would mean nothing to Juanita. She would accuse Callaghan of having thrown her at Charleston, forgetting, in the process, that you can't make anybody do anything they really do not want to do. Callaghan sighed. He foresaw a very exhausting hour in the near future when the conversation would be both one-sided and forcible.

A high wind had sprung up. The night was very dark. There was a storm hanging about, he thought, and wished that the car hood was up. Quite suddenly he remembered the letter from Thorla Riverton demanding the accounting for the five thousand, giving him the sack. She'd let herself go over that. He grinned happily.

His headlights picked up the gates of the Manor House. Callaghan swung the car through. Through the darkness, away in front of the house he could see, moving slowly in his direction, the headlights of a car. He pushed the accelerator down, increased speed to forty, speeded up the curved drive towards the headlights. Thirty yards from them he let go a fearful blast on the klaxon horn, and braked hard. He heard the squeal of the brakes on the other car as they both swerved to a standstill – the bonnets only a dozen feet apart.

Callaghan got out, his cigarette hanging out of one corner of his mouth, his face wreathed in a pleasant smile. He put his hand on the door of the open tourer, in which Thorla Riverton, bareheaded, a Persian lamb coat about her shoulders, sat, her gauntleted hands tapping impatiently on the wheel.

'Good evenin', Mrs Riverton,' said Callaghan very pleasantly. 'Goin' somewhere? You ought to get somebody to put the hood up on your car. It's goin' to rain like the dickens in a minute. You can feel it in the air.'

Her eyes flashed.

'Mr Callaghan,' she said, 'I imagine you've had my letter. You will understand that I have said *all* I intend to say to you. You will save a great deal of trouble for yourself if you leave immediately. I am in a hurry.'

He threw his cigarette end away and lit another. His smile was impudent.

'That's the trouble with people,' he said. 'They're always in too much of a hurry. They don't give themselves time to think. They go rushin' an' dashin' about all over the place bein' important. Don't you think, Mrs Riverton?'

She said icily: 'I advise you to go, Mr Callaghan. Anything that you have to say you can say to Mr Selby in his office, *if* he cares to listen!'

'No, Madame,' said Callaghan, 'I don't want to see Mr Selby. I want to have a little heart-to-heart talk with you. I can see Mr Selby any time an' when I do I never get any pleasure out of lookin' at *him*. But it's different with you. I told you once before that when you get angry you look wonderful. In fact,' he concluded, 'I'd pay a fiver any time to see you in a rage.'

She said: 'I warn you, Mr Callaghan. It will be much easier for you if you go. Kindly move your car at once.'

'An' if I don't?' he queried.

'If you do not move it immediately I shall back this car to the house, call the chauffeur and have you *thrown* out.'

'Dear me,' said Callaghan, grinning. 'It looks as if it's goin' to be a tough night for me. But I've still got to say my piece, Madame, an' you're not really in a hurry. If you'd listen to me quietly for a few minutes I could save you that journey to Ballington where you're proposin' to dash – like a merciful angel – to tell that fatuous young ass of a stepson of yours that all is well, that you've found the star witness for the defence, the feller who's goin' to prove that Riverton shot Raffano in self-defence. Well, you don't have to do it.'

She shifted the gear lever. The car began to move slowly backwards along the drive . . . slowly because of the darkness.

Callaghan walked alongside. He went on:

'An' there's another thing I wanted to see you about. I wanted to see you about that letter you wrote me. Don't you think that was a very unkind letter to write to a hard-workin' detective?'

She stopped the car.

'If you didn't like my letter you have only yourself to blame,' she said. 'It was because of your dilatory methods that this terrible situation came to a head on the *San Pedro*. It . . . '

Callaghan interrupted. 'Rubbish, Madame,' he said. 'The trouble with you is that you don't get your facts right. You jump to conclusions. You're one of those women who don't like private detectives. You start off with a preconceived notion that they've got to be no good an' you go on tryin' to prove the fact for your own self-satisfaction. The trouble with you is that you're a little stupid sometimes an' won't admit it.'

She did not reply. The car began to move backwards along the drive.

'Well,' said Callaghan, still walking, 'it's only goin' to take you a minute or two now, an' as I suppose I shall be thrown out a couple of minutes after that, I'll have to talk fast.' He nodded his head in the direction of the house. 'I suppose Mr Selby is up there?' he asked.

'He is,' she snapped. 'On my return I propose to tell him what I think of the investigator he chose to recommend.'

'Poor Mr Selby,' said Callaghan. 'That'll annoy him, won't it? You know you've had a very bad deal takin' things by and large. You've got a solicitor who recommends a lousy detective who recommends a lousy lawyer like Gagel. It's tough, *I* think.'

As the drive broadened towards the front of the house the car began to move more quickly. Callaghan jumped quickly on to the step, holding on by the top of the windscreen. He said:

'Now this is *nice* . . . much better than walkin'.'

The car stopped in front of the house. 'Get off the car and go, Mr Callaghan,' she said, trying to control her rage. 'This is your last chance.'

He could see her fingers on the wheel trembling.

He stepped off.

'Well,' he said. 'I wanted to say something about that letter you wrote me. I suppose you think I'm goin' to say that I'm sorry I made you hand over that cheque for five thousand, that I'm sorry I haven't said "Yes, ma'am", an' "No, ma'am", to everything you've thought an' said since I first came across you, that I'm goin' to try an' get you not to be too harsh on me. Well, I'm not. What I'm goin' to say is that the first time I saw you up at the Chartres Hotel in London I said you were dumb. You haven't done anything much since then to make me alter my opinion of you. You haven't even enough sense to realize that your late husband was a dam' clever feller as well as a dam' good soldier in his time, that Selby is a first-class lawyer with more experience in his little finger than you've got in the entire area of that nice-lookin' figure of yours, an' that if it was good enough for those two men to pick me to run this investigation, it was good enough for you to stay at home, keep that pretty mouth of yours shut an' like it. But no . . . you had to go stickin' your nose into things that didn't concern you. You haven't learned that in life you've got to trust *somebody sometimes.* . . .'

She said something under her breath. She sounded half a dozen short blasts on the horn.

Callaghan paused for a moment. Then he said:

'I suppose this is where the throwin' out act begins.'

He looked over his shoulder at the approaching figure of a man in a chauffeur's uniform. He sighed despairingly.

The chauffeur came up to the car. She said:

'Jelks . . . throw this man out and don't let him in again.'

Callaghan said: 'Don't you do it, Jelks. You're only about ten pounds heavier than I am, an' I'd hate to see the Riverton chauffeur with a black eye. It wouldn't go so well with that nice brown uniform of yours.'

Jelks came round the car.

'Out you go,' he said grimly.

He put up a hand as large as a plate.

As the hand touched his shoulder Callaghan's body relaxed, then straightened. Jelks gave a howl. She saw that Callaghan was merely holding Jelks' right hand between both of his own, that apparently he was not even exerting any strength. Jelks began to writhe.

'That's what they call *judo*, Madame,' said Callaghan. '*You'd* call it *ju-jitsu*, I expect. What do you want me to do about Jelks? This is hurtin' him like anything an' he can't move much because if he does he breaks his own wrist! *I* think it's one of the nicest wrist-locks there is an' . . .'

She said: 'Let Jelks go, please, Mr Callaghan.'

Callaghan released the chauffeur, who stood, looking rather stupid, rubbing his wrist and arm.

'You can go, Jelks,' she said.

The man went.

'Say what you want to say and then go,' she said.

She sat, her hands on the wheel, looking straight in front of her. A few large drops of rain fell. Callaghan looked at the sky.

'Well . . .' he said. He shrugged his shoulders. 'I don't think I want to say anything very much *now*,' he said cynically. 'Why should I? There's only one thing I would like to say, an' that is I think if the Colonel was alive he wouldn't feel so pleased to think that you – who give yourself such hoity-toity airs – would be so dam' silly an' so *infra dig* as to do a deal with a dirty crook like Gill Charleston an' give *him* twenty thousands pounds for the sole an' express purpose of makin' a dam' fool out of you!'

He began to laugh.

The storm broke suddenly. As it broke she was out of the car in a flash, her coat falling from her shoulders. The rain stung her face. She saw that he was still laughing as, her glove pulled off, she hit him across the face with the back of her hand. She noticed with an odd pleasure that her rings had cut his thin cheek, that a little stream of blood was mixing with the rain on his face.

He caught both her wrists in one hand. His fingers felt like steel bands. She gave up struggling.

Callaghan held her at arm's length. He looked her over almost insolently from top to toe. The rain swept down, soaking her thin evening gown until it clung to her like a bathing suit.

Her mouth was dry with rage. She said hoarsely:

'If I could only tell you how I *loathe* you!'

He laughed.

'That's fine,' he said pleasantly. 'I told you once before that some wise feller once said that hatred was akin to love or something like that. Well . . . you go on hatin' because it amuses me like hell. I'd rather be hated by you than have the Queen of Sheba runnin' after me. There's more kick in it. Beyond that you make me tired. . . . '

He released her wrists. Quite suddenly she felt absolutely weak . . . entirely helpless. She sat down on the steps of the car, put her hands up to her face.

Callaghan said softly: 'Good night, Madame. You'd better get in out of the rain. Don't you worry your head because you've got nothin' to worry about *now*. You can go to bed an' get your beauty sleep an' wake up in the mornin' an' be Mrs Thorla Riverton . . . the pride of the county . . . the lady with brains. . . . '

He spun round as the door of the Manor House opened. Selby, bareheaded, excited, came running down the steps.

'My God . . . ' he said. 'Callaghan . . . how did you do it . . . wonderful, my boy, wonderful . . . '

She got up, leaned against the car. She looked at Selby.

'Mr Gringall's been through from the Yard,' said Selby, the rain running down his face. 'They've got Charleston – the man who *really* killed Raffano. Wilfred is innocent. They've taken the police away from Ballington Hospital. They got Charleston outside London soon after midnight. He's admitted everything. Gringall says that we have Mr Callaghan here to thank, that . . . '

'Hold on,' said Callaghan.

He stepped forward and caught Thorla Riverton as she fell.

'Too much excitement, if you ask me,' he said. 'The feller who said that the nervous system could only stand so much had got something. It's all right . . . she's fainted, that's all . . . the rest'll do her good.'

He walked towards the entrance steps, carrying her easily.

'The devil of it is, Mr Selby,' he said, 'I'll never know whether it was your news or my *judo* that was responsible for this.'

Selby wiped the rain from his face. When he looked up he saw that Callaghan was grinning.

Callaghan stood in front of the fire in the drawing-room smoking a cigarette, and drinking four fingers of whisky neat. Selby, a cigar in his hand, sat on the other side of the fireplace.

'There wasn't any other way to play it,' Callaghan concluded. 'Charleston was holdin' the trump cards all along. Guessin's no good in criminal cases, you know that. If I'd tried to do a thing before I did, that boyo would have skipped an' we should have been in the cart. I'd got to make him think that everything was all right, that he'd got away with it.'

Selby nodded.

'It was no good my shoutin' about the Kells murder,' Callaghan went on. 'There wasn't one shred of evidence to connect Charleston with that. There was only one person who could give him away an' that was the Dixon woman. I had to work up to a situation where I could make her talk. Findin' the gun an' that blank ammunition at her place was just luck. I always thought I'd find the letter there. I've never known a dope yet who had enough sense to tear up or burn things like that.

'I knew dam' well that it *had* to be Azelda Dixon who brought young Riverton down here on the night of the shootin',' Callaghan went on. 'An' I knew that she wouldn't do it just for money. She's got some money of her own an' she makes quite a bit on the side by actin' as a professional co-respondent for slick divorce lawyers an' things like that.

'An' I *had* to put Gagel in on the job so that I could get what was practically a confession from Riverton. I knew dam' well that Gagel would want at least a thousand for doing it, an' I'd already given Jimmy Wilpins – the old boy who saw Mrs Riverton comin' off the boat – a hundred an' promised him another hundred when he wrote me a line in a month's time. So I got five thousand from her while I had the chance. I didn't know what money I was going to need.

'Once I'd got that statement from young Riverton I felt better. I showed it to Juanita, because I knew she'd tell Charleston about it. I knew that directly he knew that Riverton had practically confessed to shootin' Raffano he'd feel safe an' start puttin' the screw on Mrs Riverton for the twenty thousand. I knew that directly he knew he was going to get the twenty thousand he'd plan to make a quick getaway with Juanita, an' I knew that directly I could tell Azelda that Charleston was running out on her and *prove* it to her if necessary that she'd do anything to get her own back on Charleston. Well . . . it worked.'

Selby took a long draw at his cigar.

'You took some chances, Callaghan,' he said smilingly.

Callaghan shrugged.

'You've got to take a chance sometimes – in *my* business,' he said. He finished his whisky, took a cigarette from the box on the table and lit it. 'Well . . . I'll be gettin' along,' he said.

Selby said: 'Won't you wait? Mrs Riverton'll be down in a few minutes. She'll have a lot to say to you about all this.'

Callaghan grinned.

'No, thanks,' he said. 'I reckon that she an' I have said pretty well all we want to say to each other. Oh, by the way . . . ' He put his hand into the inside breast pocket of his jacket and brought out the twenty thousand pounds he had taken from Charleston.

'You might give her that money when you see her,' he said.

He stood looking at Selby, his eyes twinkling mischievously.

Selby counted through the notes.

'Good God!' he said. 'When did you get this from him?'

'I was waitin' outside,' said Callaghan. 'I made a deal with him – just a quiet bit of business between friends, you know – then I ran over to Falleton and telephoned Gringall.' He grinned. 'I'll see you get that account on Monday mornin',' he said. 'I'd hate you to have to sue me for it!'

Selby got up. They both began to laugh.

Selby said: 'Good night, Callaghan. Jelks has dried out your car and put the hood up. If you *must* go . . . '

'I'll get along,' said Callaghan. 'Good night.'

He was at the door when Selby said:

'The Riverton family ought to put a monument up to you for this . . . '

'Like hell!' said Callaghan. 'I think I'd prefer that writ that Mrs Riverton was threatenin'!'

The door closed behind him.

It was three o'clock. Callaghan slowed the Jaguar to a stop outside his apartment building. He walked slowly through the doors. Inside, Wilkie, the night porter, was dozing in his little glass office.

Callaghan said: 'Wake up, soldier . . . have you got a cigarette . . . a Player's?'

Wilkie stood up, felt in his pocket, produced a packet of ten. Callaghan took one.

'This'll last me until I get upstairs,' he said. 'Has anybody been through . . . anybody by the name of Juanita?'

'Yes, Mr Callaghan,' said Wilkie. 'She came through four times between one and two. She said she'd be seeing you.'

'How did she sound, Wilkie?' Callaghan asked.

'Well . . . I don't quite know,' said Wilkie. 'I think she sounded a bit fed up . . . as if she'd got something on her mind. She was pretty snappy too. She sounded . . . '

'*Ominous* is the word,' said Callaghan, grinning faintly. 'Ominous . . . Wilkie.'

He entered the lift. He stopped it at the office floor, walked along the passage, unlocked the office door and went into his own room. He took the Luger automatic out of his pocket and threw it into the bottom drawer. He rummaged in the other drawers until he found the bottle of rye whisky. He drank a good two fingers. He remembered, suddenly, the night when he and Kells had sat there drinking whisky, examining the things from Azelda Dixon's handbag.

Callaghan realized that he was tired. He got up, stretched, locked up his desk drawers and the offices, went back to the lift. He went up to his apartment.

In the bedroom, he threw off his overcoat, jacket and waistcoat and went into the bathroom. He sat on the stool and began to rub eau-de-Cologne into his hair. The sting of it on his neck felt good.

He went back into the bedroom, put on a green silk dressing-gown, went into the sitting-room, put more coal on the fire, turned on the console gramophone.

He got himself a whisky and soda and stood in front of the fire smoking, listening to the quiet music.

The house telephone rang in the bedroom. It was Wilkie.

'The lady's downstairs, sir,' said Wilkie.

Callaghan thought what the hell. If Juanita wants to get it off her chest, let her. She's in a hell of a temper and she's dying to tell me what she thinks of me. If I don't see her she'll only brood about it and when she does start in it'll be worse than ever.

He said: 'Bring her up, Wilkie.'

He walked over to the hall, opened the apartment door, left it like that, went back to the fireplace in the sitting-room.

He heard the lift come up. Then the door opened. He looked up, a contrite expression on his face.

It was Thorla Riverton.

She stood in the doorway. She was wearing the black angora frock with the ruffles under the ocelot cloak.

Callaghan said: 'Well, this is nice . . . or isn't it?'

She came into the room. She said:

'I've come to say I'm sorry. The trouble with people like me is that we're only used to meeting certain types of people – people who belong in the rather small circle in which we move ourselves. When we meet someone who is *different* – someone *outside* that circle – we don't even try to understand them. We don't realize immediately, as we should, that they probably have *infinitely* more quality in their little finger than we have in our whole bodies. . . . '

'Now I wonder what that means,' said Callaghan. 'It sounds very deep to me. And won't you sit down?'

She dropped her cloak on a settee, sat down in the big arm-chair.

'That,' she said, 'was a belated attempt at an apology. I got the whole story from Mr Selby when you'd gone. I began to understand several things I'd misunderstood. I'd have been much wiser if I'd talked to him before about you instead of coming to idiotic conclusions. I understand one thing especially.'

'Such as . . . ?' queried Callaghan.

'Such as the fact that when you told me that you'd taken your instructions originally from Colonel Riverton, and that you'd continue to take them from him – or his lawyer – you meant that your original agreement was with him, that you would see it through as he would have wanted you to, and that just as he wouldn't have allowed a foolish woman to mess things up, neither would you. I appreciate that now.'

Callaghan smiled. He said: 'Callaghan Investigations likes to live up to what Gringall says is its motto. . . . '

'Which is?' she asked.

'*We get there somehow and who the hell cares how,*' said Callaghan. 'It's not a very good motto. . . . ' He grinned. 'A poor thing, but mine own,' he concluded.

'So you've read Shakespeare too, Mr Callaghan,' she said. 'I've noticed that you are apt at quotations.'

'Am I?' said Callaghan. 'I didn't know I'd used any. An' wouldn't you like a drink after that long' – he grinned wickedly at her, mimicked the tone of voice she had once used when she had said the words – '*and unnecessary drive.*'

She laughed. 'What a fool I must have sounded,' she said. 'And I will have the drink *and* a cigarette, please.'

He mixed the drinks, gave her a cigarette.

'What was the quotation I used?' he said. 'I'm curious.'

She looked at the glowing end of her cigarette.

'Something about hatred being akin to love, I think it was,' she said very softly.

The telephone jangled.

Callaghan said: 'Excuse me.'

He went into the bedroom, closing the door behind him. He took off the receiver. It was Juanita.

'For God's sake,' said Juanita. 'You lousy *heel* . . . you stick me up for every goddam dinner an' lunch appointment I've ever made with you; you give me the air. You push me on to some goddam murderer just because you want me to stooge around an' keep the guy hanging about until you think the time's ripe for you to get him pinched; you walk out on me from a dinner appointment in order to get him pinched; you get him pinched on the night before he's supposed to marry me, an' then you have the goddam nerve to say "Hallo, Juanita", as if butter wouldn't melt in your mouth. For crying out loud! When I get my hooks into you, I'm goin' to tear you wide open . . . you heel of heels . . . you . . . ' She gasped for breath.

'Look, Juanita,' said Callaghan. 'You listen to me. You didn't want to marry Charleston, *you* know that. So isn't it a good thing you didn't? An' you've got all those clothes an' things out of it, an' what about that diamond brooch I gave you . . . didn't I tell you when I gave it to you that if ever you got into a hell of a temper with me you might take a look at it an' relax? Well . . . relax, honey. Let's have dinner one night next week.'

'Like hell,' she said. 'If ever I have dinner with you again I hope to kiss a pole-cat. Which night anyway?'

'Make it Thursday,' he said. 'Thursday night, Juanita. We'll do a show an' I'll explain everything.'

'It had better be a good explanation,' she said. 'Or else . . . Good night, you heel,' she concluded softly.

Callaghan hung up. He sighed. He went back to the sitting-room.

'What were we talkin' about?' he said.

She looked at him demurely.

'We were talking about quotations . . . the one under discussion was about love being akin to hatred.'

'Oh, yes,' said Callaghan. 'Well, I've got a theory. . . . ' He paused, his glass half-way to his mouth. 'Would it bore you to hear it?' he questioned.

'Not at all, Mr Callaghan,' she said. 'Mr Selby, who – as you pointed out when we were having our little discussion, just after you put Jelks *hors de combat* – has more experience in his little finger than I have in what you were pleased to call "the entire area of my nice figure" – I'm glad you think it nice – well, Mr Selby said that you were a person of rather extraordinary experience, that you were very, very deep, and that it was well worth while to listen to you. I should be very glad to hear an exposition from you on the "love is akin to hate" theory.'

Callaghan looked at her. Her eyes were twinkling. He was about to speak when the house telephone in the bedroom rang. He asked to be excused again, went into the bedroom. It was Wilkie.

'For the love of Mike,' said Callaghan. 'What is it now?'

'Sorry, Mr Callaghan,' said Wilkie. 'I phoned up to tell you I was just going off.'

'Right, Wilkie,' said Callaghan. 'Sleep tight. Good night.'

'Good night, Mr Callaghan,' Wilkie replied. 'Is there anything else you want?'

Callaghan looked through the half-open door into the sitting-room, saw in the firelight a dainty shoe swinging.

'No, thanks, Wilkie,' he said very quietly. 'I think I've got everything I want.'

He hung up, went into the sitting-room.